JEREMY WAGNER

For more information contact:
Riverdale Avenue Books
5676 Riverdale Avenue
Riverdale, NY 10471
www.riverdaleavebooks.com

Design by www.formatting4U.com
Cover by Scott Carpenter
Cover art and icons by Claudio Bergamin

Digital ISBN: 9781626014633
Trade Paperback ISBN: 9781626014640
Hardcover ISBN: 9781626014657

First Edition October 2018

LYRICS PERMISSIONS:
Black No. I
Word$ and Music by Peter Steele
Copyright (c) 1993 by Universal Music - MGB Songs and $nomantic Publishing
All Rights Administered by Universal Music - MGB Songs
International Copyright Secured All Rights Reserved
Reprinted by Permission of Hal Leonard LLC.

PRAISE FOR JEREMY WAGNER:

"Jeremy is a pretty impressive dude."
—Peter Straub, *New York Times* Bestselling Author,
A Dark Matter, Ghost Story

PRAISE FOR JEREMY WAGNER'S
THE ARMAGEDDON CHORD:

"Wagner debuts *THE ARMAGEDDON CHORD* with a highly entertaining blend of breakneck pacing, a cast of over-the-top characters and memorable lines..."
—Publishers Weekly

"An evil Egyptologist. A scheming billionaire. A guitar maestro. They're all there in Jeremy Wagner's, *THE ARMAGEDDON CHORD*. This is pulp fiction at its breeziest best."
—Rolling Stone

"Wagner strikes a winning heavy-metal chord in this stunning story that foretells an End of Time beyond imagination. The author's use of music as a backdrop and his development of fascinating characters make for interesting reading in this enthralling tale."
—RT Book Reviews

"*THE ARMAGEDDON CHORD* is a wild phantasmagoric thrill ride that will satisfy lovers of the darkest fantasy fiction and the heaviest of metal."
—Peter Blauner, *New York Times* bestselling author of *The Intruder, Slipping Into Darkness, Proving Ground*

"*THE ARMAGEDDON CHORD* is a kickass novel!"
—**Jonathan Maberry**, *New York Times* bestselling author of *Patient Zero and the Joe Ledger series*

"Combining the world of heavy metal with malevolent supernatural forces Wagner has created quite a fantastic read... A riveting thriller that is sure to keep readers glued to the pages until the very end... The unique blending of ancient history, religion and heavy metal make this book unlike any others I have read... If you're a reader of horror or fiction novels or if you're a musician, then *THE ARMAGEDDON CHORD* will be right up your alley. I know it kept me up turning pages into the wee hours of the morning."
—**Pure Grain Audio.com**

"*THE ARMAGEDDON CHORD* is a quick, enjoyable read full of action, violence, hell-spawned (and human) monsters and original variations of scenarios common to end-time thrillers."
—***Decibel Magazine***

"Jeremy Wagner is an up-and-coming voice in the realm of horror fiction. His talent shines through this debut novel, and I can't wait to see what his next offering will be. A real page-turner, *THE ARMAGEDDON CHORD* strikes just the right note!"
—**Yasmine Galenorn**, *New York Times/USA Today* Bestselling Author of the *Otherworld Series*

"*THE ARMAGEDDON CHORD* is like *THE DA VINCI CODE* with a heavy-metal soundtrack!"
—**Katherine Turman**, co-author of *LOUDER THAN HELL: An Unflinching Oral History of Heavy Metal*

"Wagner combines a world of classic adventure and intrigue with a dash of rock'n'roll mystique for a unique take on the thriller format."
—**Joel McIver**, Author of *JUSTICE FOR ALL: The Truth About Metallica*

"Jeremy Wagner is the king of the new breed of horror! *THE ARMAGEDDON CHORD* strikes a low chord of death right through the reader's frontal lobe."
—**Chris Barnes** of *Six Feet Under*

"[*THE ARMAGEDDON CHORD*] left vivid pictures in one's mind... There could even be a movie made about The Armageddon Chord. "
—*Valencia County News-Bulletin*

"[*THE ARMAGEDDON CHORD*] storyline is so awesome, I'm not sure why it wasn't an episode of *Buffy the Vampire Slay*er. Really. Joss Whedon is wherever he is in all his brilliance, wondering why he didn't think of this plotline. It's that good. "
—*West of Mars*

"Wagner makes the story lots of fun by taking it to the extreme."
—*Anti-music.com*

"*THE ARMAGEDDON CHORD* is a fun and thrilling combination of heavy metal music and horror. Jeremy Wagner has written a great story... This is a book that is hard to put down. Wagner has hit the ground running with his debut novel. I can't wait to see what he has in store next."
—*The Horror Fiction Review*

"[Wagner] has pioneered the genre known as 'heavy metal horror fiction' with this work, combining aspects of modern heavy metal added to a new take on the horror novel genre. Wagner has crafted an excellent, original story that no one has really ever tackled before... H. Metal fans will find the many nods and references to the real music business, the world of heavy metal music and guitars pleasing while big horror fans will love the well-crafted, unmitigated evil and gore elements. The cultural and historical facts were painstakingly researched; lending an air of authenticity to the book that rivals others in the genre."

—Metal Army America

"*THE ARMAGEDDON CHORD* is a fun, fast-paced explosion of heavy metal, Egyptian mythology, and a good taste of the occult that makes for a very engaging read. If you enjoy apocalyptic tales and epic clashes between good and evil, then the plot of this book will definitely have you hooked."

—Metal Injection

Dedication

For those who are gone but never forgotten: Dallas Mayr (aka Jack Ketchum), Rocky Wood, Katherine Ludwig, George Romero and Tobe Hooper

Acknowledgements

Big thanks goes out to Juliet Ulman—one of the greatest editors I've ever worked with who did an amazing job keeping me within the orbit of reality and sticking with making this story as amazing as possible. Thanks also to Katherine Turman for the added sanity-checks and re-reading. Grateful beyond words to Lori Perkins—my constant believer, mentor, guidance counselor, and an entrepreneur like none other. Peter Blauner—another mentor—you rule so much my friend, Ronald Malfi for constant advice, wisdom, and friendship. To my horror-brother, Kirk Hammett (monster kids rule forever!). To my badass legal team of Peter Strand and Teresa Rodriguez. And most of all to my wife Kym who's always pushed me to write constantly and who is always my first reader—and who's the first person to tell me if I'm out of my f-ing mind or not—I love you, babe.

Rabid Heart first started out as a short story for a zombie anthology St. Martin's Press was putting out. It ended up taking on a life of its own and became the novel you're reading now. This novel is Lori Perkins' fault. Any incorrect details or mistakes in this novel are my fault.

Loving you was like loving the dead,
Loving you was like loving the dead.
Loving you was like loving the dead,
Was like loving the dead...
-- Peter Steele/Type O Negative

Chapter One

Rhonda Driscoll wiped her sweaty palms on her camo as her golf cart sped along a lighted service tunnel and away from the underground armory. She could barely touch the gas pedal. The E-Z-GO cart accelerated along with her heart. The heavy cart bottomed out on a speed bump.

Jesus Christ.

Her payload of doom shifted and rattled. She glanced back anxiously as her eyes scanned the overloaded cargo of eight fully-automatic rifles, ten handguns, two RPG's, 5,000 rounds of ammo, and a case of grenades. Everything looked okay.

I'm driving a four-wheeled bomb.

She shook her head. She never signed up for this. Not long ago she'd been a happy hair stylist, newly engaged to Brad and hitting the gym and Nordstrom's when she could afford it. She was just a trusted civilian, not a soldier. But she took orders anyway, and time waited for no one, her father liked to say, and this seemed especially true today. She frowned at her zebra print watch. Sarge expected her half an hour ago, and goddamn if he didn't hate tardiness more than zombies and ISIS. She chewed her bottom lip.

The weapons were meant for newly arrived military personnel and armed civilian survivors who waited above ground at Fort Rocky Military Base: A.K.A. "Camp Deadnut." Her father ran the place.

Man, how crazy things had gotten. Had it only been six months? She'd just turned 21. Her grip tightened on the steering wheel. The fucking U.S military. And Daddy... he and his asshole Marine boys and the President sure fucked things good, didn't they? Waited until the last minute to tell everyone about a Necro-Rabies breakout in North America. Mental flashes of her mother, younger sister Beth, her friends, and her fiancé, Brad Savini, all back in Levendale... ripped to pieces by hordes of rabid, flesh-hungry zombies, the *Cujos*, along with the countless others who were merely bitten, then turned and walked among the undead.

Walking dead. Her stomach tightened. They creeped her the fuck out, all of them; walking dead, Cujos, zombies, whatever you called them.

Fuckers.

Before all TV screens on base went black six months ago, she'd watched with the rest of the country as their clever, and now deceased, president joked in an interview that the Oval Office had nicknamed the victims of the new plague "Cujos." Someone told her Cujo was actually a book by some author from Maine. Stephen Koontz was it? King, maybe? Her eyes blinked. Stevie Queen? It didn't matter. She drove her

2

cart and assumed the scary scribe had already turned Cujo himself, roaming the streets with the rest of them.

Goddamn it.

Rhonda wiped a tear from her right eye. Sure, she knew she'd been one of the lucky ones to make it out alive via a Black Hawk helicopter thanks to her dad, Colonel Kenneth Driscoll. Daddy was still alive, her only living family member, but damn him, he should've let her die with Brad. She and her babe would both be in a better place right now.

She put on a tougher face and tapped the bun of brunette hair on top of her head as the cart ascended a wide ramp into a bright day of a world above ground. Two armed soldiers in camo stood guard at the ramp's exit. A wooden-faced soldier on her left jabbed a bony finger at her. "Halt. Let me see your ID."

"C'mon, Ted. You know damn well who I am. There's only a couple hundred of us here."

Ted "Teddie" Fitch always bugged her. He acted like he was some kind of badass working Area 51 or Secret Service or some junk. She scowled at him. *Douchebag.*

She remembered Teddie from high school, back when he was just another preppy slimeball. Rhonda recalled Teddie entered military service right after graduation. Teddie was always getting into trouble, but always avoided arrest or any punishment. His old man forced him to join the Marines in hopes of straightening his ass out after Teddie allegedly slipped a date-rape drug into a girl's soda. The girl's parents threatened to sue the Fitch's but they never did anything. The girl never filed charges, something that always angered and disappointed Rhonda. It was rumored that Teddie had done this and worse before without consequence.

3

Rhonda had observed Teddie swaggering around base with a growing sense of disgust. By day, he was an insufferable tightass. At night, he chugged beer rations and hit on her whenever they crossed paths. Rhonda tasted something bad when she thought of this. Her heart belonged to Brad. Thoughts of any new man iced her insides. Thoughts of Teddie in her bed? *Gag me with a pitchfork.*

Rhonda turned to the other soldier. He looked like a skinny beaver. "Jim-Bob. Y'wanna tell Teddie here that I gotta get these weapons up top before the Colonel has another conniption and makes you both clean out the latrines?"

Jim-Bob shifted his rifle in his hands. "Yeah, Ted. Let her through, goddamn it. She's the Colonel's daughter, for cryin' out loud."

Teddie's wooden expression didn't change. He stared at Rhonda's large breasts beneath her flak-jacket and with deliberate delay, looked up into her eyes. A sly grin formed on his face before he turned away and shouted, "Coming up and out!"

Rhonda floored the golf cart and drove across Camp Deadnut to her delivery point. Camp Deadnut, home to the living, the best place in a dead world that money couldn't buy.

Two-thousand acres of Camp Deadnut's base spread throughout the gorgeous hills and country of North Carolina. Before Necro-Rabies, 5,000 Marines trained here each year in Infantry and Marine Combat. Now the camp housed only about 200 survivors; approximately 100 well-armed Marines and another hundred civilian men, women and children.

The situation could be worse. The base had

decent barracks, a clean and well-stocked kitchen, underground food storage and a chow-hall, hot showers, His and Her heads, a hospital, an airstrip, aircraft hangars, maintenance and intelligence buildings and a small chapel. But it was the two huge and fully-stocked ASA's (Ammunition Storage Areas) that Rhonda and everyone else at Camp Deadnut valued above all. These over-stocked and underground weapons warehouses also held some 100,000 gallons of regular, diesel and aircraft fuel combined.

Aboveground, additional warehouses and hangars contained two-dozen deuce-and-a-halfs, six M1A1 battle tanks, three F/A-18 Super Hornets (Rhonda learned only one dude on base knew how to fly these) and four Black Hawk helicopters. Another 15 Humvees sat parked on base near a maintenance building. Each vehicle came loaded with a weapons platform fitted with .50-Cal machine guns and MK-19 Automatic Grenade Launchers.

Rhonda parked her golf cart and approached Sergeant Harris, who was assembling his soldiers, new additions and the civilians-made-combatants, for an off-base excursion he planned.

"Sarge. The cart's loaded with plenty of firepower and ammo. Ready for distribution, sir."

Sarge studied Rhonda with his iron eyes, his grim face lined with 58 years of life IN a world full of war. He straightened his camo jacket and barked at his company, ordering them to organize, split weapons and ammo from Rhonda's cart, and prepare for new deployment. He turned his attention back to Rhonda. "Driscoll. We're set to fly out at 1300."

Rhonda glanced at her wrist. She'd be airborne in

15 minutes. She met Sarge's stare and pursed her lips. "Haven't we already picked apart every city and town in a 20-mile radius? I mean, we've saved a few, but we've lost more."

"That's why we're going out *30 miles*, Driscoll. We're going beyond and it's the first time we're going back since the Outbreak. We gotta keep looking for survivors, doctors, news, food and anything else to get that much closer to getting this shithole planet civilized. No matter what the cost."

Rhonda figured Sarge would rethink cost once their numbers dropped from 200 people to 50. She sighed. "Where we goin' this time?"

"Levendale."

Rhonda gasped. *No way.* She couldn't... no, didn't want to return to Levendale: her hometown turned horror city. Go back there? Back to that nightmare where everyone she loved, save her dad, had died? The idea made her choke. "Sarge. I don't think I can…"

"Bullshit, Driscoll. You're goin'. You think you're the only one who lost everything, New Fucking Soldier? You signed up for this shit. Every week I hear you say you wanna nuke the zombie fuckers who killed your fiancé. Here's your chance. Hell on wheels, you're going. You're the best goddamn gun-bunny we got."

Rhonda nodded. Sarge was right. She had practiced hard to become a stellar artilleryman—or *artillerywoman*. She'd shown them, hadn't she? Every Marine boy at Camp Deadnut watched her hit a paper plate with a tight, five-shot group at 100 yards with 180-grain silver bear rounds from an AK-47. Not bad for a girl who matured with shooting skills she learned in country cornfields with Daddy and his mountain of firearms.

She was a Colonel's daughter with no interest in military service. Sure, she learned soldiering and weaponry from Dad, but it was all sport to her.

Rhonda had also worked as a hair-stylist at Sylvia's Salon in downtown Levendale. Hair was another passion of hers, but like many people her age, she couldn't figure out what road to take in life. That was before the world changed. Guns were now her livelihood. Doing hair, wondering what jeans would would fit her petite frame, or hoping Brad would bring her Starbucks to work didn't matter. Other things were more important, like her ability to fieldstrip any piece of ordnance or weapon from a Colt .45 to a grenade launcher with quick speed. She gave great detail to every clean and lubricated part she took apart and reassembled. Guns and hair. She thought it sounded like a Redneck Great Clips.

I've got all kinds of skills, I guess.

She suddenly felt her resistance shift to interest. Apprehension turned into curiosity. Why not go back? What if one of her friends was alive back there, waiting for rescue? What if some of her stuff remained in her townhouse? What if fucking looters had broken into her townhouse? She had wondered about all of this before, but hadn't had the opportunity to go back to Levendale until now.

Rhonda raised her head and looked Sergeant Harris in the eye. "Nice one. And you're right, Sarge. Count me on board all the way."

Sarge's battlefield mug brightened. "Good on ya, Driscoll."

"Thanks."

"The full-bird's waiting for you at the head-shed. Wants you there yesterday."

"The *who* wants me *where?*"

"The Colonel. Your dad... wants you in the command-post before we take off for Levendale. Hurry your ass up."

Oh yeah. She remembered the term full-bird. She heard lots of military slang. It was all weird. These guys may as well speak Chinese. Rhonda shook her head. She thought she would've learned all the Marine lingo by now. She certainly heard enough of that talk in her family's house for the last 21 years. "Gotcha. I'll be back in two shakes."

Sarge frowned. "Move."

Chapter Two

Rhonda approached the 1,200-square-foot, dark-green tent. It was a modernized command post. The hum of its industrial-sized generator ran non-stop, providing the tent with electricity for computers, lights, appliances and air conditioning. Now that late fall was upon North Carolina, it would bring heat, too.

She stepped into warmth and bustling noise. Before her, soldiers in camo talked among themselves. Several of them sat at laptop computers. Rhonda knew Fort Rocky lost active Internet months ago. Every computer on base served to draft miscellaneous documents and signs, or consult old GPS files for travel strategies. She knew Daddy—Colonel Kenneth Driscoll—maintained a strict and professional military atmosphere at all times. This wasn't Afghanistan or Syria, but they were at war all the same.

Her eyes flashed on Dad, at the tent's far end. He stood in front of a large, pin-covered, marked-up map of North Carolina, surrounded by a few Marines scribbling notes as he pointed and dished out strategies and plans for various search-save-seek-and-destroy missions.

Rhonda stood at attention and watched her father, his muscular arms waving and his large hands clenched. She couldn't help but worry about the bastard's blood pressure.

"Dead Cujos are the only good Cujos." Dad waved a fist. "I want every single dead-walking, maggot-breeding, flesh-eating, inhuman, un-American, rot-smelling biped within the range of a bullet, flame-thrower, grenade or any other form of ordnance, DEAD FOR GOOD!"

High-strung as always.

The Colonel spotted her and pulled his camo hat bill to his brows, dismissing his men with a nod.

"C'mere, baby-girl." Colonel Driscoll stood straight with his left hand on his hip and his right arm extended and waved her over. "We gotta talk before you go hunting for the living and the decomposing alike."

"What d'ya wanna talk about?" Rhonda sometimes felt tempted to address Dad as Colonel or Sir, but she wasn't a soldier, and anyway, any reverence she held for him had dropped several pegs, thanks to his blatant contempt for Brad Savini, which hadn't lessened one iota now that her much-hated fiancé was dead.

"I've reviewed today's mission with Sergeant Harris and I'm sending y'all into Levendale."

"I know."

"That a problem?"

"Not really. I wasn't too keen on the idea at first, but now I'm sorta curious to see what's up there. I had hoped to get one last look at our town. To try and make sense of what happened. Maybe to say goodbye to family, and you know, Brad."

Brad's arms, reaching for her... just before Cujos nabbed him.

"Rhonda, you're alive and Brad's dead. Most of the world's dead and walking. Be glad you're here. I know you loved Brad. That you think he was your soulmate—"

"He *was*, Dad. Better believe it."

"Right. You *were* gonna get married. It's over. He's in a better place and so are you."

Rhonda didn't speak. She played with her engagement ring. Her skin had grown thick in time, thanks in part to Dad Driscoll's parenting skills.

But Brad had passed the test.

"Permission to speak freely, Dad? *Colonel?*"

"Go ahead."

"You can be a real prick about things, you know that?"

"I'm a real prick about everything." Dad offered a half-smile. "Look. Life and love are fleeting things. I'm not gonna tell you how to feel and I never would. You loved Brad... still do. Fine. I lost your mother, my youngest daughter, and my dearest friends to this Necro-shit. I lost some of my best friends in Middle East combat. I've learned to live on. Learned to stay focused, survive; and not fuck around with the small shit."

"What's your point, Dad? Can't shed a tear for your wife and kids 'cause you gotta keep conquering the world?" A pang pounded her snare-drum heart. Mom and Sis gone. Unreal. Cujos unreal. And her Brad... gone. It hurt. Would she ever get over such loss? "Nothing's small shit, Dad."

11

Dad frowned again. "My point is this: You're heading back to Levendale. You need to be extremely careful and handle all Cujos with extreme prejudice. If you see your best pal, Molly, and she's in her cheerleader outfit and eating someone's left leg, you blow her fucking head off. If you see our neighbor Jerry Jacobs strolling around looking like his head went bad in '75, you kill him. You kill 'em all."

"Dad, I—"

"You're on a mission to search for survivors and supplies. Get in, kill any Cujos you can, look for signs of real life, food, anything useful. You *do not* dilly-dally in the hometown. You *do not* visit your old hair salon. You *do not* make a sentimental visit to your old pad to fetch your hair dryer. Are we clear?"

Rhonda snorted and straightened. She gave a middle-finger salute. "Yes, Sir, Daddy, Sir!"

He waved her off. "Ahh, screw it. I could never get you to listen to shit."

"Something I always wondered; why'd you hate Brad so much? We never discussed this when he was alive. I know you hated him."

Rhonda had asked her Dad this same question numerous times and his negative answers varied. How could anyone dislike Brad? It made no sense. She knew him as a selfless and considerate young man who possessed actual class. She had observed how his popularity flourished back in high school, not just because he was a star football player for Levendale High, but also because he extended warmth to everyone he met and did wonderful deeds. He had been a rare one. In high school, Brad had spearheaded food drives for the needy and fundraisers for animal shelters. She remembered how he constantly looked after an old neighbor lady in ill-health who had no family and could barely walk. His acts of generosity and decency were endless. Yep, that was him... her kind, sweet, smart... cool as hell Brad.

He had been a hopeless romantic to boot, showering Rhonda with flowers and dinners on her birthday and Valentine's Day; he never forgot anything that was special to her. She found it easy to fall in love with him. It didn't hurt that she thought him to be a drop-dead gorgeous hunk when she'd first met him. And later, she discovered he also owned a nice cock and knew how to use it.

Rhonda thought of Brad's talents in bed whenever she touched her clit in her nighttime bunk. His hardness, his flat belly against hers, his beautiful gold-flecked eyes, how his cock and eyes all drilled into her, and his passionate words in her ears. She kept these memories fresh whenever she made herself come, always crying when she did that, bawling until she fell asleep... night after night.

Brad had been fiercely loyal. She'd seen everyone from the prom queen to teachers to mothers hit on him, but he remained untouchable. He only had eyes for her. He'd been her first and only. While her girlfriends were sowing wild oats with numerous partners and advising her to do the same, Rhonda remained happy and satisfied to stick exclusively with Brad. He'd felt the same. They had genuine chemistry. When it's right, it's right they told each other. And when he proposed marriage, well, she knew it was right.

Rhonda's mother and sister were fond of Brad, but her father wasn't. He had a hard-on for Brad since they'd first started dating. She chalked it up to her father being from some "good 'ol boy" club. The Marine Colonel who wanted the world to bend to his way.

But one other thing Rhonda loved about him was that as decent and tender as Brad was, he also took zero shit from anyone—especially from Rhonda's father. Brad never backed down from the Colonel. He was never intimidated by him. Even when Colonel Driscoll got in Brad's face, nose-to-nose, telling Brad he wasn't what was best for Rhonda, Brad didn't flinch. Brad made it clear that his love for Rhonda was forever constant. Rhonda recalled how Brad had told her father that he worshipped her beyond words and that he'd take care of her forever—that he'd love her forever. Brad had said, "That's a fucking promise, Mister Driscoll."

It was at that moment, on that declaration of love and promise, where she completely gave herself to Brad—heart, mind, body, soul—and fell so deep in love with him she thought the weight of her adoration would crush her and kill her.

Brad was her forever man... but forever didn't last as long as Rhonda had hoped. She'd never imagined living without Brad, yet here she was. How she'd been able to survive with her heart ripped out was something she'd wondered about for six months.

"Where's this coming from? Talk about out-of-the-blue. I didn't exactly hate him." Dad stepped around the table toward her. "As your father, I'm not supposed to approve of any guys who come a-knockin'. Brad was fine, I just didn't think you needed to marry the guy. Seemed rushed. Whether Father knows best, that's my two cents."

Before Rhonda could snap out a reply, Sergeant Harris entered. He saluted and turned to Rhonda. "Driscoll, Rhonda! Time to roll out!"

Rhonda turned from Sarge to her father. "Guess I gotta split. I don't want to hate you, Dad."

The Colonel gave another half-smile. "Move out, soldier."

Rhonda summoned a small smile. She kissed the air and walked away. When she neared a tent flap where Sarge waited, her father called out. "Rhonda."

She faced him. "Yeah?"

"Be careful, baby-girl." His expression softened. "Stay on this side of the grave."

Chapter Three

Rhonda checked her M4 and spare ammo magazines. Her full magazines gave her confidence, though her palms felt wet while she readied herself.

The platoon lifted off, en route to Levendale. She watched Camp Deadnut drop away and recalled her last trip out two weeks ago. At the time, she'd begged to go out. But now a twinge of despair stabbed her as she looked below, to the razor-wired security quickly receding in the distance.

From her high vantage point, she could see thousands upon thousands of Cujos circling outside every foot of Camp Deadnut's fortified enclosure.

Jesus.

Her gloom turned to irritation when Sarge paired up their eight-person group and placed her with Teddie Fitch. Rhonda protested for one second before Sarge hushed her and told her to deal with it. Oh, she'd deal with it all right. If pervo Fitch hit on her again, she'd break his damn face. She glanced at Fitch and he winked at her. Her jaw clenched and she turned away.

Fucking creep.

From his seat in the Black Hawk, Sarge explained how this small and special group would land in downtown Levendale and move out as four separate patrols of two people each. Each patrol would cover a separate part of town: North Side, South Side, East Side and West Side. Each pair was to spend only 60 minutes on their individual hunts. Sarge ordered everyone to return within his one-hour window. Those who failed to return on time or lost contact would be left behind. Before Teddie could speak, Rhonda volunteered them to take Levendale's North Side. Sarge concurred and she smiled to herself.

Rhonda peered down at the roads and woods far below that she and Brad had traveled so many times. There was Meehan Creek, where they had skinny-dipped and made love those summer nights that now seemed impossibly far away.

Sarge's sharp bark interrupted her thoughts before the tears had a chance to fall. They'd be dropping into Levendale in a matter of moments. To Rhonda's right, Levendale's urban sprawl was already blossoming beneath her. She spotted her old school, and Sylvia's Salon in downtown Levendale, where she'd spent so many days perfecting hair coloring, and gossiping. And then, before she could look away, her townhouse—no *their* townhouse—where she and Brad had lived together.

Rhonda blinked rapidly, her lashes wet. She checked her weapon's lock and load. They were descending upon Main Street. No time for sadness or tears now.

The chopper hovered several feet above the

pavement while their gunners unleashed fully-auto, M60D 7.2mm machine guns mounted to a M144 armament subsystem. The furious fire cut down every Cujo in sight like dried weeds beneath a weed-whacker. The sound was deafening.

As she often did, Rhonda found herself wondering about who the Cujos had been before—before they became the rotting monsters who shambled toward her now. They may have been teachers, office staff and happy kids once. Perhaps some were even her old clients. Who knew? The kind of people they'd been didn't matter, they weren't people anymore.

"MOVE!!! KILL ON SIGHT!!!" Sarge ordered everyone out. Rhonda scrambled with her platoon onto a corpse-strewn Main Street, where they quickly split into pairs and moved off.

Rhonda and Teddie walked north, picking their way through bones, rot and the detritus of a dead city as the helicopter rose behind them. She led them with purpose, knowing every part of town, and exactly where she wanted to go. With the roar of helicopter gone, she could hear distant reports of machine guns and excited shouts of her comrades from blocks away.

Rhonda focused her own fire on the horrors filing out from dilapidated storefronts toward her. They hissed and salivated like mad, two-legged hell-dogs. *The head makes 'em dead*, she mused, and ended them with short, controlled bursts.

Rhonda eyed her partner with contempt. Christ, such a goddamn overexcited amateur. Teddie was screaming his lungs out like a bit player in *Full Metal Jacket*, spraying rounds with reckless abandon at every Cujo in sight.

"Save your ammo. Cool it." Rhonda tried her best to yell through Teddie's fire. When he had finally blown through an entire magazine of ammo, she got her words in. "You done wasting rounds, asshole?"

"The fuckers are everywhere." His body shook and it took him three attempts to reload his M4. "I think we got 'em all. Shit. All these towns are packed. I'm sure Charlotte and Raleigh are worse."

"Probably. Let's keep moving." "Where we goin'?"

"Searching. Just like we're ordered to do."

"Where, though?"

A rogue grocery bag blew through Main Street and in front of Teddie. He jumped and fired a blast of haphazard rounds at it.

"Goddamnit, Teddie! Take it easy."

"Awww, shit. I hate this town. Always have." Teddie spat and shot her a contemptuous glare. "But you... you just love your old hometown, don'tcha?"

Muscles in Rhonda's jaw flexed. She turned her gaze away from Teddie.

I will not let this prick get to me.

"No wonder you jumped up and volunteered to take the north end of this burg. You got somethin' in mind." Teddie smirked and whistled. "Maybe you and me's gonna get some privacy for once."

"Keep dreaming, asswipe." She pointed beyond the block. "I used to work at that place."

Teddie followed her finger. "Sylvia's Salon? What'd ya do? Nails? Hair and shit?"

"Just hair. I was pretty good at color."

He smirked. "Sure you were. Don't look like this joint's doing good business."

Rhonda frowned and walked ahead. Dad told her not to visit this place, but here it was. *Oh, well*. The front door of the salon stood wide open, garbage and beauty supplies spilling out across the sidewalk. Dread pinched her. The glass of the store window, miraculously unbroken, was smeared from within with rusty brown streaks—and handprints. Her stomach roiled.

"Don't look like hair-dye to me." Teddie whistled.

"Shut your blasted mouth, Fitch." God, she'd like to use her M4 on him. Who would know, right? She adjusted her grip on her weapon and took in a deep sigh. "We gotta move on."

Surprisingly, Teddie didn't speak. He followed while she took point. They traveled about a quarter mile and shot Cujos on every block. In between kills, Rhonda poked her head in the buildings and houses that lined the street, looking for survivors and supplies.

When they reached Poplar Avenue, Rhonda led them left, walked a block further, and stopped to gaze at her light-blue townhouse; two stories high with a paved driveway and six-foot tall privacy fence around the backyard. She was happy to see it hadn't appeared to be looted or burnt. It looked no different to her, much like it did six months ago, aside from the morass of tall grass and weeds.

"What're you gawkin' at?" Teddie sounded irritated and tired. "You looking to buy a house now?"

"Fuck you, Teddie." Rhonda spoke to her townhouse. Her heart hammered away. Here it was, her and Brad's home. It felt like a century had passed since she last stood here. She turned to Teddie. "I'm going in. Why don't you wait out here or better yet, go back to the chopper."

20

"Bullshit! We're supposed to stick together and watch each other's backs and try and find other people. You ain't leavin' me alone out here." Teddie whipped his head around. "And I ain't walkin' back to the Black Hawk all by my lonesome."

Rhonda sized Teddie with her eyes. He was right. She was breaking protocol, disobeying orders, and disregarding safety measures. And for what? A stroll down memory lane? For once, Fitch was logical while she made amateur moves. She shook her head and gripped her M4 tight. "Fine, Fitch. Follow and cover me."

"Hey, I've seen this place before."

Rhonda ignored him. She walked to her front door. Her house-key remained where she'd left it under her welcome mat. Straightening, she turned around quickly and found Teddie's intense gaze fixed on her ass. *Fucking creep.*

She hoped he felt the hate in her glare. She turned to her house and inserted the key. The front door opened with ease.

"Hey... wait a minute. This is *your* place. I thought it looked familiar. Saw you and your boy-toy unloading groceries here one day. You sure jumped from high school to playing house, huh?"

Rhonda clenched her jaw and ignored him, staring into the dark interior. Okay, so she was disobeying her father's orders—the Colonel's orders. His words rang in her head. *You do not make a sentimental visit to your old love-nest to fetch your old hair dryer.*

"Whatever," she murmured.

"What's that?"

"Nothing. Let's go." Rhonda entered her house. Behind her, Teddie jumped at nothing. Jittery bastard.

21

Could he breathe any harder? Her front door opened into her living room. A staircase to her right led to a second floor. She paused, clicked the safety off, and carefully scanned for Cujos lurking in shadow. Everything looked clear. A few blinds and drapes remained drawn. All furnishings looked as she'd left it.

Nice and stale. Place could use some Febreze. The old brown hand-me-down sofa with the balled-up snuggle blanket she and Brad cuddled under when they watched movies together was against a wall. In front of her sofa, a small wooden coffee table covered with magazines and some empty Chinese food containers. She walked to her fireplace and gazed at cobweb-covered pictures on the dusty mantel. In every picture she found a happy face. In every picture they posed together in love.

"Bet you're missin' some lovin', huh?" Teddie stood right behind Rhonda. His hot breath blasted her neck.

Rhonda whirled and clipped Teddie's chin with her M4's front sight. "You need to shut your fucking mouth before I make you a casualty. It'd be easy to kill you and leave you for dead in Levendale. No one's gonna care about your body. My word is golden. Not another thing outta you. Got it, creep?"

"Cut my chin? Damn bitch." Teddie rubbed his chin and eyed a small streak of blood on his hand. He glared at Rhonda and looked like he might say something, but a glance at her M4's black barrel quelled any unwise words.

Rhonda scrutinized everything in her first-floor walk-through. Nothing seemed out of the ordinary. She had always kept her house neat and clean, and aside from a good amount of dust layered on every surface from floorboard to ceiling fan, she didn't see evidence of any disturbance. But when she reached her old kitchen, she noted the back door open a crack.

Had she or Brad locked this door six months ago? She couldn't remember. Her palm felt moist as she opened it inward with slow and deliberate care. She found a key in the lock. Someone opened it from outside? She pulled the key and tucked it in her pants pocket before quietly closing the door and locking it from inside.

She tested kitchen light switches, even though she knew the electricity was dead. In semi-darkness, she scanned the kitchen with her gun raised and felt a shiver course through her. Something wasn't right.

"You gonna do somethin' here or not? I wanna get." Teddie entered and rubbed his chin with apparent boredom.

"I wish you'd just—" Rhonda halted. She heard something. Had a floorboard creaked from upstairs? Above her head?

My bedroom... right over the kitchen.

"What was that?" Teddie whispered uncertainly. He stared upward and waved his machine gun in wide and unsafe arcs. "Holy fuck. What if a Cujo's up there?"

"Dunno. But we're gonna find out."

"Fuck this. Let's get out of here."

"I'm going up. This is my place. It's probably just a raccoon." Please. A raccoon would be welcome. Anything but a Cujo. All spookiness she felt, she kept to herself. "You can go if you want. Take your chances out there. I'm gonna check out the upstairs."

"Awww, shit. Fine. You go on up first and I'll follow. It's *your* place after all."

She pushed past Teddie to the staircase near the

23

front door. She turned to him and put an index finger to her pursed lips. *Keep your trap shut.* She turned and ascended with gun raised, cautiously sweeping from side-to-side.

Upstairs, her small bathroom waited in front of her. She peeked inside and found nothing other than scattered makeup on the sink, dirty towels and a shower stall and toilet in need of a scrub. She backed out and proceeded through the hallway to her left. Aside from her bathroom, only a guest bedroom and her master bedroom at the end of the hall occupied the second floor. Rhonda crept quietly along the carpeted hallway. When she reached the guest bedroom, she put an ear to the door, but she didn't hear anything behind it. She opened the door quickly and did an immediate sweep inside.

Empty? Good. It looked neat and well made. She heard Teddie in the hall and stepped out and gave him the okay sign.

She turned to the closed door of the master bedroom, her heart heavy. Here it was, the gateway to the special sanctuary she once shared with Brad. She pressed her left ear against her door and listened. Had something just thumped in her bedroom? By Teddie's uneasy expression, he'd heard it, too. Again she listened, but no further sounds came from behind the door. What made the noise? No matter what she'd told Teddie, no way raccoons entered a house with a key and shut doors behind them.

Teddie snuck along the hallway toward her. He appeared nervous and slippery. "Go on. Move in."

Rhonda stepped away from the door and spoke in a low and controlled voice. "Wait at the top of the stairs. You're too squirrelly and I don't wanna get shot."

Teddie frowned at her. He opened his mouth as if to blurt something, and then shut it. He glared a moment longer before he retreated to the other end of the hall with a huff.

Rhonda watched Teddie take his place near the stairs. With a damp hand, she gripped the brass knob of her master bedroom door and turned it slowly. The door opened with her gentle push. Her M4 felt heavy as she raised it. The creak of the hinges sounded like a scream in the silence. She winced.

Jesus. She chewed on her bottom lip and stood in the doorway. With her breath held, she paused and listened before stepping in quickly, her heart racing and her finger on the trigger. She flattened her back against a wall and made a fast, visual inspection of her bedroom, sweeping her room with her M4 and her eyes. Everything looked clear, if in disarray. Her bed was unmade, sheets and blankets kicked to the side. Two dressers stood with drawers open and clothes scattered around the room. Inside her open closet, she spied nice dresses, blouses, and scattered designer shoes she'd left behind.

We sure took off fast.

She remembered the stern face of the MP who'd come by their house to fetch them on the Colonel's orders. Necro-Rabies owned Levendale, the MP said. *What the fuck is Necro-Rabies?* She and Brad didn't know then, they only knew they needed to leave. Rhonda had ripped their bedroom apart and packed a suitcase with everything she could stuff. If only she stuffed Brad into the Black Hawk, or her suitcase he'd be safe and sound right now.

Her bedroom windows remained closed. No signs

of animal scat or damage. But what was that nasty smell? Maybe the scent came from six-month-old snack food gone bad? What about the creak she'd heard from the kitchen? And the other sound she heard just a few minutes ago? Perhaps the house was settling.

Yeah, right.

She took a deep breath and finally lowered her gun.

"What's going on in there?" Teddie's voice registered alarm and bounced on hallway walls.

"All good here." Why he couldn't keep his mouth shut? So much for stealth.

Goddamn, any Cujo within earshot's gonna be lured here.

Hairspray bottles and perfumes covered the vanity top. She wiped her dusty mirror clear and looked at herself. Oh, how she longed to let her jet-black hair down and get into civilian clothes. Six months without cosmetics? Did she even remember how to put it on?

She spied a bottle of Brad's cologne. *Cool Water.* She'd spray it on her own clothes back then, so she could take his scent with her everywhere.

I know I'm gonna cry once this hits my nose. Fuck it. She'd spray her entire bedroom and refresh this special place. She'd kill whatever rotten stench hung here, too.

Then, before she could spray one droplet, Teddie busted in and broke the spell.

Oh my God. This asshole!

She felt almost violated, having him here in her bedroom, in this moment.

Teddie chuckled. "My, oh, my. These are real sweet. Bet ya looked hot as hell with these coverin' that sweet ass."

Her heart thumped against her ribs liked a caged gorilla. Her hands shook and she set the bottle down. Rhonda stood but didn't turn around, staring at Teddie in the mirror. He stood a few feet behind her, twirling a pair of her panties on his M4's barrel with a disgusting grin on his face.

"You play hard to get, girl. You're just teasing me with these undies." Teddie kept his eyes fixed on her G-string. "Your old boyfriend must've really—"

Rhonda spun around and silenced him with a hard, open-palmed slap to his face.

Teddie dropped his gun and grabbed his cheek. His eyes watered and he gasped at her with an expression of pained shock.

Good.

"You fucking creep. Don't you *ever* touch my things, harass me, and never, *ever* talk about my fiancé again." She turned back to her vanity and pocketed Brad's bottle of cologne. "I swear to God I'll put a round in your dome and leave you here."

Rhonda began to exit her bedroom when a bright flash of light exploded in her head. Stars and pain bloomed. She fell into her vanity with a loud bang, catching herself before her face hit the furniture. She blinked and her eyes found Teddie's predatory reflection in her mirror. He snarled and stood behind her with his gun raised and the folding stock level to the back of her skull.

Creep hit me. Knew better than to trust—

Again, he slammed the stock into her skull.

"High-falutin' cock tease. How about I leave you here with one in your dome?"

Teddie's second bash to her head made a bright

27

flash go to black. She blinked away the black. Her sight wavered. Somehow she remained on her feet. She heard the crackle of their radios and Sarge's voice yapping away, asking where they were. And goddamn it, Teddie ignored Sarge's questions. Teddie only laughed. Then she heard him dump his gun before both of his hands squeezed around her throat from behind.

No...

His rank breath, hot on her neck. His repulsive, wet tongue molested her right ear.

"Slap me? Diss me? Gonna leave me here, bitch? I don't think so." Teddie panted hard and fast. "I've never killed a living person before, but it's a whole new world now, ain't it?" He laughed. "*You're* gonna be the one left here when I'm done. No one's gonna look for ya. Maybe dear old Dad, but he won't find shit when I leave you for the Cujos."

She cried out when Teddie released her throat and yanked her head back by her hair. All of her strength vanished. Her eyes winked with pain. It was so difficult to focus. Mirrored reflections came and went. She caught Teddie in snapshot blinks. He looked crazy. She cringed. And how he howled when he undid her pants and pulled them down. How could she have let her guard down? She imagined Dad would say her situation was one she could've predicted. It was almost laughable. Hang out with a predator and prepare to be preyed upon.

So this was it? She had no doubt he'd kill her... after he finished. Goddamn, just two firm whacks to her head had stolen every molecule of fight in her, rendering her defenseless and weak. Her legs stayed strong and she remained standing and stared into the mirror. She looked at herself and Teddie as he held her head up by her hair.

Did she just see something? She blinked again and again and caught reflected movement behind Teddy. Through blurring vision she watched the hanging outfits in her closet *move*. Was she seeing things?

A ghost-white arm appeared from between her blouses and dresses. Another disembodied arm reached out from the closet, connected to a longhaired Cujo in tattered clothes.

Oh, Jesus.

It walked with a slow, ungraceful stride toward Teddie.

"Gonna show you things, whore." Teddie was frenzied. He cursed and spit on her, but Rhonda only cared about the thing moving toward Teddie.

I'm going to die here.

Rhonda began to pass out. Teddie's hands throttled her throat again. He choked her tighter. Then his hands were off her. She fell forward into the vanity as she heard Teddie scream. Rhonda's head hung as she gulped in air. She heard a violent struggle behind her... sounds of Teddie's feet kicking fiercely as he was dragged away, his shrill screams never pausing.

Escape. That was her first thought amidst a mix of confusion adrenalized panic. She quickly pulled her pants up as Teddie's screams quieted to liquid gurgles.

Holy shit.

Her awareness returned, albeit no less foggy. Her former partner lay on his back. Somehow his camo pants had pulled down to his knees during the fracas. His legs kicked in spastic death jerks while the Cujo ripped out chunks of Teddie's throat and windpipe

29

with ravenous ferocity. Aghast and relieved, she watched as it performed mouth-to-mouth, sans resuscitation. It consumed Teddie's lips and tongue.

Blood erupted into the Cujo's face and spread across the bedroom carpet. *I'll never get that out*, Rhonda thought, absently. Faintness hit her again. She stumbled into her soft bed.

Rhonda collapsed on her mattress. Things didn't look any better. The Cujo rose and set its undead gaze on her. Its bloody face fearsome. A threatening hiss issued from its crimson maw. It walked toward her, step by shaky zombie step.

Why couldn't she scream? Goddamn, her head pounded like a hateful bitch.

The undead terror loomed above her. Its hair hung in a long and dirty mop, its dead eyes dyed milky-white. Yet, behind the blood and gore-plastered mask, she knew that face.

Wait a minute...

"Brad?" She spoke with great effort and slipped into darkness.

Chapter Four

Rhonda roused minutes later and found undead Brad above her. She screamed with surprise. She straightened in bed, suddenly no longer weak or disoriented. All pain in her head departed as fear and shock seized her.

Brad stood motionless, staring at her with eyes clouded with white. She refused to understand. *Why doesn't he blink? Why doesn't his chest move?*

Brad's head cocked to his right. His crypt eyes stayed on her.

Even in her terror, her heart spread. *Poor baby.* His skin was cadaver-pale, his hair and fingernails filthy and long. His face and clothes were dirty, covered with bloodstains and god-knew-what. He no longer looked like the Levendale high-school hunk who'd taken her to senior prom, nor the man who'd proposed two years later.

So, Brad had turned Cujo along with everyone else. She'd wanted better for him—she'd allowed herself to hope for something like eternal death and peace—yet here he stood. Was this his destiny, to return from the grave just to stare at her?

He still hadn't moved. Gradually, her adrenaline waned and her breathing slowed. Staring into his lifeless eyes, she felt almost... safe?

"Brad? Can you hear me?" She mustered a gentle tone. "It's me, baby. It's Rhonda."

Brad's head cocked to his left and his brows pinched together. Rhonda studied him. Did electricity exist in his undead brain? Did something arc there, reawakening synapses and reanimating dead memories?

Brad's open mouth released a soft moan-hiss. He reached out with his right index finger and pointed at her.

"That's right, baby. Rhonda. Your fiancé."

Did he recognize her? His finger still pointed at her, surely a deliberate motor action and not some random reflex. It had to be, right? Brad's arm dropped to his side. His slack features shifted in a slow-motion movement and it looked as if he wanted to say something.

"Rrrrnnndaahh."

"Yeah, that's my name. I'm *your* Rhonda."

She scooted across the mattress and eased off the bed. *Careful and cautious now.* He turned and followed her with his ever-open and dreary eyes, but took no other action. Rhonda steadied to her feet. She moved slowly and walked around Brad to grab her M4 from the vanity top.

Brad hissed. Did he identify her gun as a bad thing? He sure didn't seem to like it. He advanced toward her and she aimed the barrel away, toward the ceiling. How could she ever shoot him? Fear and heartbreak set in. Her limbs trembled as Brad reached her. He stopped inches from her. She held her breath. Christ, he smelled God-awful.

"Brad. Baby. Please don't make me shoot you." Tears came. No, she couldn't handle this. In her heart, she accepted Brad's death for months. Why'd she have to come here and find him Cujo-fied in their old house? Dad had told her not to...

Brad reached out with his right hand again. Rhonda death-gripped her M4, prepared to fire point-blank into his rotten noggin. His cold hand touched her cheek. She flinched.

Oh, Brad.

His touch set off a stream of hot, heavy tears she couldn't contain. Those hands, they once set her on fire.

Brad moaned and drooled and gave her a cadaveric smile. He garbled something.

Did he just say, Love you? Damn, if she didn't want to believe it. "I love you, too, baby."

She closed her eyes. What had she wished for so many times? To be with her man again? Yes, anything for that. How often she'd longed to return to his arms, to smell him one last time, to tell him she loved him.

Now here, in their bedroom, Brad's touch returned to her.

I'm still in love. Dead or not.

Her wishes, albeit imperfectly, had been granted, and she found herself grateful. Fuck it if he'd turned Cujo. This moment was better than nothing, was more than most people got. Here, in this room, they had each other. She had more than just her memories...

Rhonda blinked and sighed. *I'm a selfish bitch.* Damn it all, he must be miserable as a Cujo. Who in the hell wanted to be walking undead, feeding on other human beings? Was Brad in torment right now? Craving release from a necro-purgatory, and looking to her to end it?

God, I'm confused.

A crackle from her two-way radio interrupted her thoughts. Teddie's radio also crackled from the floor. Brad withdrew his hand and his features slackened. Sarge's unhappy voice sounded from the radios. "Driscoll and Fitch. I'm sick of asking for you both. Time's up! Everyone's at the chopper. Goddamn it, where you at?"

Rhonda was surprised Sarge hadn't left already. She looked at Brad and put her right index finger to her lips. Christ, like was gonna say anything. *Duh.* "On the North Side, Sarge."

"You got anyone? Supplies?"

"Ummm... negative on all that."

"Fitch, you got anything to add or cat got your Goddamn tongue?"

Teddie's tongue was definitely gone, but no Goddamn cat had it. "Fitch's dead, Sarge. Group of Cujos jumped us. They got him."

A pause. "Can we recover the Private's body?"

Rhonda stared at Fitch's mutilated corpse. He was unrecognizable. Nothing but meaty clumps in a puddle of blood between the bottom of his nose and collarbone. She swallowed acid. "Negative, Sarge. I'm afraid he was ripped to pieces. There's nothing left."

Sounds of heavy gunfire filled the radio. After a few seconds, Sarge returned. "Driscoll, your ass is grass and my foot's the lawnmower! I'm gonna skedaddle. You're already late!"

"Sorry, sir! Don't leave!"

"MOVE!"

Rhonda moved quickly. *Brad baby.* Her brain went on autopilot. She couldn't leave him. She had to find a way to bring him back with her. Somehow. What did she need? Clothes for sure. Hairspray would help.

"Brad?" She spoke as calmly as she could. "Be good for me, 'kay?"

God, he reeked. He embodied physical filth. She held her breath while she put him into a Cult concert T-shirt and black shorts. He moved and moaned. "Stay still, dammit."

She applied generous amounts of hairspray to his blonde feral locks, then combed and slicked his long hair into an obscene pompadour.

She used a stray blouse to wipe blood and drool from his mug. Brad snarled.

"Watch it, buddy." She didn't back off until she cleaned his entire face as best she could. What could she do about his eyes? Where were those damn aviators? She dug around and found a pair of chrome sunglasses with mirrored lenses.

Right on.

She placed the sunglasses over his ghoulish peepers. Precious minutes had passed and she knew she was in for a good ass-chewing by Sarge. She needed to hustle or be left behind, but she wanted just a couple other items she knew were inside the shoebox of adult toys they kept under the bed. She pulled it out and retrieved a red gagball and a pair of handcuffs covered in dark red and fluffy fur.

"Sorry, baby, gotta do this." Rhonda forced Brad's arms together, in front of him, and cuffed his wrists.

Brad hissed once before his features relaxed. Rhonda worked the gagball into Brad's rank mouth. "I'm so sorry."

Gosh, he looked so sad. Reluctantly, she shoved the ball behind his teeth with great care and fastened the gag straps around his head, muzzling him.

"Okay, babe?"

Brad didn't answer.

"Right." She frowned at her creation; Brad's slick new hairdo, his summer wear and aviators, restrained by a gagball and furry handcuffs. In another time, she would've found this scenario hilarious, but she didn't feel it here. No, she only felt pity for him. Her poor, live-undead lover.

This is so fucking nuts. How am I gonna get away with this?

She checked her ammo and M4. One last thing. She covered Teddie's body with a sheet. "Stay dead, creep."

With her M4 out front, she led Brad to the first floor. He offered no resistance and placidly followed her outside.

What would Sarge, Colonel Daddy Driscoll, and everyone else at good 'ol Camp Deadnut say or do when she arrived with blighted Brad? Who ever said Sarge would even let them on the chopper? She was bringing them a zombie in a gagball and fuzzy handcuffs, after all.

God help me.

Chapter Five

Rhonda winced. Goddamnit, if Teddie Fitch wasn't the gift that just kept on giving. Sudden, sharp aches coursed through her head.

Shake it off, lady. Gotta move.

She worked her way back to the chopper, block after block, and Brad followed her every step. No need to pull or push him along. He kept up like an obedient dog.

Good Cujo.

Brad stayed back, not moving, when she finished off aggressive, animated dead with her M4. There were a few she dispatched with her Ka-Bar knife, and another few she kicked away with surprising force.

None of this was good. It seemed the crowd of Cujos had grown since her platoon had landed. No doubt the Cujo-zombie bastards were drawn to machine gun fire around town. For sure, the thundering motors of the Black Hawk didn't help keep the soldiers on the down-low. Cujos, she learned, were attracted to noise and bright lights.

Her heart rate and adrenaline rushed as she blasted away.

On the move, she approached Main Street from a side avenue. Black Hawk rotors sounded nearby, along with heavy-duty salvo from the chopper's M60D 7.62mm machine guns. A new war indeed. She envisioned waves of Cujos at the chopper.

But how would she get through? Constant chopper racket mixed with machine gun screams and other sounds of Cujo chaos. She bit her bottom lip. This was the type of shit where a person could quickly become a casualty of friendly fire.

With a vise-grip on her M4, she leaned against the corner of a bookstore and squeezed her eyes shut.

Gotta calm down.

She yelled into her two-way radio. "Driscoll here. I'm coming to you from the North Side. I have a civilian with me. Repeat. Rhonda Driscoll here. I'm approaching from Levendale's North Side. I'm coming to the chopper from Main Street."

Sarge's voice barked through the radio. "You said you had no survivors. What gives?"

"Found him on the way." Rhonda didn't want to lie, but she sure as hell wasn't going to come clean about her visit to the old Driscoll-Savini love-shack. Nor recant her lie about Teddie's bloody death. No, she'd keep that shit to herself. "I'm coming in. Don't shoot me."

"Hurry the hell up, Driscoll! We'll cover you."

"C'mon, lover. We gotta move." Rhonda grabbed Brad by his cuffed wrists. Through crowds of Cujos, she

shot, stabbed, and kicked her way through to the Black
Hawk. She hadn't fought this many Cujos on her own
before, but she cut them down, and to her surprise, she
did so unscathed. The cover from the M144 armament
subsystem's relentless barrage helped.

Rhonda pushed Brad forward and helpful hands
pulled them both inside. She buckled Brad in and then
herself as the Black Hawk lifted high from Levendale.

Sarge sat across from Rhonda and glared.
"Driscoll! What the fuck is *that*?"

Rhonda found herself suddenly lost for words.
What had she done?

"Why does this civilian have a goddamn *gagball*
in his mouth?"

Jesus Christ, her face felt hotter than hell. Had all
her blood rushed to her head? It sure felt like it.
Sudden self-consciousness rattled her. Through this
whole crazy plan, the last thing she'd expected was to
feel *mortified*.

Sarge's face contorted into an expression of
contempt. "And what's with the hairy handcuffs?"

"It's Brad, sir. My fiancé. I found him in town
and I'm bringing him back to Fort Rocky. He's,
ummm... a Cujo, Sarge."

Sarge released a string of obscenities furious
enough to make a jailbird blush. A few people in her
platoon jumped at her news and they aimed their guns
at her and Brad. Someone cried out, "Awww, hell no!"

"Easy, everyone." Rhonda raised her hands,
open-palmed, in a gesture of surrender. "Please. Relax
and lower your weapons. He's harmless. Really."

Sarge leaned forward. "You're insane. I'll throw
loverboy out of this chopper right fucking now."

Sarge planted the tip of his M4 barrel on the shiny gagball and slid it up to Brad's nose.

"Wait." Rhonda reached out to Sarge. "Please. Don't hurt him. Look, I've got Brad secured. He's got a seatbelt on. No one's gonna get hurt."

Sarge just stared at her. He didn't speak or lower his automatic rifle.

Rhonda swallowed. "Hell, I hate the undead as much as any of you. But this is different, Sarge. This is personal. I'm begging you, just let me get Brad to Doc. Please... just this one time."

"I never point a weapon at anything I don't intend to shoot." Sarge's fierce eyes burrowed into Rhonda, flicked to Brad and returned to her. "Goddammit, if this ain't a clusterfuck!" He pulled his M4 away.

Rhonda offered a smile to Sarge and her platoon. They all shook their heads at her. "Thanks, Sarge. I really—"

"Save it, Driscoll." Sarge's tone grew harder. "I'm letting it slide against every instinct of my Marine ass. But the Colonel ain't gonna be happy 'bout this. He's the boss. You're outta my hands now."

"Okay." Rhonda sat back in her seat and glanced out the side door. Camp Deadnut revealed itself in the distance. Her father's command-post looked tiny. Rhonda spoke, but didn't look at Sarge. "No disrespect, sir, but I'll handle the Colonel."

Chapter Six

Sarge radioed Fort Rocky's command post. "Platoon dropping in minutes. Confirmation of one casualty. Private Fitch. Killed and eaten in Levendale. Soldier's remains and dog-tags MIA. We got a Cujo on board."

Oh, this was great. No doubt, before she stepped off the chopper, every Deadnut would know that she'd dragged her Cujo-fied fiancé back to base.

Rhonda's father waited outside the helicopter pad. Two officers stood at attention behind him. She watched Doc Brightmore run up with clipboard in hand. She liked old Doc. Everyone did. But goddamn, she wasn't looking forward to a face-off with Dad.

Rhonda's platoon departed. Every bona fide and civilian-recruited soldier saluted Colonel Driscoll on exit. Rhonda watched Sarge brief her father. Sarge turned and glowered at her. *Yikes.* She blinked and bit her bottom lip as he walked away.

Colonel Driscoll stood straight; hands behind

him, his camouflage uniform neat and crisp, combat boots spotless. His usual commanding pose, Rhonda thought. He sure looked pissed. Dad's face was a mixture of unhappiness and disappointment as he looked upon her and Brad.

Dad launched into her like a mortar. "Rhonda. Just what in the name of Sam Peckinpah d'ya think you're doing?"

"Bringing Brad back to Doc."

"I didn't give you authorization to bring a Cujo back to Deadnut."

"No. But I didn't plan this, Dad. It's Brad."

"I don't care if it was your mother, God rest her soul. You acted with insanely reckless behavior with this horseshit you pulled. Bringing infection into the base. A goddamned Cujo. What were you thinking?"

Her hands began to shake. "I don't know. Maybe I was thinking this world is screwed. This is a half-assed military base, Dad. Fort Rocky's surrounded by Cujos just outside the fence. It's all up for grabs. Everything. You think anyone else is out there operating like us? Have you seen any other soldiers, people or planes? Have you received any communication? No. It's been six months and we seem to be the only people alive. Pretty soon, being civilized with procedures won't mean shit."

Colonel Driscoll's words snapped loud and made her jump. "Watch the attitude. Everything you're saying doesn't explain your selfish and crazy behavior. It's not about authority, being civilized, or anything else. It's about common sense. What happened to Teddie Fitch? He was with you and now he's dead and not to be seen again. And you brought a Cujo boyfriend back here." He adjusted his hat. "You mindlessly endangered everyone here. You violated our sanctuary."

"I wasn't trying to violate anything, Dad. I didn't mean to... look, it's *Brad*, Dad. I muzzled him and kept him safe from everyone. Maybe we can do something." Rhonda watched Doc Brightmore join them. Doc saluted and looked anxious. She knew she was reaching. "Dad, let Doc work on Brad."

"You know I have some good ideas on pacifying Cujos, Colonel." Doc sifted through papers and diagrams on his clipboard. "I think I'm onto something."

"You're onto horseshit." Colonel Driscoll aimed his authoritative voice and attention at Doc. "You can't fix a monster. It's a waste of time and resources. Not to mention it's goddamn dangerous to everyone here."

"Colonel, I'm thinking, maybe if I can give these lively cadavers a proper lobotomy, then—"

"*You* need a lobotomy." Colonel Driscoll jabbed a finger at Doc's face. "We found you over in Dulcimer, hiding inside an OBGYN clinic. You're a gynecologist, Doc, not a brain surgeon. I'd have better luck opening heads with a bullet. Lead lobotomies. Now that'll get results."

Rhonda watched Sarge shaking his head and looking absolutely disgusted.

Doc tugged his thin, gray hair and scratched his head. "This world needs a chance to get right again. I want to help."

"I know you do, Doc, but I've humored you enough with your half-assed delusions of messing with animated corpses." Colonel Driscoll frowned at Rhonda. He shook his head and looked at Brad with an expression of pure disdain. "Christ, he looks like zombie-Elvis in bondage. I must be as reckless as you for not blasting Brad to hell right here and now. Go. Take your 'lively cadaver' of a fiancé to the infirmary. Doc can play with him. But I already know nothing miraculous is going to happen. Loverboy's gonna serve as our new target at the firing range sooner than later."

Asshole.

She could punch him in the face. Not a good idea, though. Time to simmer, for Brad's sake. Gynecologist or not, maybe Doc could make a breakthrough. She hoped. "Okay, Dad. I'll help Doc and keep Brad out of everyone's hair."

The Colonel frowned. "Just remember, this is very temporary, baby-girl. You got more important things to do than playin' house-nurse to a Cujo, fiancé or no. Carry on."

Rhonda watched her Dad turn and leave with his officers. He didn't salute. His words echoed in her head, and in her empty stomach and heart.

Doc put a gentle hand on her shoulder. He smiled. "Let's see what we can do."

Rhonda cast a glance toward Camp Deadnut's large and razor-wired fence. She heard numerous Cujos on the other side; their cemetery moans rode on the fall wind. She shivered. An orange October sun made long and haunting shadows. Afternoon would be night soon.

Chapter Seven

Inside Camp Deadnut's hospital, Rhonda and Doc sat Brad down. His mouth remained gagged and his hands restrained in fuzzy sex-cuffs. He maintained his primitive forms of affection toward her. She wondered if he'd ever snap back into typical zombie-mode. Maybe he didn't actually want to hurt anyone. Back at their townhouse, she thought he was only trying to protect her. Still, she was troubled that Cujo-fied Brad killed and ate people. She'd give anything to have her old Brad back.

Doc examined Rhonda. He tended to lumps on her head and to sore spots on her body: everywhere Teddie Fitch had nailed her with his gun-stock and fists.

Rhonda eyed a large, gray hospital safe against a wall. She knew Doc kept pharmaceutical drugs locked in there. Only Doc could manage and distribute prescriptions. Some of Rhonda's fellow Deadnuts had substance abuse problems even before the world went to shit. Doc kept everyone straight. He opened the safe and passed her a Vicodin.

"Thanks." Rhonda swallowed her pill with a mouthful of bottled water. "Rough day."

"Fell down stairs you say?" Doc narrowed his skeptical gaze.

"Yeah. I'm lucky. Coulda been worse." Rhonda gave Doc a half-smile. She doubted he bought her bullshit.

Doc patted her hand. "That should help ease the pain a bit. I'm gonna lock up the stash and get your boy a fresh gown before I examine him."

"I can get Brad cleaned up and ready for you."

Doc nodded and walked into an adjoining hospital room. Rhonda removed Brad's Cult T-shirt and black shorts and gave him a sponge bath. She held her breath. He stunk like a dead woodchuck in high summer, but his body appeared well-preserved.

She sponged Brad from his hairspray-shellacked head to his crusty toes. What to do about his fucked up hair?

"Good to go?" Doc Brightmore returned, a fresh hospital gown in his hands, open and ready for Brad.

"Yeah. Cleaned him best I could."

Rhonda scanned Brad's body. He smelled a little better. She removed his cuffs, but left the gagball in his mouth. She couldn't take the chance. He didn't struggle.

Good boy.

She and Doc dressed Brad in his gown, gently lifting his heavy limbs.

Doc motioned. "We'll strap him to this bed."

"What's the plan, Doc?" Rhonda guided Brad to the brightly lit operating area, where Doc helped strap him down.

"I'm going to examine Brad. I'm still learning what Necro-Rabies does. I'm hopeful it can be cured."

"If you wanna know what this virus does, just pick my dad's brain, pun intended. The Colonel knows the military made it."

"Been down that road. He acknowledged the source of it all—the military as you say—but doesn't know a cure, obviously. He said if he did, we'd be curing them all now. The Colonel only knows what we all do; the virus makes people rabid and undead and extremely aggressive."

Rhonda sighed. She held mixed emotions about it all. For months she hadn't given a damn about Doc's crazy Cujo cure. She wanted them all nuked. Now, with her Cujo-fied fiancé in her care, she wanted him saved. Sure, her reasons were selfish. Anyone else in her position would want the same, right? "You think there's any hope here?"

Doc shrugged. "I'm not sure. I've been a physician in the field of female health for my entire career. My expertise in female reproductive systems is one thing, acting as an impromptu brain digger is a whole 'nother deal. I might be the only doctor left in the world. And one working on the walking dead, to boot. I'm sure as hell gonna try my best."

"What's your theory on what makes the dead walk? I mean, normal rabies certainly doesn't reanimate dead people."

"No, rabies doesn't make anything undead. Necro-Rabies works like a regular rabies virus. Rabies travels to the brain by following the peripheral nerves. When infection reaches the central nervous system, symptoms begin to show. Normal rabies infection is usually fatal within days. It's a neurotropic virus."

"Neurotropic?"

"It's a virus capable of infecting nerve cells. By avoiding the bloodstream, neuroinvasive viruses like rabies evade the usual immune response and dig themselves deep into the host body's nervous system. Like normal rabies, Necro-Rabies is prevalent in the nerves and saliva of a symptomatic Cujo. The route of infection starts with a bite. Getting bit by a Cujo can turn you into one."

"Or if you actually ingest the saliva, right?"

"Not necessarily. You might risk something if you ingest Necro-saliva, but I really think it's a bite that does the direct damage. If you're bitten, you're screwed. Of course, then you may not have to worry about getting infected at all because you're being eaten alive."

"Why don't they eat each other?"

"No idea. They seem to like fresh blood and some type of 'undead appetite' compels them to eat live human flesh."

Rhonda looked at Brad strapped helplessly to the bed. He sure didn't seem to be hostile like every other Cujo she encountered. "Necro-Rabies kicks up Cujo's violent nature, huh? That's why they attack like wild dogs."

Doc nodded. "Like rabid animals, infected Cujos are exceptionally aggressive. They attack without provocation and exhibit uncharacteristic behavior."

Rhonda remembered enraged Cujos charging straight into gunfire and flamethrowers. No matter what you threw at them, they never stopped until their heads were destroyed.

She could see Doc was entering lecture mode.

"The name *rabies* is Latin. It means 'madness.'

Or the word, *raberes*, which means 'to rage.' Same stuff." Doc adjusted his glasses. "Typical symptoms of rabies are violent movements and uncontrolled excitement. The primary cause of death from rabies is respiratory insufficiency. But, of course, Cujos don't breathe. Death from normal rabies invariably results two to ten days after the first symptoms. The humans who've ever survived rabies were left with severe brain damage. Cujos don't drop dead because they're, in fact, already dead."

"That's so goddamn crazy. It's like we're living in a horror movie, but no one's yelling, '*cut!*'"

Doc smiled. "These folks don't suffer from rigor mortis, though. You're right. Embalming would certainly preserve human remains. But these corpses, these *Cujos*, they walk, and ever-so-slowly they rot."

"Wouldn't they eventually fall apart into nasty pieces until they were bone?"

"One would think so. I theorize the muscles, ligaments, and all tissues would disintegrate. Skeletons would lose all support. But we're already six months into this Necro-Rabies pandemic and I have yet to see a Cujo eroded to the point of collapse. The progress of decomposition seems to be nearly static."

Rhonda nodded. She'd been a part of this same subject discussion many times over six months. Why are they? How can they be dead and alive? Why aren't they totally rotting away like a normal corpse? Always the same questions, never any answers.

Doc looked grim. "Your father told me that Necro-Rabies was produced from a unique rabies culture that was synthesized into something they called a *reanimation agent*. This stuff was injected into dead rats at a military

49

lab—only a few miles from this base. Supposedly the NR was gonna be a 'battle drug' developed for warfare, supposedly used to reactivate fallen soldiers on the battlefield. Kinda like regaining health points in a video game. Evidently, the dead rat's lifeless brains jump-started and they attacked military scientists and everyone else in the labs. Everyone there contracted NR and died... and then came right back. Virus spread. About 10,000 of the little bastards broke loose, attacking and biting anything that moved; people, cats, dogs, you name it. From shrew to elephant. Necro-Rabid animals bit humans, and before you knew it, the world turned mad in mere days. Levendale was ground zero."

"I know. I've heard the same story for half a year now." Rhonda folded her arms. "Sorry. Didn't mean to sound rude. It's just... things are hopeless. Dad always said he thought we'd end up being in World War Three with North Korea instead of being at war with the undead."

"This is like the Black Death of our time. Vermin spreading Necro-Rabies aren't much different than black rats of yore on old merchant ships, spreading the plague throughout Old World Europe. Y'know?"

Rhonda shrugged. "I suck real bad at history, Doc."

"Well, it was one of the deadliest pandemics in human history. When all was said and done, it killed about 60 percent of Europe's population. Necro-Rabies has worked four times faster than the Black Death."

Jesus. She'd been so busy trying to survive, she'd never taken time to process the true magnitude of their situation until now. "We were just talking about hope a little while back. The more I hear you talk, the less hope I feel."

Doc Brightmore came around the bed and stood in front of her. He set a tender hand on Rhonda's shoulder. "The Black Death fizzled out and this will too. Rabies always resulted in death until a vaccine was developed. The rabies vaccine was harvested from infected rabbits. Who knows? Maybe we'll find a scientist who might create something that cures an infected person who isn't too far gone. Bring some back from the dead. Maybe they'll make a gas that specifically wipes out all of the infected worldwide in one shot. Or maybe someone will make an Anti-Necro-Rabies vaccine for the living. But then, maybe I can stop wishing for things that'll never happen."

They both laughed. Rhonda asked, "Can't you come up with something?"

Doc frowned and shook his head. "I'm just a guy who went from cervixes and babies to Cujo study."

"Geez, Doc."

"And don't ignore your female health, dear." Doc smiled. "As for Cujos, if we can't reverse 'em back to normal or diffuse them, I only hope bacteria gnaws them to bones. Until then, I'll keep playing Doctor Frankenstein."

"Why'd you mention lobotomies earlier to my dad?"

"It's just an idea. Honestly, I'm bored as hell here and need to at least try something with my time. No one else is. Ultimately, I'd like to disable some of the circuitry in the gray matter. Hoping to make 'em docile."

Rhonda frowned at her poor fiancé, helpless and strapped to the bed. Gagged, drool flowing down his chin. What if his original personality could be resurrected? She didn't want to chance losing it. She

51

turned to Doc Brightmore. "Do me a favor, don't cut into Brad until we talk about it. I wanna help him. I wanna help you, too. It's just... I don't wanna lose any more of him than I already have. Don't rewire him until it's absolutely a last resort. Y'know what I mean?"

Doc nodded. "Don't worry. I'm just doing an examination. I'm taking notes and will see if I can't get an MRI and some scans done. If I want to try anything else, I'll consult you first. Okay?"

"Thanks, Doc." She hugged him and stepped away. "I'm gonna cruise back to the barracks and crash. I'm tired and hurting. I'll meet you in the chow-hall for breakfast. We'll talk progress then."

"What's on the morning menu?"

"Pancakes, I think."

"Really? I just might be first in line." Doc smiled. He looked at Brad and returned his bright gaze to Rhonda. "He's in good hands. We'll see you tomorrow."

Rhonda felt a pang. Brad, poor thing, all alone for months in a cold, dead world. She wished she could offer him some kind of comfort. Something more than her tears. She moved toward Brad's face and Doc raised his hands in a cautionary gesture. But seeing her expression, he stopped and didn't say anything as she leaned in and kissed Brad's forehead. "I love you baby. Be good."

Brad rolled his dead-white eyes in slow circles. "Rrrrnnndaahh."

"That's right, baby. That's my name." She stood, eyes stinging. She blinked and looked at Doc. "See, he remembers."

Doc nodded. "Yes. There's something there."

Rhonda wiped her eyes. "First thing tomorrow."

"Breakfast at eight. I'll be there."

Rhonda grabbed her things and walked toward her barracks. She longed for her bed. She wanted this hell of a day behind her. She replayed the day's crazy events in her mind. Brad had returned to her life in the most fucked up way. What would tomorrow bring? She thought of that. She also reflected on Teddie Fitch and Dad and the rest of the inhabitants of Camp Deadnut. She rolled over and knew she'd never rest.

Chapter Eight

Rhonda awoke to the blare of her alarm clock at 0800. She hated military time and disliked the concept of "early to bed, early to rise." She'd meant to get up over an hour ago to get her morning workout in but had clearly smacked her snooze button again and again in her sleep.

"Shit. Doc's waiting." She didn't want to miss Doc or breakfast. At Camp Deadnut, breakfast, lunch, and dinner waited for no one.

After Rhonda had collapsed in bed, she'd been kept awake by a barrage of thoughts, and only drifted off just after two in the morning. Awake now, she nixed a shower. Instead, she tied her hair into a ponytail, brushed her teeth and slipped into military garb. She checked her Ka-Bar knife, .45 automatic sidearm, M4, and six, 30-round magazines and lit out for the chow hall. She and everyone at Fort Rocky were required to remain armed at all times. The world turned, a blue marble full of chaos and billions of Cujos. Countless walking-rabid-dead waited outside Camp Deadnut's reinforced walls.

Rhonda entered the chow hall, dozens of soldiers and other Deadnuts filing in with her. The clatter from busy dinnerware echoed through the huge hall.

Wow. Sad to think this place once hosted thousands of hungry soldiers. Now only hundreds of survivors ate here. She frowned. She walked to the far end and entered the kitchen through large, double-swing doors.

Smells of bacon and fresh coffee and the chatter and bustle of a busy kitchen filled Rhonda's senses.

It smells like the normal world.

Rhonda paused as everyone sat bowed in prayer while the Marine Chaplain, Jimmy Johnson, said grace and blessed everyone at Fort Rocky. After Chaplain Johnson finished, Rhonda walked among tables. Where was Doc?

Some of her fellow Deadnutians greeted Rhonda with smiles while others looked at her with wary stares. Of course Brad's arrival would have made folks worry, and those same worrywarts might be concerned about her state of mind. No doubt her fellow Deadnuts had been discussing Colonel Driscoll's daughter and her undead fiancé all night. It made for hot new gossip, right? Water-cooler talk about the horror of it all, and good Lord, what'll happen next? Cujo cohabitation?

Fuck 'em. Nothing mattered, only Brad.

A voice called her name from somewhere in the chow hall and she ignored it. The voice called Rhonda again, closer, and she turned, surprised, as Chaplain Johnson stood near.

"Rhonda Driscoll. Good morning." Chaplain Johnson smiled at her with yellow teeth. "Can I have a word?"

What was it about the man? She could never put her finger on it. He sure looked like an upright military dude, with his gray flattop and Marine attire and Semper Fi expression in the jowls and eyes of his creased face. And he sounded like a priest when he opened his yap and kicked in with holy talk and impromptu prayers given to those who cared to listen both in and out of Camp Deadnut's chapel. But she always seemed to sense something else, something uneasy. An air of arrogance, perhaps? She couldn't place it, but it always rubbed her wrong.

"Sure Chaplain, but I'd sure like to eat soon."

"Lord, yes. The living need sustenance in these trying times." Chaplain Johnson produced a good-natured smile and gestured toward the far end of the chow hall. "Let's talk... over there in private. Just for a moment and then you can feed your hungry soul."

Freak.

Rhonda walked with Chaplain Johnson. When they stopped she folded her arms and gave him her best no-bullshit stare. A wariness jumped inside her. He seemed friendly enough, but in recent months, she'd seen him go off on a number of Deadnuts he deemed blasphemous, adulterous or corrupted. What would *he* have to say about Brad?

"What's up, Chaplain?"

"Your father. The Colonel." Chaplain Johnson started slowly, like he was searching for a lost piece of a planned spiel. He cleared his throat. "He asked me to talk with you about this *situation* with your fiancé, Brent."

"His name is *Brad.*" Fuck. Don't let him see you fret. *Simmer.* Chaplain Johnson was a priest after all, right? Part of her felt this demanded a pinch of respect in these dark days. Maybe Chaplain Johnson was the only priest left in the whole wide and rabid world.

"Brad, right."

"Go ahead."

"God's putting us through Revelation as we speak. This disease that's taken over the world, it's part of His plan. He's already taken the chosen souls to Heaven and left behind soulless husks on the Earth for the Devil to play with."

"This isn't the Rapture or whatever."

"Oh, it is. It's all about the End Days now." Chaplain Johnson's voice raised and spittle cleared his yellowed teeth. He looked around and quieted his tone. "We're living Biblical prophecies right now."

Rhonda retained little from Sunday school. Anything holy or specific to organized religious beliefs didn't interest her. She kept her own version of faith in her heart. Mom and Dad made her and her younger sister go to church every Sunday. Good 'ol Colonel Driscoll had wanted God and the American Way constant in the Driscoll family's lives.

What a joke.

"If this is the End Days, or some Rapture, then why the *hell* are we still here?" A laugh bubbled up and threatened to snort out. She held her breath for a second. "Y'know, most folks here are God-fearing and you're a priest, so we should all be called home if what you say is true."

"Well... "

Well, fucking what? She almost asked. Good 'ol Chaplain Johnson didn't seem to have a reply.

57

Chaplain Johnson again cleared his throat. "True, many of us are servants to Christ, and we're still here and haven't been called home. It's part of the Lord's plan. It's—"

"Save it." Rhonda found it difficult to corral her irritation. "I don't have time for a church sermon right now. I'm hungry."

"Wait." Chaplain Johnson's voice firmed with urgency. "Your father personally wanted me to talk to you about the impious road you're going down with your zombie fiancé."

"What's that supposed to mean?"

"Rhonda, look. You brought your undead fiancé back here. A Cujo. Sweet Jesus. You think that witch doctor Brightmore is going to make Brad a living man again? That's a misguided hope of a most sinful variety. Your father's worried about it and so am I. It sends the wrong message to everyone here. This gives people hope for something that'll never be. Soon other folks'll want to find their zombie kin and lovers. In the eyes of God, it's not natural or holy."

"You're starting to piss me off. Irreverence intended."

"I implore you. Listen to what we're saying." Chaplain Johnson spread his arms out, palms open. "Brad's long gone. He's with God. There's your Rapture... his soul is in heaven and that thing you love is an evil shell. What you've got locked up in that hospital is nothing more than a walking unmentionable, totally devoid of spirit and filled with evil. The real Brad's gone. You've got nothing more than a rotting cannibal with no soul. He must be destroyed. All of them must be."

Rhonda ground her teeth hard. What would happen if she punched the priest in his fucking nose? Would she get locked in the hole? Would she go straight to hell? Chaplain Johnson was talking blessed smack about the love of her life. Cujo or not, she refused to allow anyone—even a priest—to trash her man.

Soulless? Bullshit. Brad Savini was her soulmate for eternity, and she'd scream it from Johnson's precious chapel pews. She gave a hazardous stare and lifted her clenched fists. Chaplain Johnson looked startled and stepped away from her.

Rhonda was about to give Chaplain Johnson explicit instructions on where to stick his holy opinions when the main doors of the chow hall opened and the noisy chatter died. She turned to see her father enter the hall, flanked by a few officers in front and behind him. Several soldiers at picnic tables stood and saluted, while the civilians or those who no longer gave a shit remained seated and stuffed their faces.

Colonel Driscoll stopped and locked eyes with his daughter. His gaze flicked to Chaplain Johnson before he frowned at both of them. Rhonda glared back, drilled her stare into him like an invisible ray of unhealthy resentment. Her father turned away and took a seat at an officer's picnic table.

Rhonda pointed a finger in Chaplain Johnson's face. "Don't ever tell me how to live my life or what to do with Brad. Got it? I love him and I'm gonna do everything in my power to save him. I'll be with him for as long as we live. I don't give a good goddamn what you, the Colonel or your Lord has to say about it. Now get outta my way."

"Uhhh." Chaplain Johnson's mouth opened and closed like a startled guppy. He didn't budge until Rhonda moved away to find Doc.

The nerve of these assholes.

Her head throbbed. Here she was waiting for flapjacks while her fiancé lay alone and scared, strapped to a bed in a desolate military operating room.

She finally reached the picnic table where Doc Brightmore sat alone before an empty plate. Damn, he looked frazzled. His hair was wild and unkempt and his lab coat soiled. "Doc, you look beat up. Want some coffee? Pancakes?"

Doc looked at her with tired eyes. His lids dropped and when he spoke, he seemed drained. "I have to talk to you, Rhonda. I came by to give you some news."

Doc's demeanor alarmed her. What had happened to Brad?

Doc glanced over his shoulder before turning back to whisper to her. "The Colonel and Sarge and some soldiers came to see me before sunup. They roused me from bed and escorted me to the operating room."

Uh oh. Her blood pounded in her temples. If they had hurt one long hair on Brad's head...

"They asked me questions about your fiancé. I explained that I was evaluating Brad. Just taking pictures and notes. I hoped to rewire him or explore another avenue that might yield better results." Doc looked over his shoulder again. "The Colonel ordered me to stop everything. Now I'm supposed to quietly terminate Brad and give his corpse to a disposal crew by noon. I'm keeping my promise to you... consulting you before doing a thing. I'm telling you this in case you want to put Brad down yourself. Sorry."

Rhonda bit her lip until she tasted blood. She looked across the chow hall. There was Dad, joking with his officers. How nice, the fucker laughed and fed his Marine mug without a care in the world.

Chaplain Johnson walked by and whispered in Colonel Driscoll's ear before he sat next to him. Dad scanned the chow hall and found Rhonda's eyes. He frowned and shook his head, then returned his attention to men around him.

Fucking schmuck.

Her father had always begrudged Brad and their engagement. Bad enough he had already threatened to hurt Brad, but now, Dad planned to murder her fiancé behind her back.

When he said Brad's stay was temporary, he wasn't kidding.

No one's disposing of Brad. Not while *she* breathed. Brad might be Cujo-fied, but he remained her fiancé. She'd be damned if she'd allow anyone to terminate him.

Simmer. Just simmer.

She held her breath and counted to ten. She admired her engagement ring and allowed her heart rate to slow. She looked to a large clock with a US Marine crest on its face. Damn. Was it almost 9:30? High noon was coming. She knew she needed to work quickly. Her window of opportunity was rapidly narrowing.

She spoke evenly. "Doc. I'll be slipping out the back door. Meet me in the hospital in 30 minutes."

"What exactly are you thinking? Putting him

down?" Doc acted agitated. "If it's something else, I don't need to tell you that we're under constant military watch here, and no one's going to let either of us off the hook if you do something stupid with Cujo-Brad. You can't save him unless you can sweet talk the Colonel, and he doesn't strike me as a man who listens to anyone."

Rhonda licked blood from her lip. "Just meet me in that goddamn hospital."

Chapter Nine

Rhonda hustled through the kitchen and made haste toward the underground storeroom. Opening the storeroom door, she hurriedly flicked on half a dozen light switches before jumping to the bottom of the stairs. Taking a quick visual inventory, she pulled two empty banana boxes from the floor. She filled the first box with nearby provisions; deli meats, coffee, various canned soups, rice and beans, sugar, bread and peanut butter, and several mega-bars of milk chocolate. She entered a frosty fridge and grabbed a case of Heineken along with several cans of Diet Coke and a fifth of Jack Daniels, and placed them in the other box.

She carried the stacked boxes upstairs and out of the storeroom. Good thing she had stuck to some kind of workout routine. No way she'd ever be able to lug all this food and drink in one run otherwise.

Rhonda breathed hard. Sweat ran from her pits to her ankles. She safety-checked the hallway and fast walked to the back door. Exiting, she stashed her boxes near a dumpster and moved on.

She jogged to her barracks, grabbed a duffel bag and filled it with her meager belongings. From the barracks, she made for a military garage wedged between two maintenance buildings.

There sat Fort Rocky's fleet of Humvees, parked in five neat rows of three on a parking pad beside the garage. She could see .50-Cal machine guns and MK-19 Automatic Grenade Launchers, paired together atop of each Humvee. She knew every heavy weapon came armed and max-loaded with ammunition; a mandatory rule. She hoped the Humvees held full tanks of gas.

Rhonda memorized a six-digit number painted on the hood of the first Humvee in the front row: #006969.

She slowed her pace and neared the garage. Okay, just *act casual*. Someone had left the large overhead door of the garage wide open. "Hello?" Rhonda yelled inside but no one answered. Was everyone still at breakfast? She hoped so.

Rhonda entered and walked to the mechanics' office. Sure enough, there she found a small locker bolted to a wall. She opened it and grabbed a set of Humvee keys with a laminated tag printed with numbers: 006969.

With a growing sense of urgency, Rhonda performed a dummy-check around the office and garage. God forbid she missed something important. She found nothing of interest and slipped outside to the parking pad.

The Humvee started right up. Rhonda checked the gas gauge and adjusted the mirrors and seat to suit her. She noted a two-way radio, and a car stereo built into the dash. Out of habit, she turned the radio on, and as expected, found no active radio stations. She pushed the CD button and AC/DC hammered out, *For Those About To Rock, We Salute You.* This put a smile on her face. She silently thanked the unknown Marine who'd left the CD. Thanks to the rock gods, she wasn't stuck with a Disney soundtrack or something worse.

Rhonda drove behind the chow hall and loaded the boxes of provisions into the Humvee. Next stop, Fort Rocky Hospital.

She expected to raise eyebrows. Shit, she never drove Humvees anywhere except for around the inside of the base to pick up and drop off people and supplies. Plus, no other vehicles were moving on base right now except for maybe a perimeter guard.

She glanced at the clock on the dash. 10:15 already? An hour had somehow blown by. Damn it all, she had to get Brad before anyone else did.

She parked in front of Camp Deadnut's hospital and spotted many of her co-inhabitants in the distance. To her relief, no one seemed to be paying attention to her or the Humvee. Soldiers and civilian Deadnuts walked and talked amongst themselves, oblivious.

Rhonda walked past the reception area and found Doc Brightmore on his way, leading Brad by his elbow toward the front door. Brad was back in his Cult T-shirt and black shorts. Doc must've changed him. Brad remained placidly gagged and cuffed.

She looked straight into her fiancé's dead eyes. His brows arched. Did he recognize her? She grabbed Brad's arm gently and turned to Doc. "Did you have any trouble getting him dressed and cuffing him?"

Doc shook his head. "No. I kept the handcuff

keys you gave me and slipped them right on. Surprisingly enough, all he did was hiss. No problem. Every Cujo I've ever encountered has been highly aggressive. Brad's amazingly docile, though I wouldn't trust him right now without that gag."

"Yeah." Rhonda thought about the bloody job Brad had done on Teddie Fitch. "Muzzles and safety first. Let's hustle."

"What's the plan?" Doc helped Rhonda walk Brad along with brisk steps.

"I've got a Humvee. I'm going to get off base and get him away from here."

Doc looked alarmed. "You'll never make it. The world's crawling with Cujos. They'll eat you alive. I've seen mobs of 'em roll trucks over just to get to folks inside. The odds of escaping on open terrain are very bad."

"I know. I'm really fucking nervous. And I'm out of my mind about what I'm pulling here." An uneasy laugh slipped from her lips. "But I've handled plenty of Cujos in my time."

Doc Brightmore gave Rhonda a quizzical look. "You've had only months to fight Cujos—and you did so alongside other people with heavy weapons. You're not Rambo. And I'm not your dad. So... go do whatever. I didn't expect you to take the insane route when I gave you that head's up about your dad's plans for Brad. So if you don't mind, I'd just as soon play ignorant and not know you did this."

Rhonda walked Brad to the Humvee and buckled him into a backseat while Doc stood a few yards away looking around nervously. "Thanks, Doc. I really appreciate your help." Rhonda walked up and pecked his cheek. "I hope you're gonna be okay after I'm outta here."

"Me, too." Doc smiled at Rhonda and maintained cover. "Be safe. For the love of God be safe... and maybe think about what you're doing."

Rhonda shook her head. "I haven't been thinking straight for half a year. You take care of yourself."

Doc nodded and Rhonda drove toward the front gate. She glanced in her rear-view mirror and watched Doc disappear behind a building.

"Rrrrnnndaahh."

Rhonda's gaze flicked to Brad's face in her rear-view. He stared at her. "Yeah, baby. We're getting the hell outta this place. Or die trying."

She drove around the complex until she reached a service road she knew led to the front gate. She put her .45 in her lap and fingered the trigger.

Chapter Ten

Rhonda slowed the Humvee some 50 feet before Camp Deadnut's front gate—tall and super-reinforced like the rest of the high-impact, razor-wired security wall built to protect every square foot of the military base. No terrestrial vehicles and no one on foot, Cujo or otherwise, entered Camp Deadnut without clearance from soldiers who guarded this main entryway.

On either side of the inner gate, Rhonda spotted sheet-metal guard shacks with small mountains of sandbags stacked in front of them. She also noted the pair of high guard towers on either side of the inner gate. In each tower a sniper-lookout stood watch.

Before her, two identical soldiers with squarish, chiseled features in green MP helmets stood armed to their buzzed ears with automatic assault rifles. They gestured for her to halt with their raised palms. She stopped and gripped the steering wheel with nervous excitement. Damn, she needed to pee.

To Rhonda's right, a soldier in camo stood with his rifle slung over his field jacket. The twin soldier to her left approached, his gloved right hand gripped on his rifle. What the hell was she going to tell these guys? She found herself fresh out of bullshit.

The soldier on her left tapped the glass on Rhonda's driver's side door. "Roll down your window."

"Morning." Rhonda smiled. This situation seemed familiar, kind of like all the times the North Carolina State Troopers pulled her over. Lucky her, she'd escaped every speed stop with only warnings, thanks perhaps, to her gift of gab and pretty eyes. Now, she wasn't sure she'd get away with anything. "How are ya?"

"Fine."

Okay then.

The soldier before her looked like pure business. Rhonda recognized his face but his name eluded her. Goddamn, she was terrible with names.

"License and registration." The soldier extended his hand through Rhonda's open window.

"What?"

The soldier's granite-cut face cracked as he guffawed. "Gotcha! Hey, do I look like a cop?"

Rhonda jumped at his sudden change in attitude. Surprised, she felt her heart race and didn't know what to say. The soldier looked at his partner and they both chortled. Rhonda swallowed and managed to produce a chuckle. "Good one."

"I kill myself sometimes." He slapped the roof with a heavy hand. "Gotta have a sense of humor in these dark days. Know what I mean?"

"I hear ya."

"Seriously, though, where the hell d'ya think you're going?" His laughter died.

Rhonda swallowed. "I've got orders to check the perimeter. Doing a full circle around Deadnut."

"Sarge didn't say nothin' about it." The soldier pursed his lips and looked uncertain. "You got papers for this run?"

"No." *Papers? What fucking papers?* She tensed, struggling to untangle her vague memories of protocol. She grasped for something. *What did Sarge call Dad?* "This comes from the full-bird."

The soldier looked surprised. "The Colonel?"

"You got it."

He looked troubled. "Kinda strange the full-bird wouldn't send this through Sarge. Even stranger the Colonel would send a civvie to do this. Shit, even stranger you ain't doing it in a tank."

"Guess they want the right woman for the job." Rhonda flashed a bright smile. "No worries. I'm armed."

The soldier laughed and looked at his colleague. "Whaddya think, Cap?"

The other soldier shrugged.

The soldier nearest Rhonda returned her gaze before looking past her and into the backseat. Her heart went into overdrive.

Oh shit.

"Hey. Who the hell's that?" The soldier pointed, no doubt surprised to find her ghost-pale passenger.

"Him? Oh, just another Deadnut. He was ordered to assist me."

Here we go... just let it flow.

"Hmmm. He don't look too good." The soldier furrowed his brow. "His eyes look zombified. Dead."

"No. No, no, no." Rhonda generated a light laugh and tried to scrub the anxiety from her voice. Those freaking aviators. Where were they? Why hadn't she asked Doc about the goddamn mirrored sunglasses? Did this soldier know about a certain Cujo-zombie dropped into Camp Deadnut yesterday?

Her words gushed as she talked faster than she wanted to. "That's Brad. He's been up all night. That's why he looks like shit. Ha! Look, he's my boyfriend, okay? We do all kinds of drills together."

"Drills, huh?" He didn't keep his eyes off Brad. "What kinda drill involves him chewing on that rubber ball nonstop?"

"He's got an oral fixation." Rhonda blurted. Why did she have to say that? Oh, how she wanted to scream.

"Lucky you." The soldier stepped back from Rhonda's door. He didn't bat an eye. "I'm gonna call this in to Sarge. Not that I don't trust you, but this ain't procedure. Once I clear it, I'll—"

He stopped and looked at Rhonda. Had he read something on her face?

To her surprise, the soldier's scowl transformed into a friendly smile. "Wait a minute. You're the Colonel's daughter."

"Rrrrnnndaahh." Brad moaned through his rubber sphere.

"Yeah, Rhonda." The soldier nodded and laughed. "You cut hair for the troops a few times."

"That's me." Rhonda smiled.

Can I scream now? Maybe these guys hadn't heard the news about her bringing a Cujo back to base? *Please, please.*

"Why didn't you tell me?" The soldier straightened.

71

"Name's Fred. We'll get ya right out. We gotta check for undead hostiles outside before we give you a clean break. When you come back, radio first so we can watch for ya from the towers. We'll clear you in. Be goddamn careful out there, now. Those nasties'll do things to you that hell couldn't dream up."

"Yeah, I know it. I'm well-armed and ready to mow 'em down."

"Hold tight." Soldier Fred slapped the Humvee's roof and strolled back to his military partner.

Rhonda watched them talk. They gestured and nodded before parting to separate guard towers, stopping at each tower to shout to the soldiers above.

Her hands moistened. Nausea and increased nervousness washed over her. Time, precious time was running out. Surely, this charade would end here at the gate. If so, she figured they'd shoot first and ask questions later.

Brad made new, uneasy noises behind her. Maybe he knew their luck had pushed too far. Rhonda turned to put a trembling hand on his knee. "Don't worry, baby. We're getting outta here. Even if I gotta jump that fucking wall."

Brad didn't respond or blink. He just stared at her. If only she could be alone with him. A million miles from Camp Deadnut would be nice.

Sudden gunfire from sniper towers startled her. She jumped in her seat and stared out the windshield. Soldier Fred ran to her while his MP partner, Soldier Cap, opened a slot in the gate to peer outside.

Holy shit.

Rhonda watched Cujo arms punch through the open space at Soldier Cap's face. Soldier Cap jumped and recoiled before he rammed his machine-gun barrel through the slot and unloaded his magazine.

"We're clearing the gate for ya." Soldier Fred motioned toward the gate and the gunfire. He jacked a round into his rifle. "Our guys are sniping and Cap's blasting. This is kinda fun, to be honest. We get pretty bored out here. Wasting these Necro-fucks is a nice distraction."

Rhonda hoped Soldier Fred and his trigger-happy pals remained unwise to the "Necro-fuck" in her backseat. Funny how only yesterday she'd been ready to waste every Cujo she saw, just like them. Now she sat here trying to save her undead fiancé. Boy, she sure turned into a hypocrite, quick—and a selfish one, too.

"Give us a couple minutes. Once we signal, we're gonna open the gate. You gotta fly out like hell-hounds are on your ass." Soldier Fred puffed his chest out. "Run over anything in your way. Got that?"

Rhonda nodded. "You don't gotta tell me twice."

"One other piece of advice. I don't recommend you and your boy getting out of this Humvee for any hanky-panky. We lost a pilot that way. Flyboy thought he'd have a quickie with a civvie while on patrol in a department store. They set their guns down, started going at it, and got torn apart."

"We're staying in the vehicle, thanks. Just checking the perimeter for anything unusual."

"Yeahhh. Well, let's hope your boy's gagball stays put." Soldier Fred raised his eyebrows and snickered. "Anyways, don't forget to radio ahead so we can getcha back in clear."

"Thanks, Fred. I'll do that."

Soldier Fred quick-saluted with his index finger and jogged to the gate to join his buddies. He shoved his own rifle through the gate slot and fired auto bursts. Rhonda shifted into drive and crept forward. She checked her rear-view mirror for trouble. A few faces looked her way, perhaps their attention momentarily caught by the gunfire. But they soon turned away, uninterested in activity at the gate.

Nothing to see here.

Rhonda waited. Couldn't they clear the gate faster? Time moved slowly; the minutes seemed like hours. This was it. Whatever lucky horseshoe might be crammed in her ass was gone. By some providence, she had lifted a Humvee and food without any problem. But now, she felt she'd pushed things too far.

Rhonda drummed her fingers on the steering wheel. Finally, silence. She watched Soldier Cap run to an exterior electric box on the left-side guard shack. He pushed a button and the massive reinforced steel gate ahead slid sideways.

Soldier Fred turned toward her and yelled, "Get ready!"

The gate opened all the way. *It's now or never.* She revved the engine.

Soldier Fred nodded. "Be safe."

Rhonda winked. "Tell 'em I'm sorry for the trouble. 'Kay?"

"Huh?"

Rhonda accelerated and almost clipped Soldier Cap on her way out.

Whoops!

Adrenalized, she nailed three Cujos who crossed the gateway. They dropped under her wheels, sending nasty vibrations through the floor as their emaciated bodies broke and burst.

Faster, she raced down the short service road. This road, her link to freedom, connected Fort Rocky to a main highway.

"Christ!" She spotted muzzle flashes in her rear-view mirror and ducked. On second glance, she felt relief. The soldiers weren't shooting at her. More flashes and dozens of Cujos fell before the gate shut far behind her.

At the main highway, Rhonda turned left and hit another rotten Cujo. It exploded on the Humvee grill like a bag of bad tomatoes.

"Oh my God, that's fucking nasty." Rhonda turned the wipers on and drowned the glass with windshield fluid until every putrid bit washed away.

A billboard-sized wooden sign in the turf to her left declared:

Fort Rocky Military Base.
United States Proud. Marine Proud.
God Bless America.

"God bless America? There's no America. And God? Where the hell are you anyway?" Rhonda didn't expect God or anyone else, aside from Brad, would hear her.

"Rrrrrrrrr."

"Right here, baby." Rhonda looked in her rear-view and smiled at Brad. He looked safe, all buckled in, the drool-covered gag secure in his mouth.

She focused on the road ahead. What angry hornet's nest stirred inside Camp Deadnut right now? No doubt some pissed-off soldiers would want their pound of flesh. She hoped they wouldn't take it out of Doc's backside. And Dad? Yeah, he'd blow a gasket and a half when he found out what had happened back there.

Rhonda couldn't worry about it. Colonel Jerkwad had given her no choice.

Not today, Daddy.

On this apocalyptic planet, love was now as rare as fresh fruit. Whether Brad rolled as a warm-blooded hunk or a life-impaired dreamboat, none of it mattered. She would never quit on him.

The highway was an almost clutter-free route as she drove south. She encountered occasional Cujos and turned them into roadkill. She maneuvered around infrequent abandoned vehicles, but nothing slowed her progress.

What was she thinking? Dad and his Black Hawk helicopters and soldiers would cover a lot of ground fast. Shit, they'd find her if they knew what direction she went in. Maybe they'd think she was stupid enough to go back to Levendale. They wouldn't come for her right away... she hoped. She just needed time to formulate a concrete game plan, to keep Brad and herself safe—and hidden somewhere.

A scary, nightmarish world awaited her, and she didn't kid herself about it. No longer would an armed platoon have her back. No more Fort Rocky fortress to keep her safe at night. Damn, if she hadn't just dived head-first into a land of pure hell. Yeah, time to get serious about her future, real fast.

She glanced back at Brad in her rear-view. He gazed non-stop at her with an expression of dead innocence.

"Rrrrnnndaahh."

"I love you, baby." Rhonda felt giddy. "Y'know what? I think we just eloped."

Chapter Eleven

Rhonda passed a few towns and then spotted a sign for Levendale's city limits. She drove past it. Six months gone AND now she'd been near her old hometown twice in 48 hours. She cruised with slow and deliberate caution. Visions from yesterday's dangerous visit popped in her head.

What was Levendale's population, anyway? 20,000? A city infected with Necro-Rabies. She stayed on the highway and avoided downtown.

Her zebra print watch read 2:00. Only a few hours of daylight remained before she'd need to hit the headlights and find a place to sleep later. Day or night, she must always stay on guard, 24/7. Rhonda felt a cold tickle of fear. This new world creeped her out. Her thick skin chilled as she thought of driving into a midnight sea filled with the living dead.

Levendale looked like a haunted ghost town. Rhonda passed abandoned schools and playgrounds, all of which she'd grew up in and on, along with numerous and forsaken houses and cars along her route.

The world is dead.

As she drew closer to Levendale, the walking corpses grew more plentiful on the main road and moved through the streets she'd spied from her seat. Ghastly faces stared at her from sidewalks, yards and streets. In her rear-view mirror, Cujos chased her Humvee.

She bypassed Levendale and eased on to another country highway that would take her around the town and eventually to the Interstate. She didn't stop.

What about her short-and-long-term plans? She didn't want anyone from Fort Rocky to get her. Boy, was she sick of North Carolina. Of course, her plans all depended on fuel and electricity, and she hoped to find all the working pumps and gas she could fill along her way.

Florida. Florida sounded damn good.

Rhonda loved Florida. Naples and the Gulf of Mexico were in her heart since childhood. Her parents took her and her sister to Naples whenever her father was on leave, or during holidays and occasional spring breaks. Heat and a beach sounded super great right now—though she didn't rule out Cujos roaming in sun and surf.

Thoughts of her family tugged at her heart. She began to weep and shudder from memories. All the loss and the constant death surrounding her sometimes felt too much to bear. Doc told her one day that he was sure she suffered from PTSD thanks to the day her family, friends and Brad had all been decimated by Cujos. That, and being forced to fight in the front-lines against zombies every week for half a year rattled something in her brain. She didn't need Doc to tell her that. Sometimes she cried or screamed for no reason. Sometimes she felt indifferent to the world and consequences to herself or anyone else.

She loved her father. He was now her only living kin, and she hated what they'd become. Her deep resentment, their dysfunction, all created from spats about her fiancé—when he had been alive and now undead. Why did it have to be like this?

"Gotta get out of here." Rhonda wiped wetness from her eyes. "We're on a road trip. This honeymoon's just starting, love."

Rhonda wanted to reach over and touch Brad on his pale cheek. Instead, Rhonda turned on the CB radio. It came to life with crackles and her father's voice.

"... read?" Colonel Driscoll's disembodied voice said. "Repeat. Do you read me, Rhonda? Do you read? Rhonda, just say something. Over."

Rhonda's heart slam-danced. Dad was on the line? *Oh, shit.* She stared at the CB like it was a snake.

No doubt her lack of response worried her father even more. She imagined he'd put men on the two-way day and night in an effort to find her. She wanted to love him for that, yet still wanted to punch him.

She listened for a few minutes to her dad's non-stop requests for a reply before she finally relented and clicked over.

"Yeah?" She released a heavy sigh. "What d'ya want?"

"Where did you go? I've been worried to death about you. Over."

Yeah right. "You're not worried about me, Dad. I

heard about your plans for Brad and I wasn't gonna just wait around for you to turn my fiancé into a casualty."

He cleared his throat through the static. "Fiancé? This joke needs to stop. I get your love for Brad, okay? Hell, I loved your mother more than anything and woulda done almost anything to get her back. But let me be perfectly clear, I wouldn't think twice about neutralizing Mom if she came back as some *thing* from a horror flick."

"You don't get it."

"Oh, I get it plenty. *You* don't seem to get it, baby-girl. Brad's no different than a vegetable who got damaged in a car wreck... long gone with just a shell remaining. You gotta pull the plug. It's the humane thing to do. It ain't fair to Brad."

"He's not a vegetable, Dad. He smiles at me. He even tries saying my name. He's never attacked me. We're just running away to live happily ever after."

"You what? Hang on! You've gotta be fucking kidding me. You got a death-wish?"

"No, I've got a love-wish, Dad." Rhonda paused and thought how corny she sounded. "I was engaged and happy once. I was looking forward to growing old with Brad before your military brainiacs turned the world into a giant cemetery. That life was ruined. But now Brad's been given back to me, and I'm never lettin' him go."

Dad cleared his throat again and spoke with slow emphasis, as if speaking to a feeble-minded child. "He's a *Cujo*, Rhonda. Zombified as all get out. He's not even really alive. Might I add, he's lethal and full of Necro-Rabies. Whatever passive behavior he's exhibiting is temporary. You've seen it yourself. When his trigger's pulled, he won't hesitate to rip your pretty blue eyes out with his teeth."

"Let me worry about that. I've been with Brad for days now and I'm pretty confident he's more teddy bear than terror."

"You need help, baby-girl. A lotta folks have experienced traumatic stress with this apocalyptic clusterfuck. Plus, being holed up at Fort Rocky most of the time couldn't have done you any mental favors."

She thought of the PTSD diagnosis Doc had given her. She didn't want to think of herself as damaged as she probably had become. "I'm a lot saner than the entire group of bumbling civilians and soldiers you've got under your watch."

"You're sure not acting sane. For Christ's sakes, the next thing I know, you'll tell me you slept with a dead man."

"You think I'm so cuckoo that I'd get into necrophilia, Dad?" She looked over at Brad, and though she still adored him to the moon and back, the thought of fucking him had never occurred to her, and the idea suddenly made her sick. "I don't need you to get *this*."

Colonel Driscoll's voice took on an impatient timbre. "I want you to get back here and I want you to get some help."

"Help? I don't remember a shrink being in residence at Camp Deadnut." Rhonda now remembered Doc Brightmore. "You gonna have Doc counsel me?"

"Not so soon. He's locked up right now. You know I can't tolerate that kind of subordination."

Guilt smothered her. "I made him help me. He's innocent."

"That's not the report I got." Colonel Driscoll cleared his throat. "When you get back here, and after I get you some help, you're gonna have to answer for the theft of a US military vehicle. I've taught you better than this. Rhonda, you're deficient on pure common sense."

"And you're lacking in the Dad Department." Again she thought of how corny her argument sounded.

He paused for a long moment. Rhonda heard only static from the radio and the soft drone of the Humvee's engine. When he returned, his voice was firm. "Marines don't give up and Driscolls never give up. If your mother was here she'd put a boot up your ass."

"She's not here, though, is she?" Rhonda felt the urge to start bawling again. She mourned her mother and also wanted to sob from the urge to hurl hurtful words at her father. It felt as if her heart existed only to be ripped out and kicked again and again. She composed herself. "Sorry, Dad. Call me crazy, but I'm holding on to the one last thing in this hell that makes me happy. Brad and I are goin' away."

"You stay put. I'm comin' to fetch you." Colonel Driscoll's voice grew louder through the CB. "You need some major straightening out and you need to get away from that goddamn Cujo."

Rhonda flushed with anger. She put her lips to the microphone. "Fetch this, Dad: *FUCK OFF!*"

If Colonel Driscoll responded, she didn't hear him. She turned the two-way off and glanced back at Brad. "Sorry about that, baby. I'm sick of his bullshit, y'know?"

Brad didn't respond, though he twisted his lips and presented a crooked grin.

Rhonda turned in her seat. She looked through the windshield and gripped the steering wheel until her knuckles turned white. Why'd he have to be such a fucking asshole? Why couldn't he see how much Brad meant to her?

The AC/DC CD began to replay as a Cujo-fied mailman stepped in front of her, a soiled mailbag hanging from its emaciated neck. Peeling skin and hair hung off its scalp in nasty strips. Its skull-like face contained a pair of yellow eyes. Its nose and bottom jaw were gone, and a long, leathery tongue drooped to its chest like an obscene tie.

She stomped on the gas pedal. At point-of-contact, she braked hard and sent the undead mailman airborne. It flew and smashed into the road in front of her. Its mailbag exploded on impact, sending numerous pieces of junk mail and grubby letters into the street. The Cujo pushed up and rose on its arms, pulling its broken body across blacktop toward her Humvee. It came on, its tongue dragging across the pavement, its ghoulish eyes set on Rhonda.

"You picked the wrong time to cross my path, dude." Rhonda glared from behind her wheel, her anger fresh and hot. The Cujo crawled and disappeared somewhere below her bumper. Her steering wheel felt breakable in her rigid grip. Everywhere she looked, something ruined this godforsaken world for her. No, she couldn't leave fast enough. The Cujo remained out of sight, but she heard it bustling somewhere under the Humvee. "This is what you get for delivering mail on Sundays."

Rhonda hit the gas and felt the Cujo crunch under one of her wheels. She reversed then drove forward and reversed again, and again, until nothing but a bloody smear and a gore-stained postal uniform painted the pavement.

Relaxation set in. She felt calm and satisfied.

Rhonda drove on and a new peace filled her. She welcomed it like a special guest. Highways and states unfolded ahead in her mind's eye. The road was telling her what she already knew... it was time to get on with her life.

Chapter Twelve

An hour later, with many miles behind her, Rhonda found herself cruising on the same empty country road. She would've preferred to be on a large highway, but it couldn't be avoided—this was the best route to the Interstate. No other cars or people appeared. Dead brush and tall weeds grew beside and in the cracked blacktop.

Rhonda had driven this old road to the coast before. She and Brad had often taken long weekends in Kitty Hawk and Nags Head, and the Outer Banks that one time. Myrtle Beach, too. These memories in her head and heart filled her with tender nostalgia and melancholy, knowing she'd never have those moments again.

But I have Brad again, don't I?

Her Humvee didn't have navigation or even a lousy state map in the glovebox, but Rhonda knew she didn't need either. She knew she'd run into Interstate 95, and once she hit it, she'd take it straight to Florida. I-95, she recalled, passed through more states than any other

Interstate highway. Hell, she could travel the whole Eastern Seaboard on one unbroken stretch of road.

Rhonda glanced at Brad in her rear-view mirror. He had remained quiet and sat stock-still since they'd left Levendale. He hadn't said her name even once. From his seat, he'd maintained a perpetual gaze out his window and watched the countryside pass by without a blink.

What mental transmissions occurred in his head? What thoughts could a Cujo have? Something must be happening inside their squalid circuit boards. Cujo motion, like normal human activity, called for some dynamic, operational brain processes in order to function, right? Nothing in this world made sense to her anymore.

Hot blood, she knew, didn't flow through their veins. The precious fluid just sat there, like noxious oil inside their veins. Cujos didn't breathe and their stomachs and intestines remained inactive organs, like their dead heart and lungs.

If Cujos somehow digested the flesh they ate, she didn't want to know about it. And she didn't want to think about Brad being one of those things. A frown formed on her face and she held her breath in reflex.

"Gross."

The interruption of her own voice did nothing to pause the all-new high-resolution cerebral proofs on display behind her eyes. What would Brad excrete if he took a zombie dump? The thought made bile rise in Rhonda's throat and she swallowed hot sandpaper. Why the hell couldn't she hypnotize herself and avoid these types of make-believe scenarios?

Rhonda's eyes and thoughts lingered on Brad. With her focus off the road, and with her thoughts consumed with Cujos, her mind and reflexes didn't process the big thing in front of her. She didn't have time to brake or identify the dark shape that flashed in her peripheral vision for only a millisecond before impact.

She hit the Hereford bull at 80 miles per hour. She screamed and squeezed her eyes shut as her ungoverned and armored Humvee T-boned a 2000-plus-pound wall of beef.

Rhonda's eyes opened just in time to see the body break and burst under force. The bull sailed upward, and flipped into and over the Humvee. Its horned head hit her bullet-resistant windshield with considerable force and webbed the high-tech polycarbonate with dozens of spider web-like cracks.

Rhonda bounced hard off the steering wheel and was slammed into her seat. The Humvee careened out-of-control. Her high-tech vehicle didn't have anti-lock brakes. She couldn't slow down at this speed, and she screamed as her Humvee flew off the road and nose-dived into a steep ditch. Her seatbelt damn near ripped her to pieces and cut into her waist and upper torso but the restraints kept her from eating the steering column when the Humvee came to a brutal halt.

Rhonda didn't move. She sat, she quivered, and tried not to freak. An insistent car horn blare sounded as her achy forehead rested on the center of the steering wheel. Thankful for her seatbelt, Rhonda cursed the military for lack of airbags.

She heard Brad hissing loudly from the backseat while the horn wailed and hard rock blasted her ears. Her heart jackhammered and she thought, yes, she might've pissed herself.

"Christ. A cow? A goddamn cow?"

Her words disappeared under the loud horn and

music. The blaring horn stopped as she straightened in her seat. She silenced the stereo. With shaky hands, she shifted to park and let the engine run. Through her windshield and past the hood, she saw tall ditch weeds.

"Fuuuuck."

Oh, God. Brad.

She removed her seatbelt and turned around to check him. Thank the gods, he looked fine and remained buckled in his seat. He looked at her with wide Cujo eyes and seemed to ask, *now what?*

"I really did it this time." Rhonda's voice trembled. She felt sick.

She left the Humvee to get some air and assess her predicament. She also needed to see the bull. If the poor animal lived, she'd shoot it.

She slammed her driver's door shut behind her and scaled the muddy slope of the ditch to worn county blacktop above. Holy shit, the Humvee certainly hadn't escaped the collision unscathed. The massive bull had not only fucked up her windshield, but its carcass had torn off the entire weapons platform, the .50-Cal machine gun and MK-19 Automatic Grenade Launcher, the whole goddamn thing. So much for the weapons accessory being USA tough. Bull one, Humvee zero.

Rhonda turned. Behind her, she saw large and small hunks of metal scattered across the county road.

Hunks of the *bull* also littered a stretch of asphalt. A hundred feet of fresh blood glistened over the centerline, legs and internal organs strewn along the way. She spied the rest of the carcass balled in a truncated heap off to the side of the road. It looked like Godzilla had chewed and spit out the Hereford.

Rhonda felt horrible. The whole stupid accident could've been avoided. In this new and dangerous world, she knew better than to daydream.

Unhappy with herself, Rhonda looked away from the roadkill and spotted other red and white Hereford cows grazing in a field farther up the road. They appeared normal and rabies-free. She caught a whiff of old manure and liked it.

Among properties near the fields, Rhonda took in buildings and grain silos of a forlorn dairy farm with a long gravel driveway. Everything felt Halloween-ish in October's incandescent glow that covered the countryside. She turned and looked behind her. She thought it was a gorgeous rural scene. Nice and tranquil... before Cujos ruined it for her.

She counted ten. Most ambled with a slow gait, like handicapped horrors, but a few, to her dismay, moved at a faster speed and were sprinting quickly toward her. Panic punched her gut when Cujos reached the field's far edge and disappeared into the corn. The rabid and rotten bastards were moving somewhere in the unharvested crop between the road and farm. Well, if she didn't piss herself before, she was about to now.

She whirled at sounds of mooing from startled cows behind her. The herd scattered and ran across a field and into the county road. Sonofabitch, six new Cujos from the neighbor farm across the way were making haste toward her.

On instinct, Rhonda reached for her M4 and her sidearm, but she carried no weapons. "Shit!" She'd left her firearms on the passenger seat and she doubted they were still there since the accident.

Not my day.

She ran and jumped into the ditch. Cold mud covered her boots and she grabbed her driver's side door handle. Locked. She swore and ran to the passenger door. It wouldn't open. Brad was out of his seatbelt and crawled around inside. He stopped and stared at her with milky eyes and without expression.

"Open the door, babe." Rhonda jabbed her finger at the driver's side door and desperately hoped he understood. "The door."

Brad put a white palm to the window and offered a crooked Cujo smile, but made no effort to unlock anything.

"Shit! Shit! Shit!"

Rhonda ran around and frantically tried all other doors. To her alarm, they were all locked. She realized she'd left her keys in the ignition with the Humvee running when she went to survey the accident. Did Brad hit something and lock all the doors? Perhaps her collision with the bull and impact with the ditch caused some internal glitch with the doors. She knew she didn't have time to speculate. Corpses in motion emerged from the cornfield before her and from the road above.

She clambered onto the Humvee's hood, and damn near slipped off when her muddy boots didn't bite. She fell forward onto her knees and hit hard with a metallic bang. She pushed her pain somewhere else and sprang from her sore knees.

With feet firm on the Humvee, she used her right foot and kicked the windshield with all the power she possessed. It wouldn't give, of course. She might as well have kicked a brick wall. All she wanted to do was bust through and get behind the wheel. Again, entry denied. Though the glass layers of the laminated windshield had shattered into countless bits from the impact of the bull's head, the high-strength plastic contained every piece of broken glass and refused to yield to anything else.

Cujos from both farms filled the ditch and approached her Humvee. Rhonda hysterically scrambled onto the roof. Maybe she could crawl through the roof hatch where the weapons platform had been. But again, the day was out to fuck her. The thick steel now bent over the hatch like a giant beer-tab.

She stared in angry awe, amazed at how sheer Herford mass had managed to twist armor and tear off the entire weapons platform.

Damn cow's worse than an IED.

From where she stood on the angled roof, she surveyed the nearby farms and the wide countryside beyond the deep ditch. Ten Cujos circled her Humvee, hissing and eyeballing her with milky orbs full of ill intent while six other Cujos helped themselves to the fresh roadkill several yards away. Engrossed in consuming bull pieces on the road and the mangled Hereford carcass, they didn't seem particularly interested in this little chick in distress.

Then she did a double-take. What was that one doing?

No... Really? That's just wrong.

She watched a Cujo crawl into the gape of the bull's cleaved belly and disappear deep inside, somewhere behind the bull's chest cavity. For a second, she glimpsed the Cujo's dirty ankles, exposed in late afternoon sunshine before they followed their owner and slipped inside the beefy carcass.

Rhonda blinked her eyes away and flicked her gaze to the .50 caliber machine gun lying in the middle of the road like a discarded piece of scrap metal, just a few yards from where carnivorous corpses fed. She might be able to make the distance and get her hands on the weapon—if she moved fast enough.

The Cujos around the Humvee grew agitated, straining and swiping their clawed hands at her. One particularly nasty fellow's putrid shirt emblazoned: LIFE'S TOO SHORT TO EAT STORE BOUGHT MEAT.

If there's redneck zombies, it's these guys.

These undead neither confirmed or denied the accusations. But two Cujos near the front of the Humvee managed to scramble onto the hood. They found their balance and came at her. Rhonda turned, and in one fast motion, she kicked and her boots connected with the Cujos and sent them tumbling into tall grass near the grounded Humvee's grill.

She slipped again, pin wheeling her arms before catching herself, and stood firm.

Fuck it.

With a running start she jumped off the Humvee, only to land a foot shy of the shoulder. She kissed gravel. But with one more step, she made pavement—and began running as fast as she could.

She heard hisses from behind her, but didn't look back. She imagined rural Cujos from the ditch in hot pursuit. The .50-Cal rested a few yards ahead. However, now the Cujos at the roadside bull-buffet had taken notice of the commotion and were headed her way.

The .50-Cal was on its side, a lengthy piece of ammo belt hanging from the feed chamber, disconnected from ammunition cans. A long piece of intestine also dangled from the gun like a huge fleshy hose. Rhonda ignored the guts. Only the couple hundred belted rounds mattered to her.

Rhonda kicked aside a blood-spattered and dented ammunition can and lifted the machine-gun by its grips. It was heavier than she anticipated. She'd only fired these kinds of guns mounted before.

With the large gun finally in her hands, Rhonda faced a dilemma. First, she needed to dispatch 16 Cujos. Yeah, right. Second, the .50-Cal didn't have a stock or a traditional trigger. She couldn't aim the gun or shoot from her hip since both butterfly triggers were placed at the far end of the gun. How would she do it? She required a fucking base, some kind of support to give her a platform to fire from. In the middle of this country road, she didn't see anything to help her.

All around her, Cujos drew near.

Rhonda cried out. On fear and adrenaline, she used all the power she could muster and spun herself counter-clockwise, dragging the gun barrel and bullet-belt with her. The Cujos were closing in. She spun harder and faster. Finally she built up enough momentum and the heavy gun rose up to her waist. While she rotated, she depressed both butterfly triggers and force-fed bullets to every Cujo around her.

A few Cujos in closest proximity Rhonda first took the solid machine-gun barrel to their bashed and putrefied faces before losing their entire heads to point-blank shots.

Rhonda whipped her hefty .50-Cal around. It screamed and pummeled her with insane recoil. Her teeth clenched. Was she going to break under the stress and strain of it all? It felt like it. Cujos blurred as she spun and blasted away. Cujo heads exploded and disappeared in reddish-black puffs of flesh and bone. Undead bodies blew in half and backwards with basketball-sized holes in their bodies.

In seconds, Rhonda wasted a dozen Cujos and burned most of her bullets. She slowed and stopped, her body tottering with dizziness. Her ears now rang worse than ever. She dropped the .50-Cal to the pavement and bent over to catch her breath. With hands on her knees, Rhonda looked ahead where three Cujos approached her. Her eyes flicked to a fourth and last Cujo, rolling in a large pile of Hereford offal, oblivious to recent gunfire and liquidation of its brethren. Rhonda noted one of the Cujos, a middle-aged woman in a worn-out blue dress, didn't have arms. Blackish-red fluid oozed from ragged stumps at its shoulders. It didn't appear bothered by this and came at Rhonda with intense, white-washed eyes and black teeth.

Far across the blacktop, and behind these road Cujos, Rhonda noticed movement. She watched as the gorging Cujo finally emerged from the remains of the Hereford. Rhonda's mouth dropped with disgust. It backed out of a huge red hole somewhere between the bull's sinewy, visible ribs and the animal's road-ravaged rump to birth into the open like a repugnant breech-baby.

It rose and stood next to the dead bull, and Rhonda wished she could teleport the fuck out of there. From scalp to heel, red shiny bowel-goo covered the Cujo, matting its sparse hair and soaking through its already tainted rags. It chewed on something gruesome.

The Cujo was holding something bloody. Was that a hunk of beef in its hands? It was oddly shaped.

Then the creepy bastard spotted her. Its rotted mouth opened to hiss angrily, dropping half-chewed chunks of Hereford meat to the road.

I've gotta bad feeling about this fucker.

While the other three Cujos in the road turned and looked at their loud, gore-slicked friend, Rhonda picked up her .50-Cal and walked backwards toward her Humvee. Her gun scratched a white line in the road as she retreated, her eyes focused on the Cujos.

The bull-birthed Cujo hissed louder and began speed-walked toward Rhonda, clutching its meaty prize.

Rhonda turned and jumped off the shoulder. She dug her boots into the grade and used the ditch and road edge as a level vantage point to shoot from. She rested the machine gun barrel on a disconnected Cujo head and coordinated her axis of motion. Leveraged and prepared to fire, she glanced at her bullet-belt: maybe a dozen rounds remained.

Gotta make 'em count.

The last four Cujos came at her and she fired the .50-Cal with deliberate care. The decapitated Cujo head absorbed the recoil and stayed in place. Every shot hit.

Her next target was the carnage-covered Cujo quickly closing in on her. But when she squeezed both triggers, Rhonda realized—*too late*—that her undead mark held something catastrophic. In a nanosecond, the late day exploded into a burning sun.

The Cujo hadn't been holding chunk of meat at all. No, the fucker clutched a gore-plastered, 48 round can of primary ammunition for the MK-19 Automatic Grenade Launcher. About 50 pounds of grenades were packed in the ammo can, and Rhonda shot it.

Sarge had taught her how the immediate impact from MK's high explosive, dual-purpose M430 grenades would kill anyone within five meters; and wound everyone else within a radius of 15 meters.

She didn't need to be Stephen-freaking-Hawking to know anything within 45 feet of a detonated M430 grenade got fucked. Part of all civilian and soldier "post-Necro-Rabies defense training" at Camp Deadnut involved use of an MK-19 launcher on decrepit Army tanks. Rhonda had personally witnessed a lone M430 grenade rip through two inches of rolled homogenous armor.

Her bullet hit the grenade-box dead-center.

A roar of white light swallowed the day's end. The Cujo corpses in the road blasted into charred atoms. All of this Rhonda caught in a flash of time before she ducked her head and the mountain of hot energy propelled her into the bottom of the ditch.

Am I alive?

Rhonda opened her eyes and found herself on her backside, next to the Humvee's ass end. The vehicle idled. She groaned. Her head pounded and her ears rang painfully. Her dad had always said she'd get tinnitus from all the hard rock she jammed on. She'd be lucky to even hear music again after this.

She shakily rose to her feet and a blanket of dirt fell off her. The late afternoon sun hung low like a footnote in the sky. She shook dirt from her hair and patted debris from her clothes. Brad remained safe and quiet in his backseat. He fixed her with his constant zombie-gaze. If only she could read his thoughts.

Rhonda climbed the steep ditch to the road above.

Her body felt wrecked and her head hummed. She

drew a deep breath and tried to calm herself. How many lives did she have left now? Not many, she figured. She must have some kind of luck to be alive. Hell, she had avoided pure incineration. Not to mention shrapnel from the massive detonation could've cut her to bits.

Christ, she didn't feel good. She couldn't smell manure in the air anymore. Everything smelled burnt. The air itself smelled cooked.

This is what war must smell like.

Rhonda gazed at a smoky crater, spread out from the county road and into the ditches on both sides. Every last Cujo and chunk of bull, along with a large section of road, had vaporized into micro-particles. What if she had remained on the pavement, closer to the grenade-carrying Cujo? No doubt, if she'd been a little closer, she'd be fertilizer for bygone cornfields by now.

"Someone get me the fuck outta here already."

She turned from the scorched earth and walked back to the Humvee, drained and exhausted like never before. She hurt. Every muscle throbbed in pain when she leaned and once again heaved the .50-Cal machine gun from the ground. She wasn't sure it ranked as her favorite weapon-of-choice anymore. Sure, she knew this mean motherfucker saved her tush, but what an absolute bitch to handle without a tripod. Nonetheless, she had one last mission for it.

Rhonda remembered a tidbit of trivia Sarge had taught her, relevant to strengths and breaking points of bulletproof glass. Bulletproof glass was manufactured as a glass/polycarbonate laminate combo, a high-strength plastic similar to airplane windows.

But if multiple bullets hit a compromised area, they'd punch right through. She was banking on it.

The bulletproof glass on her driver's side window was rated resistant to 7.62mm AK-47 rounds, but she knew damn well it wouldn't stop a black-tipped, armor-piercing .50 caliber bullet.

Rhonda faced Brad. "Hold your balls and cover your ears, baby. This is gonna be loud."

With a grunt, she lifted her .50-Cal and pressed the barrel against her drivers-side window. With gun grips firm in each hand, her fingers hovered above each butterfly trigger.

She eyed the barrel position and made sure it aimed straight through her window with a clear shot through the front passenger window-glass, hoping she didn't do something stupid like shoot through seats or the dashboard, only to have those rounds continue into the engine block or tranny.

With her gun aimed straight, she turned her face away, squeezed her eyes shut, and fired. The .50-Cal jacked in her hands. She let off the triggers as the gun barrel pushed through open air and into her Humvee. She yanked the .50 out and dropped it. Both driver's and passenger side windows obliterated to tiny chips. She reached her hand through her glassless door and unlocked it.

"Meaner than a Slim-Jim. Huh, baby?"

Far beyond tired, she'd kill a platoon of Cujos for a hot shower and a soft bed right about now.

She sucked it up and climbed gingerly behind the wheel. She needed to get the Humvee out of this ditch if she ever hoped to make Florida. She shifted into drive and reversed, going forward and back again and again to build traction. Dad had taught her how to do this when they got stuck in a winter storm while driving to Washington D.C. a few years back.

I kinda wish he was here.

An hour later and into nightfall, she finally freed her vehicle. Too tired to celebrate, she continued on her journey, this time more slowly, the frigid night air from windowless doors biting at her mile after tortuous mile.

Chapter Thirteen

Sometime in the night, she hit I-95 South. Later, she crossed into South Carolina. I-95 was smooth, only the occasional wrecked car and the dead—both walking and not.

Nothing interrupted her journey. She kept her speed down.

Rhonda forced herself to drive through the dark night, her visibility handicapped by the shattered and blood-splashed windshield. To her displeasure, she found her windshield wipers had been torn off in the crash, leaving her with no way to wash away the blood. though she knew wipers and wiper fluid wouldn't help her see any better anyway through countless, crisscrossed bits of broken glass.

She continued into the Palmetto State during the night and found safe shelter in a Motel 6 somewhere south of Timmonsville. Rhonda locked herself and Brad in a room with two twin beds. She tucked Brad into bed and then sat in the other bed with her bag of booty. She pulled out some of the goods stolen from Camp Deadnut and made a ham and peanut butter sandwich and sucked down a warm Heineken and a shot of Jack. Then she plummeted into deep and troubled slumber.

Bright images of Brad filled her REM sleep. In her dreams, he was normal and un-Cujo-fied, dressed in his high school football jacket. He held Rhonda's hands and looked at her with love; his smile appeared movie star radiant.

In her dream, Brad spoke. "I love you."

"Oh, God, I love you too, baby." She looked at him and felt her heart hammer.

Rhonda stood on tiptoes to kiss him. Brad leaned in and met her mouth. In dreamland, they made out and soon their clothes disappeared and her dreams took an erotic turn. She gazed into his gorgeous face above her, a face filled with such tenderness and pleasure, and saw the sunny dream-sky behind him turned dark. A chill of dread crept upon her as she watched the black clouds roil and churn.

Brad moved in her, oblivious.

"*Loveeee.*" The word erupted on carrion breath, his pronunciation distorted by a rotten tongue.

In this dream-turned-nightmare, Rhonda screamed. A spoiled corpse fucked her. Brad's golden flesh had turned to rot, her smiling fiancé now a hideously animated heap of decomposing flesh with a rancid hard-on.

Rhonda bolted upright in her hotel bed as nightmarish and rotten Brad bit into her face, and as his fetid phallus broke off inside her during his necrotic climax. She reached for Brad, the *real* Brad, but he was no longer beside her. She panted in confusion and tried to grasp solid reality. Christ, she still felt imaginary thrusts of her lover's rigor-mortis member. Somewhere between worlds of fantasy and veracity, she seemed to detect rot from between her legs.

Brad sat in a corner of the room. "There you are." Relief flooded her. He wasn't the Dawn of the Dead version of her nightmare. He waited for her as he always had, ever handsome and undead.

Bright sunshine sifted through dirty blinds, illuminating particles in languid constellations.

"Rrrrnnndaahh."

Brad's voice brought Rhonda out of her daydreams. She smiled. The memory made her stomach turn.

With a long yawn and a wide stretch, Rhonda stood and gathered her small inventory of belongings. Ah, she missed the old days, when she woke with Brad, both of them nude, with her head on his broad chest and with her hair spread across his skin and their linens. Back then, daybreak often began with drowsy and slow sex followed by a light breakfast and coffee before she went off to work.

She longed for coffee. And not that shit she'd been drinking for six months. She hated Camp Deadnut coffee. *I miss Starbucks.* She'd give her right tit for a venti vanilla latte right about now.

The fall air felt crisp and cool as Rhonda stepped out of Motel 6 and into bright sunshine. It looked to be another gorgeous day in Cujoland. Beneath morning light, her blood-caked and battered Humvee looked like it had been driven through Hamburger Hill. Poor thing deserved a Purple Heart.

She buckled Brad in. He gazed at her through cloudy, dead-fish eyes. Bright sun couldn't even bring out the original color and sparkle of his orbs. Rhonda found herself blinking back tears.

"Another drive, baby." Rhonda smiled for Brad. "I promise, things'll be better once we're on a beach in Florida."

Suddenly it hit her. The beach? Would ultraviolet rays do a real number on cadaveric skin? She'd worry about that later. She shut his passenger door.

Rhonda opened her own door to a vehicle filled with morning dew. She stepped back and took a good look at the beat-up Motel 6. It didn't appear so sinister in daylight; just neglected and sad. In a world without maintenance men and landscapers, foliage was overtaking man's static creations and the elements were extracting their due.

Eons split continents and whittled mountains to dust. So, why wouldn't every trace of man's artificial and unnatural existence eventually be erased? Who cared anymore? Dates and time didn't mean shit now. In a hundred years it all would all be forgotten.

On this, she raised her wrist to look at her watch. Near 11:00 in the morning. Another day she'd slept in, another late start.

Oh, well.

Rhonda took off her watch and chucked it across the unkempt parking lot. Only Brad gave meaning to her place in time in this crazy world.

She started crying again as she continued south.

Chapter Fourteen

The road. It felt strange being out here on the Interstate with no other travelers. No 18-wheelers roared by. No cars, buses, RV's or any other vehicles in motion around her. Nothing on wheels moved in any traffic lanes.

With I-95 desolate and clear of traffic, she could damn well speed if she pleased. Nice thought, but unrealistic since the Humvee's smashed windshield made it difficult for her to see clearly. Also, the blown-out windows made for a loud and chilly ride at any speed above 40. The wind also made it hard to enjoy her music. It fucking sucked.

Why, why, why did she have to hit the bull? She felt ashamed. How stupid, losing herself in random thoughts as she took her eyes off the road to stare at Brad. And what had it gotten her? A mangled car, that's what, and nearly a piece taken out of her by some backwoods-ass undead. Not to mention the pack of grenades that she shot. It was a miracle she'd survived.

Rhonda shook her head and cast a quick glance at Brad.

Deadbeat.

She laughed out loud at that. Yeah, she loved him. They'd once talked of getting married and having kids. Children weren't ever going to happen, but maybe she'd marry Brad her own way. Perhaps she'd find a courthouse and pull out a Bible. Hell, she'd do all the vows and swear them in. Maybe do some ring exchange thing and declare them wed. Why not? She didn't care how or where she did it; she'd make it happen. Rules went out the window six months ago.

Rhonda checked her gas gauge. It was on a quarter tank.

Need to find a gas station, pronto.

The Humvee sucked gas like a vacuum. She had stopped for gas a number of times without incident. She had to figure out how to turn the pumps on from inside each station since credit cards and prepay weren't going to work. Each time she'd been able to fill her tank.

Rhonda knew she should've traded this wreck in for a new car. The thought had been on her mind since the accident, but she didn't want to fuck around in car dealerships. It was already bad enough she had to stop for gas. She guessed her chances of staying safe were greater if she just kept rolling: plus, the Humvee was still armored. Stopping for gas was already making her stomach flip-flop. Once she got to her Florida destination, she didn't care if she ever drove again. She planned to make a stand there. She'd gather weapons and ammo, make a fortress in a condo and scavenge or learn to live off the land. They'd make a life of sorts.

Semper Fi, Daddy.

They were passing dead cars and bleached bones every couple miles. Did the bones belong to folks who had succumbed to Necro-Rabies and withered away? Or, were they victims, ripped apart by cannibalistic walking, or running, dead?

It didn't make her feel real positive about any *Homo sapiens* chances surviving. It sure didn't look good. No doubt, a new stone age lay ahead. Everything they had built propelled backward until mankind itself became a nondescript blip on the electrocardiogram of this planet. It felt like one of those *Twilight Zone* episodes.

What of other countries and people around the world? How were Europe and Asia and Australia and all nations around the globe handling this? She had to assume the plague had reached the rest of the globe. There weren't any planes in the skies and no foreign nations had moved in to assess or seize the United States since it went down the shitter. No, the rest of the world was probably dealing with their own hordes of Cujo-fied Mexicans, Koreans, Chileans and maybe, God forbid, zombie Eskimos.

She couldn't find it in her to laugh. Humankind had brought this plague upon itself. The end was just around the corner. All the more reason to run away with Brad. They'd meet the final days together.

* * *

"What the hell is *that*?" Rhonda had just crossed into the Peach State of Georgia when she caught movement in the middle of the highway.

A large, black-bearded man stood on the centerline and waving his arms. Rhonda braked and stopped a few yards in front of the guy, and through her broken windshield, gave the stranger closer inspection. Tall and wide, he was dressed in dirty green coveralls and a grubby John Deere cap. He looked middle-aged. His long black beard bore a streak of white whiskers down the middle, like a skunk's tail. His bright blue eyes looked normal.

Normal? Rhonda knew normal didn't mean ordinary these days. Normal just described this guy or anyone else who wasn't Cujo-fied; but didn't mean they weren't batshit cuckoo. Months ago, on her first flight out of Camp Deadnut to find survivors and supplies, both Daddy and Sarge told her: out here, those who survived in these forsaken lands endured by their wits... and their willingness to do unspeakable things. She had heard of non-Cujo cannibals who ate other normal, healthy people. It was said those same living monsters, always men it seemed, held women and children hostage and enslaved them for grunt work... and worse.

Yes, she'd learned fast, even the smallest catastrophe turned regular Joes into wretched and sadistic creatures. Evil lurked inside of men, seemingly only waiting for an excuse, be it a war or a zombie apocalypse, to shake free the reins of conscience.

"Can you help us out?" The big man called out in a deep Southern drawl, then dropped his arms. Through windshield cracks, Rhonda watched him approach her driver's side window.

Rhonda shifted into reverse and backed away. She parked and raised her open palm to the broken windshield to signal the man to stop. Her Ka-Bar knife was under her seat while her M4 and the six 30-round magazines waited on her Humvee's floor. No worries, she favored her sidearm for the moment. She pulled out her .45 and stepped outside. Using her driver's side door for a shield, she centered her gun on his chest. "Stop right there."

"Okay." The stranger froze and raised his hands. His deep voice lightened with a tone of appeal while he jerked his head in a direction behind him. "I got kids over yonder. Locked themselves in the trunk-a my car. I need tools. Got tools?"

Got soap?

She guessed she could smell him from a mile away. No surprise. Anyone living out here wouldn't find it easy to stay clean. The spatters of deep red on his coveralls worried her, however. *What the fuck has he been up to?*

"I don't have tools, mister." Rhonda commanded her toughest voice. "Can't help you."

His hairy face transformed into a grimace of heartache. He motioned around with his big arms. "My whole car's locked up. Kids got the keys. Please. We're stuck bad out here. You know what it's like. Cujos could get wind of us anytime. Rabid animals everywhere. Packs of 'em. Please! My kids... my damn kids."

Transients were instant red flags for her. She didn't trust *anybody*, period. Dad's agenda and Teddie Fitch's assault had ensured that.

She studied the wretch in front of her. How would a cop handle a situation like this? Why was this guy without a weapon in his hands? Why were there

108

kids in a trunk and how had they gotten in there? Why was his whole car locked and why'd the kids have the keys? It sure as hell didn't smell or sound right at all.

"Show me where your car is." Rhonda kept her .45 on the stranger while she took her keys from the Humvee's ignition and tucked them in a pants pocket. She shut her driver's side door and shot a glance to Brad. He stared at her with his mouth open and soundless. Turning from the Humvee, she advanced on the stranger, gun drawn. "You go ahead and I'll follow."

"Who's your friend in the car? Maybe he can help."

"Just worry about your kids and walk."

The man squinted and stared at Brad, then turned and began walking. Rhonda kept herself 20 steps behind him.

Glancing back occasionally to make sure she was still following, the man made his way to an exit ramp further up the road.

The stranger in front of her moved with a quick step for such a large man. Well, who could blame him for hurrying with kids trapped 'n all. She descended the ramp behind him and saw land spread out for miles before her. A small oasis of gas stations, fast food joints and lodging banked together along each side of the road below. Deserted vehicles of all shapes and sizes lay scattered in and along the road and at the bottom of the ramp. Rhonda noted an 18-wheeler below, toppled on its side like a child's toy. Contents from the rig had been left to the elements; hundreds of cardboard boxes lay scattered everywhere, blown out the trailer's ass-end.

"Right over here." The big bearded man pointed to a late model Volkswagen Passat parked a few yards away, off the right shoulder of the exit ramp. "They're in the trunk."

Rhonda shook her head. She told the guy she didn't have tools, and if the trunk was broken, what did he expect to accomplish with their bare hands? She stopped and kept her gun on the stranger when he reached the car. The Volkswagen looked like it had been sitting here for a long time, weather-beaten and filthy, kind of like its owner. It didn't look like it been driven in months.

The hairs on the back of her neck raised.

She remembered she'd been locked out of the Humvee when she had her accident, but she blamed Brad for that. But how'd *this* guy manage to lock himself out of his car? And why would his kids jump in the trunk with the keys and lock themselves in?

Her skin prickled.

She crossed to the other side of the ramp and scanned the embankment below with her sidearm ready, keeping an eye out for anyone who might be in wait. She crossed back over and did the same spot check.

"What're you doin'?"

"You can't be too careful." She didn't like his tone. "Go over to the trunk and knock on it. Let's see how your kids are doing."

The stranger paused, and seemed uncertain. She waved her gun toward the car and he walked to the trunk and rapped on it with the side of his clenched fist. "Hey! Daddy's here. You kids okay?"

Rhonda heard muffled voices.

"Oh, please, Daddy. Get us out of here!" A cry spoke from inside the trunk.

"It's hard to breathe, Daddy. It's dark in here," another voice whimpered words from within the Passat. "Hurry before Cujos come."

Rhonda stared at the trunk, then she looked at the man and maintained her distance, her .45 pointed straight out. "Hit the trunk again. See if it'll pop."

"I've hit it a hundred times, lady. My hand hurts bad." He waved a large and beefy mitt at her. "Tried everything. Rocks. You name it."

Rhonda looked at the dented trunk again. The dents appeared rusty and old. No, it didn't look like anyone had been pounding the trunk—not in recent days, anyway. She reserved suspicion and turned toward him. "If the car's locked up, why don't you just bust a window and pop the trunk from the inside?"

"What kind of fool busts their own car window just to get inside?"

What kind of asshole wouldn't smash a window to save their kids?

She was walking toward the driver's door to smash the window herself when—

"I think we found a handle in here, Daddy." The sudden cry from the trunk stopped Rhonda. "Should we pull it?"

"Oh yeah." The big stranger tugged at his beard. "I plumb forgot that lever in the trunk can open the darn thing. Gosh-damn I'm a knuckle-head sometimes."

Rhonda stared at the man. She certainly couldn't argue with that. She walked closer to the trunk. "Tell them how to pull it and push up on the trunk at the same time."

"Who's that, Daddy?"

Rhonda heard fear in there.

"A helpful lady, Patty. Come to get you and your brother outta there."

Patty, huh? A daughter. "What's your other kid's name?"

The stranger paused and looked away from Rhonda's gaze. He tugged and stroked his skunk beard then faced her, showing a grin full of shoddy green teeth. "Randy. Son's name is Randy."

Rhonda smelled a skunk and it wasn't from the dude's nasty beard. He was acting odd. She backed away and kept her distance a few yards behind the rear bumper.

Rhonda kept her gun and a watchful eye on the stranger. He wasn't instructing the kids and she didn't have time to keep fucking around. "Patty and Randy? This is Rhonda. I think you might've found the emergency handle to open the trunk. Inside the top of the trunk, right?"

"Yeah." Two uneasy voices spoke in unison from within.

"Okay. Pull on that sucker and push up on the roof of the trunk from the inside. Do that and you should be free."

"You sure you ain't a Cujo?" A voice squeaked from inside.

"Who's asking?" Rhonda said.

"Randy. I'm asking 'cause I don't like Cujos."

Rhonda smiled. "I promise you. I'm no Cujo. Your dad's right here and he'll tell ya the same."

The stranger nodded. "She's all good, kids. No Cujos here."

"Okay." The voices inside spoke together.

"Ready?" Rhonda spoke louder. "Count of three."

"Okay." This time one voice answered and again Rhonda wasn't sure if it was a boy or girl.

Rhonda pointed to the stranger. "If you can, get your fingers in the groove of the trunk and bumper on that corner and I'll get this corner. Just in case it doesn't spring up all the way."

The large stranger nodded and grunted while he put his fat and dirty fingertips into the space between the trunk and bumper near the Passat's rear left panel. Rhonda stayed back and observed.

She lowered her gun began her count. "Here we go. One. Two. Three!"

When the trunk flew wide open with no effort at all, Rhonda recoiled at the sight of the kids inside.

What the fuck? They're NOT kids!

Sure, they were the height of grade-schoolers, but the undersized man and woman before her were wrinkled and filthy middle-aged things with dark eyes and bad teeth.

The little man inside bared mule teeth at Rhonda while the tiny red-haired woman leapt out, running and pointing something at her. She muttered, "Dumb bitch."

Rhonda raised her .45 to fire but wasn't fast enough. Instant pain from pepper-spray blasted her eyes and ravaged her nose, throat, and mouth. It blinded her. She couldn't scream as she retched and coughed and whirled around in the road. She fought an urge to press her hands into her eyes. Rhonda had trained with mace and pepper-spray and learned not to touch an affected area to avoid spreading irritants, but it took all the self-restraint she had.

"Grab her! Get her! Get the gun and get the bitch before she tumbles down the ditch!"

113

In pain, blinded, and fearful, Rhonda knew she couldn't escape.

"That's a good lady. Don't even think-a runnin' from me." The big stranger's voice boomed right behind Rhonda. Even through the pepper-spray, she smelled his strong and noxious breath on her head. "Let's get her put away before her friend gets on to us."

"What friend?" A high-pitched voice said.

"She left someone behind in one of them Hummer deals up there on the road," the man answered. "We'd best get into our place before we get shot or somethin'. I'll deal with 'em later."

"You fuckers!" Rhonda cried out in pain and despair. She felt her .45 yank away and a pair of huge arms bear-hugged her from behind, lifting her off the ground to whisk her away... to a fate she couldn't see coming.

Chapter Fifteen

Oh, God. Where were they taking her? She couldn't see anything, but she knew they had placed her in a small room. It felt claustrophobic.

Her eyes burned and she coughed in fits. She assumed her abductors had made a beeline to the oasis at the bottom of the exit ramp.

She overheard the little people and big bearded man discuss a number of unsavory plans for her. Her captors debated: Would they make her a sex-slave or into a stew? The little people and the big guy argued over having her for sex, dinner or both. Every suggestion made Rhonda feel sick.

Brad! Oh, God, he was still buckled in his seat, all alone on the highway. She batted her eyes. Slowly her new environment came to light, though her throat was still raw from coughing fits and her face burned.

Rhonda moaned in a combination of pain, frustration and frank fury. These scumbags were good as dead. But if they harmed Brad, she'd do them slow.

She seemed to be in some kind of broom closet. A door, several feet in front of her, stood ajar, allowing daylight to cut in a narrow beam. Gray metal storage shelves stood from floor to ceiling on either side of her, bare save for some yellowed newspapers from another world.

The closet door opened wider, and in the watery light, Rhonda made out silhouettes of two short and stout forms. Yes, she remembered these two: Patty and Randy. Were their names even real? No matter, she didn't give a shit. They held blurry objects in their tiny hands. She thought they might be batons or pipes, or maybe her trusty sidearm.

"She don't look too damaged." Randy's squeaky voice came from Rhonda's left. "Her eyes are fucked-up is all."

"I'm not interested in her eyes." Patty scoffed. "I wanna see what this pretty young thing's tongue can do."

"That all you think about? Eyes make good eatin,' I say."

"And I says I want her t'do a number on me. You boys can eat when I'm done with my fun."

Great. Rhonda grimaced through her facial sting. *Vertically challenged cannibals. A dyke cannibal to boot. How do I get into this shit?*

"Wait." Rhonda raised a hand. *Gotta stall 'em until my vision returns.*

"Wait nothin', dumb bitch." Patty barked and released a malicious cackle. "You're eating pussy or else you're getting the mace again. Want that?"

Rhonda shook her head. No, she definitely didn't want to take spray to her eyes again.

"She'll eat you, and then we eat her." Randy guffawed, nudging Patty.

With each new disgusting threat, Rhonda's fury rose one hot notch at a time. She'd be damned if she'd be anyone's dinner, or taste this wee bitch's fire crotch.

Fuck them.

Rhonda made a nonchalant pass with her hands and remembered her .45 automatic had been stripped from her.

"Hey." Rhonda did her best to smile and sound upbeat. "Randy and Patty, right?"

The little people paused. Patty spat. "Maybe. What's it to you?"

"Just curious is all." Rhonda blinked. Shit, Patty held Rhonda's .45 in her child-sized hands, though she appeared to be handling the firearm with some difficulty.

"Curiosity killed the cunt." Randy sounded amused by his brand of wit.

Rhonda coughed, her trachea raw. "I just wanna know why y'all wanna eat me and hurt me. Aren't things bad enough out here? People need to stick together. To fight Cujos and to survive."

Randy stopped and scratched his head. He turned to Patty. "Don't you just love these naïve ones?"

"Shut-up, dummy." Patty spat and held the handgun out with her stumpy arms. "Dumb bitch thinks like a dumb bitch. Ain't nothin' t'do but take care of your own neck."

"Every man for himself now. I want to keep her, pretty girl like that. Don't have to eat her." Randy nodded at Rhonda. "Roy's easy. He'll agree."

Roy, huh? Rhonda committed all their names to memory.

"Roy's horny *and* hungry. He wants to fuck, but he'll want to fill his belly before the next one rolls along. I'm sure on that one." Patty frowned. "'Sides, we can't afford to feed another mouth here. Pretty slut or not. Not with us 'n Roy *and* those two little brats."

Little brats? Rhonda's heart jumped. Were there real kids out here, around these monsters? The thought was chilling.

"Where's Roy?" Rhonda started to rise.

"Sit your ass down and don't mind where Roy is." Patty stepped closer with the bulky handgun in her mitts. "He went up to the highway to take care of your friend."

Blood drained from her face and rushed to Rhonda's heart. Poor Brad, still strapped in his seat, waiting for her, confused. Roy would kill him easy as a trapped animal. She whimpered.

"Awww. You worried 'bout someone special up there?" Patty grinned. "Well, Roy's gonna kill 'em and we're gonna eat 'em."

Rhonda gritted her teeth. Patty's voice vexed her. Her vision finally back to normal, she glared into Patty and Randy's small and wrinkled faces. Her inflamed eyes met theirs. "If Roy's so much as mussed up Brad's hair, I'm gonna blow his balls off. And I'll feed you pieces of yourselves until nothin's left."

Patty and Randy giggled together, shaking their heads.

"Sure you will, pretty. And Brad? That name's gayer than my sister here." Randy giggled his way into further high-pitched guffaws.

"Shut it, idiot." Patty yipped at Randy through her giggles. She bore an expression of contempt. "You

118

ain't blowin' off or feeding anyone nothin'. We're running this show."

Rhonda couldn't end this crap fast enough. She jumped to her feet, only to freeze fast when Patty rammed the .45 into Rhonda's crotch.

"Hold it, bitch." Patty snarled, flashing tiny, discolored and square teeth. She fumbled with Rhonda's .45, twisting the barrel into Rhonda's pubic bone. "How 'bout I blow something off of you? Randy! Tape her wrists together."

With a snort, Randy switched his rusted metal pipe from one hand to another. He reached into his raggedy, cutoff pants and pulled out a battered roll of duct tape. What else did he keep in his pockets?

"Put your arms out and down in front of ya' or I'll brain ya' with this pipe." Randy raised his right arm and shook the pipe at Rhonda.

This Munchkin enforcer, what a joke. If it wasn't for the dangerous placement of a .45 to her holiest-of-holies, Rhonda thought she could take Randy and Patty down.

Randy wrapped silver-colored tape around Rhonda's wrists while Patty held the gun in place. With her arms bound tight, the little people led Rhonda from the closet and into a deserted gas station mini-mart.

Rhonda's eyes ached, but she saw well enough. The unoccupied station smelled like old oil and food grease. She noticed shelves stocked plenty with expired snacks and food. No doubt, this stuff was valued like gold out here. Behind the bulletproof glass of the old attendant partition, she saw rolls of old scratch-off lottery tickets, phone cards, cartons of

119

cigarettes and bottles of cheap booze. Everything was covered in dust.

"Looks like you got a good stash here." Rhonda scanned more dirty and stocked shelves as she walked down an aisle. "Plenty to eat and party with."

"We claimed the exit and this entire stretch of fast food joints and gas stations months ago." Randy bragged as he pushed Rhonda along. "There ain't animals 'round here to hunt. Most got Necro in 'em anyways. We're saving all this stale shit in here for when things get *real* bad. So far, we've had plenty of food from the other joints, and thanks to dumb-fucks like you, we get fresh meat just about once a week."

Just half a year and here we are. Half a year and people become cannibals and casual rapists.

"And this stash ain't for partying." Patty spoke from behind. She pushed Rhonda forward with the .45 planted into her tailbone. "Roy 'n Randy 'n me stay away from booze and all that bad shit. We don't smoke and we don't drink out here."

"Oh, of course not." Rhonda feigned laughter. "You're living the good and pure life with all of your raping and people eating."

Patty pushed the .45 harder into Rhonda's coccyx. "You need to fuckin' shut it."

Randy turned to Rhonda when they reached the station's front doors. "We'll see which side of the coin your purty ass lands on. Heads we eat. Tails we screw. Since we make the rules, we might do both."

Rhonda found Randy's threat to be one part ridiculous and one part creepy. They led her outside and into the fading amber light of the day. She frowned at a lofty BP sign high above her for all eyes to see.

Oil spills or Necro-Rabies. We sure shit in our nest. Rhonda gazed at the flower-like corporate logo with distaste.

"Move it." Patty shoved Rhonda forward.

"Where we goin'?" Rhonda looked around. Everywhere were things left behind from a vanished civilization; rigs and cars, an abandoned McDonald's and Waffle House across the road, dejected gas pumps nearby, an adult toy store and a fireworks stand—everything left to rot.

What about Brad? What was going on up there? Rhonda shot a concerned glance at the highway, now ahead and high above her. She spotted the Passat-trap parked on the exit ramp, and above it, the dark shape of her Humvee's top poking above a highway guard-wall. She didn't see any movement.

"We got a real nice place over yonder." Randy walked ahead. He pointed at a five-story building with a big sign in cursive script: *Ruthie's Inn.*

"Except you ain't getting a suite at this place, bitch." Patty sneered. "We're taking you to the slave pen. Should've put you in there already. You'll stay there 'til we decide what t'do with ya'."

Rhonda's eyes widened.

What the fuck was a slave pen?

Chapter Sixteen

They forced Rhonda into the darkened, green-tiled foyer of Ruthie's Inn. A terrible reek bombarded her nose, acrid smells of carrion and human excrement... and old urine everywhere. She raised her taped wrists to her face and covered her nose with cupped hands.

"Smells like home." Randy inhaled deep. He walked quickly into a long hallway and motioned to Rhonda and Patty. "C'mon. Follow the leader."

Rhonda followed and noted the hotel's dusty and neglected interior. She stepped over suitcases and bags, the foyer and reception area littered with countless pieces of assorted luggage. Everything appeared rummaged through, clothing and personal items spread about in disarray. Perhaps these personal effects belonged to those who had fallen victim to Roy and these undersized psychopaths.

In a corner, near a tall and cobwebbed faux palm tree, she glimpsed piles of dark turds and shit-smeared rags and papers.

Shitting in the nest again.

Patty and Randy escorted Rhonda along a dark hallway flanked by multiple rooms on either side. Many rooms waited with doors open wide, and in these doorways, she glimpsed human remains scattered within; some skeletal and others covered with leathery flesh. Not a single one was complete.

If this isn't a hotel of horrors, I don't know what is.

"We like to keep all them body parts piled inside to make any riff-raff think twice about coming in here." Patty's tiny voice sounded winded from her walk. "When we use up the parts we want, we chuck what's left around here. Scares off undesirables."

The idea of Patty calling anyone else "undesirables" was almost enough to make Rhonda laugh, but the .45 at her back kept her tongue in check.

Deep red bloodstains saturated the hallway carpet. As daylight faded, she discovered gory evidence with every step, and envisioned bloody bodies, or parts of bodies, dragged through this corridor toward fates sane people wouldn't think of... or ever want to.

"Why would you wanna prey on people?" Rhonda blinked and focused on a door at the end of the hall. "You must remember what it was like to be normal people. Good people."

Randy stopped and scowled at Rhonda. "Who says we was ever normal or good?"

On this, Randy began a new round of high-pitch giggles. It seemed infectious as Patty also went into a fit of staccato giggles. Rhonda's minikin abductors led her through the hallway door and through a blood-smeared Texas Chainsaw kitchen. They stopped at a

123

formidable beige metal door posted with a Maintenance Only sign.

In gloom, Rhonda squinted. Someone had secured the door with a stainless steel deadbolt, and below it, a stainless steel door-latch with a hefty steel padlock added extra security.

Randy fished around in his pants pockets and pulled out a ring packed with keys of all sizes. Metal rattled as he flipped through them and scrutinized, murmuring and cursing to himself. Finally he paused with a large key between his fat thumb and index finger. He smacked his lips once and walked to the door.

Rhonda watched Randy climb a tallboy chair near the door. Standing tiptoe on the chair seat, he raised his hands and slid the key into a padlock above his head with a grunt. He unlocked the shackle and dropped the padlock on the seat of the chair, then raised up again to open the deadbolt. With everything unlocked, Randy jumped from the chair and swung open the door with a flourish.

"We're gonna need flashlights soon." Patty pushed Rhonda through the open doorway. "It's gonna be darker than a boxcar full of cocksuckers 'round here."

Maybe Patty worked as a truck driver or steel worker in her former life. The little bull-dyke sure wielded a huge and ferocious mouth. Rhonda wanted to kick her teeth in.

"I left a lantern and Maglite with the kids. They got 'em down in the basement." Randy held the door open and ushered Rhonda and Patty to the stairs.

Rhonda heard Randy slam the door shut behind them as she descended the dark stairway. She couldn't see anything but a faint glow of yellowish light farther below. It smelled terrible here, much like all smells throughout Ruthie's Inn: A miasma of putrefaction mixed with a pungent stench of shit and piss. Maybe another blast of mace, straight to her nose, wouldn't be so bad.

Near the bottom she noticed the glow grew brighter. Her ears detected weird sounds. Things below rustled and grunted, then something hissed. A fetid stink hung in this dead air and she knew it: the unmistakable fragrance of zombie rot and undead B.O.

What the fuck? They have Cujos down here?

Rhonda stopped cold.

"I didn't tell ya' to stop." Patty barked from above and kicked the back of Rhonda's neck with a tiny boot.

Patty's kick was weak and didn't hurt, but it pissed Rhonda off. She didn't like being walloped any more than she liked a handgun drilled into her vertebrae. With her wrists taped together, her captors held the advantage, for now. She turned, and in the dim light cast from the nearby glow, she made out Patty's small and round body a few steps above her. She whispered through clenched teeth. "There's fucking Cujos down here, you stupid assholes."

Patty's shadowy figure shrugged. "So what? Tell us somethin' we don't know. And we don't call 'em Cujo's. That's the stupidest fucking name for these undead bastards. They're Fleshfucks. *Flesh* plus *fucks.* Got it?"

From darkness behind Patty, Randy's shrill and impatient voice spoke. "Move goddammit. We got stuff t'do."

On Randy's last word, Patty kicked Rhonda again, but this time her little foot connected hard with Rhonda's chin, sending a blast of stars and pain through Rhonda's head. Surprised and caught off guard, and with her wrists taped together in front of her, Rhonda couldn't catch her balance and fell backwards. On reflex, she jumped off the stairs and hoped to land on her feet somewhere in the gloom below.

Rhonda didn't fall far, but landed roughly and did a backwards jig, her legs kicking out like a showgirl's as she fought to keep from taking a spill in the dark. A blast of pain rocked her when she stopped hard, her back and ass slammed against a cinderblock wall. She groaned.

Okay, you fuckers.

"Careful. We don't want you gettin' all messed up now." Patty stepped off the stairs. She stood in front of Rhonda and pushed the .45 into Rhonda's belly. "We got plans for you still."

Randy followed Patty and stood next to her. He leered at Rhonda. "We'll mess ya' up later when we're done with ya'."

Rhonda exhaled. She hated them. Leaning against the wall, she saw everything better thanks to the mysterious glow. Where did it come from? She looked to her right and saw it then, light from a room at the end of a short utility passage.

The little couple moved Rhonda along and they all entered the room. The illumination came from a large kerosene lantern placed amongst rusty tools and knives on top of a rusted metal worktable centered inside. The concrete floor was strewn with yellowish, gristle-knotted human bones, and it suddenly occurred to her that human remains could draw fucking rats; and rats meant Necro-Rabies.

Patty pushed Rhonda toward the messy worktable. New dread filled her and for a second she wished she was back with her dad at Camp Deadnut. She wished she was with Brad and wondered what predicament he might be in.

Worry about that later.

She noted stacks of moldy cardboard boxes piled on several decrepit skids along every wall. A set of rusty lockers and a dirty twin bed with a stained pillow and a navy blanket in one corner. Worst of all, against a far wall, two Cujos hissed and lashed out from behind a floor-to-ceiling chain-link pen, the door secured with a large padlock.

Rhonda observed the emaciated Cujos. On her left stood a semi-decomposed adult male dressed in a dirty and crumbly polo shirt and shorts get-up. Beside the undead dude stood a young, Cujo-fied woman, naked and in a state of inert rot, smeared with red and black, like a mixture of blood and grease. The Cujo-fied pair hissed and showed large, blackish-yellow teeth poking out of black and receded gumlines.

"Our putrid pets." Patty withdrew the gun from Rhonda's back and walked to the worktable. She tucked the gun into her waistband at the back of her pants and grabbed a piece of metal pipe from the tabletop. At this, the Cujos hissed louder, rattling their cage with agitation. Patty strolled over and stopped inches from the chain-link. "We keep 'em around for fun. Feed 'em fresh meat sometimes, once we're done with our share. Get back ya' nasty fuckers!"

Patty cursed and swatted undead fingers with her pipe, but the Cujos didn't withdraw their hands, just clutched and shook their cage non-stop. Rhonda worried as they became more and more pissed off. Their hisses rose and abundant amounts of Cujo drool trickled from their mouths. Patty jabbed her pipe through the fence and nailed the female Cujo in her pronounced ribcage. The blow tore a cruel hole in bad flesh.

"Hey! Roy likes that one." Randy's falsetto voice rose. He walked to Patty.

Patty turned from the pen and raised her pipe at Randy. "I don't give a shit what Roy likes. Roy'll fuck anything, and 'round here, *anything* is *nothing* and nothing 'round here lasts long. He'll find another one."

"Your buddy rapes that Cujo girl?" Rhonda looked at the rabid corpse behind the fence, then cast a disgusted expression at the little people.

The pint-sized pair shrugged and returned to the middle of the room, on the other side of the worktable. They glared at Rhonda, their crabapple faces visible just above the tabletop, their compressed features filled with malevolence, beady eyes flickering in lantern light.

"Any port in a storm, Roy says." Randy flashed his tiny teeth. "You're in our world. Learn it, live it, love it."

"Yeah, our *buddy* fucks girls. Dead or alive. Eats 'em, too. So what? We all do." Patty banged her steel pipe on the table.

It wasn't such a surprise that Roy or anyone in this miserable land would fuck the dead, motionless or animated. Rhonda knew such things happened outside of Fort Rocky. She thought of Brad and how anyone would view him as an object to be defiled.

He's my true love. Not a plaything...

Rhonda put her thoughts away as Randy suddenly stopped and raised a hand. She watched his face bunch into a scowl, like he smelled noxious gas. He turned to Patty and his high-pitched voice rose like a siren. "Where're the fucking kids?"

"Settle down, dumbshit." Patty tossed her pipe and it landed on the tabletop with a clang. She pushed past Randy and duck-walked toward the twin bed in a corner of the room.

Patty squatted, breaking wind like a pack of firecrackers. Rhonda didn't think the room could smell any worse.

"Come out here ya' little shits." Patty shouted into darkness beneath the bed.

A moment passed and nothing happened. Everything beneath the small bed remained quiet and unstirred. Then, Rhonda watched a sudden flashlight beam cut through blackness under the bed. This beam first spotlighted Patty before turning and tilting upward to point at Randy and Rhonda.

A child's cautious voice spoke from beneath the bed. "You got another bad person with you. We don't wanna get hurt."

"You're gonna get hurt if you don't get your asses out from under there." Patty stood and kicked the metal bed frame. "We didn't bring no Cujo with us. Now get outta there!"

Rhonda watched two kids, around nine to 11 years old, crawl out. A boy with light blonde hair, in dirty jeans and a soiled white T-shirt, clutching a long and large black Maglite. The other kid, a girl with long blonde hair, wore filthy overalls and a dirty top beneath. They both looked at Patty and Randy before their gaze shifted to Rhonda. She saw terror on their dirt-blotched faces.

Rhonda presented a large, kind smile. She raised her taped wrists and wiggled her fingers at the kids. She hoped they saw her like them: innocent and kidnapped.

The boy paused on his hands and knees with his gaze on Rhonda. His eyes opened wide.

Rhonda cleared her throat and tried to make her voice sound cheerful and non-threatening. "Hi guys. Don't worry about me. I'm no monster. Not like these guys."

"Shut your slut-hole. Next time you open your yap, you're lickin' me." Patty frowned and spat at Rhonda. She turned to the boy, then reached and pulled the boy to his feet by his hair. He appeared a good inch or two taller than Patty. She snarled in his face and slapped him with her free hand. "I told you and your sister, there ain't no place to hide."

"We'll eat ya' 'n throw your scraps to the Fleshfucks. Maybe jes' feed you to 'em. Ha!" Randy chimed in and pointed at the Cujo pen.

The girl gripped her brother's arm and buried her face into his shoulder. It broke Rhonda's heart. These poor kids, the lives they must lead. It reminded Rhonda of Hansel and Gretel, except instead of falling prey to a cannibal witch in a forest, they were held hostage by a pair of psycho-sexual, flesh-hungry deviant halflings.

Rhonda observed the boy, who stood rigid while

his sister snuggled into his arm. Rhonda noted Patty's fresh handprint, printed in dirt on the boy's cheek. It looked like it stung. Yet the boy didn't offer any tears. Instead, Rhonda observed, he glared at Patty with hate in his eyes, his chest puffing in steady breaths and his bottom lip out.

"You eyeballin' me, boy?" Patty pulled the .45 out from her waistband and raised it to his face. "Awwww... ya' look so mad. Too bad. That slap wasn't the first or last, boy."

The boy's shaky words came out fast. "Go to hell."

Randy's mouth dropped open while Rhonda watched, surprised by the kid's courage.

"Tough guy? *Really?*" Patty spoke in her tiny and sinister voice. "You ain't no tough guy. You ain't nothin' but a little shit with a smart mouth." With an uneasy, one-handed grip, Patty shoved the gun barrel hard into the boy's chest and pushed him backward with it, grabbing his sister and yanking her away with her free hand. "How about I throw your sister in the slave pen with the Cujos? Maybe that'll teach ya' to stand down."

"*Nooo!* Tyler, help me!" The girl wriggled and screamed while Patty dragged her to the Cujo pen.

Rhonda already held an ocean of undiluted anger and disgust at these horrible little fucks. She was ready to jump in to help the girl at any cost, her bound hands be damned. But before she could leap into action, the boy set new events in motion on his own.

Despite her tape-bound arms and sore eyes and shadowy lantern light, Rhonda was bent on kicking her tiny captors to death. But the boy, Tyler, beat her to the proverbial kick.

As Patty dragged the young girl toward the Cujo pen, Rhonda watched in surprise as Tyler ran past Randy and the worktable, and came up behind Patty with his arms raised high and the large Maglite clutched in his hands. Exerting savage speed and force, he walloped Patty's red-haired dome with the flashlight.

Patty screeched in pain as her scalp and burgundy locks parted in a wide gash. A vibrant spray of blood followed the blow as Maglite metal met cranial bone.

I bet that fucking smarts.

Tyler clubbed Patty again and Patty screamed, releasing the girl as she stumbled from the blow and reached for her split head. She also dropped the .45 to the floor where it spun underneath the table.

Randy released an outraged bellow, took a step forward next to Rhonda, and then froze. He looked confused and scared.

"You're not the boss of us! You're not the boss of us! You... hobbit... bitch!" Tyler chased Patty and pinned her. He stood over her and beat her again with the Maglite.

Rhonda couldn't imagine what horrors Tyler and his sister had been through, but just one hour down here was hell. She was surprised the kid hadn't snapped and beat his captors silly before today. No matter, payback had arrived.

Rhonda turned to Randy. His shrieks cut off when he saw her liberated .45 automatic spinning under the table. Randy flicked his gaze to Rhonda's eyes, and she found desperation and uncertainty in his beady little orbs. He scowled and bared his mule teeth at her.

"Don't do it."

Rhonda gave Randy a clear order, but unsurprisingly, the little creep didn't heed her. He squealed and dove toward the worktable, attempting to get his small mitts on the sidearm. Rhonda kicked her foot out and the toe of her boot caught Randy under the chin and slammed his head hard into the table's underside, forcing Randy and the heavy table to flip together, scattering junk across the floor, lost among human remains.

"Whoops." Rhonda watched the dislodged lantern smash as she went for her .45. Kerosene spread and burned over the floor. Unbound flames flickered and popped, adding an eerie and sinister glow to the chamber of horrors.

Randy landed on his back. He rolled and staggered to his feet, holding his head and jaw. Blood poured from his small mouth and Rhonda watched him try to speak. He bellowed forth words carried on a spray of red. "*I it nigh uuung!*"

Fucker must've bit his tongue. Perhaps, she hoped, it was severed in two.

Tyler continued his Maglite assault on Patty's back as she wailed for mercy. Beyond Tyler and Patty, Rhonda spied Tyler's terrified young sister. The girl hid in a corner, crouching with her face pressed into a wall. The Cujos were going nuts in their slave pen, perhaps frenzied by the bloody action before them.

Rhonda went for her .45 and caught Randy's movement. She faced him as kerosene flames grew larger. She watched Randy spit out a large blob of stringy blood that reflected the flickering firelight. He bared crimson-smeared mule teeth at her before snatching a large knife from the detritus of the bone-littered floor. He shrieked and waved a dirty and pitted blade at Rhonda as he charged. Desperate. He again dove for Rhonda's unsecured sidearm. This break, and Randy's awkward gait, gave Rhonda time to move. She stepped to her .45 and dipped with ease and rose again with her sidearm gripped in her bound hands like a fishing stork with a powerful, high-caliber frog.

Randy belly-flopped in front of Rhonda and landed hard on his ample gut, expelling a painful, bloody bark. Having missed his chance to get the gun, he wailed and swiped at Rhonda with his knife, but caught only the toes of her combat boots with the blade tip.

Rhonda aimed at his head, but he twisted and she ended up blowing a large hole through Randy's right shoulder. He released the knife and roared in a high-pitched, caterwaul of misery. Remarkable, how such a small man could make such noise.

Rhonda kicked Randy's knife away and sought the kids.

Gotta get them out of this hellhole.

Heavy kerosene smoke had begun filling the room as the flames licked and ignited the molding cardboard boxes and skids along the walls.

"Tyler! Stop! Grab your sister." Rhonda pushed her voice above the little people's screams. Tyler didn't seem to hear her, so she kicked Patty out of the way and faced him.

"We're gettin' the fuck outta this place. Get your sister and head upstairs. Use your flashlight."

Tyler looked confused for a moment, and then snapped to attention and nodded. He appeared winded, no doubt from the beat-down he'd dished out. He clutched his Maglite like a war club and stood down as Patty bled and crawled to her collaborator, who remained face down on the floor moaning in agony.

Rhonda glanced at the girl balled in the corner of the psychotic realm. Tyler ran to her and pulled her to her feet. "C'mon, Ellen. We're running away."

Tyler led Ellen toward the stairs and Rhonda watched the kids until they disappeared into the small and dark corridor and staircase beyond. Fire crackled and something moved behind her. She spun and thrust her taped wrists out with her .45 pointed straight ahead.

Patty and Randy stood, albeit unsteadily, in front of the Cujo pen, their tiny forms flashing yellow and red in firelight. Their pet Cujos hissed behind them and attacked their enclosure with mindless fury. Patty had reclaimed her pipe and Randy his knife. Their eyes sparkled in faces twisted by hate.

"You ain't gettin' away with this." Patty's voice was rife with absolute anger and pain. She waved her pipe. "You dumb bitch."

"Oooo ucknn cunnn!" Randy strained words through his crimson mouth. The bullet-hole in the front of his right shoulder bubbled with blood.

On Randy's last and unintelligible word, he and Patty threw their respective weapons at Rhonda. Patty's pipe missed Rhonda's head by inches, but Randy's rusty knife found a final destination in Rhonda's right leg above the knee. The blade cut clean through her camo pants and flesh with ease. It *thwacked* inside her, every sharp and filthy inch penetrating deep in her muscle.

"Fuuuuck!" Rhonda's leg failed her, and she

fired as she fell to the floor. She landed hard on her right knee. A sudden warm and sharp pain flamed between her kneecap and crotch.

Rhonda's sudden loss of balance had knocked her aim off and she missed the stunted sadists. Despite being an expert markswoman back at Camp Deadnut, firing at moving targets with bound wrists while falling with a knife in her leg was a whole new dilemma.

Patty and Randy scattered, but Rhonda saw a different opportunity. Blinking away pain, and with precise aim, she fired a round into the padlock on the Cujo pen. The lock exploded into fragments.

Patty and Randy whipped their heads around to the Cujo pen with new expressions of alarm on their sour apple faces. The captive Cujos shook their pen and Rhonda watched the undead cellmates pause in their rage. They turned their attention to their cage door, which slowly opened on its own with a loud metallic squeak.

Some type of comprehension sparked in their deceased gray matter and Rhonda watched their bile-colored eyes widen as their cell door opened... and they found their captors within biting distance.

"I'm outta here!" Patty power-waddled to escape.

"*Fuuuuuugggghhh!*" Randy's terrified bellow filled the burning horror chamber. He limped behind Patty and followed her toward nearby freedom.

"No fucking way." Rhonda forced all her weight onto her left leg; as Patty moved in range, Rhonda side-kicked the little beast with her wounded right leg. Despite the knife blade sticking out of her agonized leg, Rhonda nailed Patty's throat as hard as she could with her combat boot. "Who's the fucking *DUMB BITCH* now?"

Patty's broken body slammed into Randy, and both tumbled back into the fiery room to rest at the freed Cujos' feet.

Rhonda turned and limped toward the stairs as quickly as her wounded leg would carry her. She didn't look back, ignoring the horrible noises coming from behind her.

Go. Almost there.

Halfway up the staircase, a flashlight beam hit her face. She raised a hand and shielded her eyes. Tyler's voice yelled to her. "C'mon lady. Get up here!"

I'm fucking trying. Rhonda willed herself to move faster. With taped wrists and a wounded leg, she ascended stairs the hard way.

Rhonda finally made it and the kids grabbed her arms and pulled her into the hotel kitchen. On the floor, she rolled on her back and looked toward the Maintenance door. It stood wide open, vomiting clouds of black smoke into the kitchen.

"Shut and lock that door! Hurry!" Rhonda tried to stand, but her bad leg betrayed her.

Tyler slammed the door shut. Standing on the chair near the door, he secured the padlock with a loud click and slid the deadbolt home.

Rhonda's leg hurt but she didn't care. She smiled in the dark kitchen. "You kids got a lotta guts. Way more than those little monsters down there."

"I hate them." Ellen looked at her feet.

The sound of young Ellen's voice shocked Rhonda more than her knife wound. She reached a hand out to a shadowy form and touched the girl.

"Hey, I hate 'em, too. Don't worry, those teeny monsters now have big monsters to straighten them out."

Tyler stepped near. In semi-darkness, right outside his Maglite beam, Rhonda could see the shape of a large butcher knife in his hand. "Put your hands and arms up."

Rhonda, on her back, raised her achy, shaky arms, still clutching the .45. Tyler slid a blade between her wrists to cut the tape and helped unwind it off Rhonda's forearms. Her hands felt weird. The sensation of her free arms made her shudder. "Thanks."

"Let's get out of this place. Please?" Tyler aimed a long beam of light across the kitchen to a doorway across the room.

"Sounds great to me." Rhonda inhaled deeply and stood on her strong left leg. Holstering her sidearm, she grabbed both kids' hands.

As they made their kitchen exit, there was a sudden slam against the Maintenance door, followed by intense pounding and high-pitched screams... then Cujo hisses and the pitter-patter of little feet in the stairwell.

"Just keep walking." Rhonda painfully led them on.

Chapter Seventeen

Once free of the hotel, they moved a few doors down until they reached the BP gas mart. Rhonda rested on a curb at the station's main entrance. Her leg alarmed her. It bled and throbbed with new intensity. She'd need to remove the damn knife before she tried to ascend the exit ramp. The highway seemed so far away. She'd just wait awhile. Get her strength and wits back.

And Brad? What had happened to him?

Please be alive. Dead alive... at least undead and okay.

Rhonda felt ill. What if Brad was unharmed, but now wandered Cujoland alone?

Rhonda sat with the kids long enough to watch Ruthie's Inn turn into an inferno and took a small amount of satisfaction in knowing she'd delivered as promised to those abhorrent sickos. Roy, however, remained unaccounted for.

One problem. She needed to get a jump on Roy

before he spotted her and the kids. Any element of surprise posed a challenge while Ruthie's Inn blazed hot and bright in the fall night. What if he now had her M4 and ammo? If this insane fire hadn't already gotten Roy's attention and drawn him into action, it would no doubt draw every undead in a five-mile radius.

Against her better judgment, indeed against her desire to get moving as soon as possible, Rhonda needed to tend to her wound, and she needed the kids' help. "Tyler and Ellen. Go into the station and get me some paper towels, rubbing alcohol... anything that looks like first aid stuff. Do it fast, please."

The kids nodded and left her.

Rhonda hated to ask Tyler and Ellen to enter a dark and abandoned gas station by themselves, but she needed to stop moving before she did irreparable damage to her leg. Her leg had better heal quickly. Being helpless got old really fast.

You out there watching us, Roy? She stared at the ramp and the darkness beyond with her .45 in hand as she waited for the kids.

The kids returned within minutes, their arms full of bagged goods. They spread their discoveries next to Rhonda and she sorted through it.

Rhonda rummaged through the bags and there was more than she hoped for; scissors, gauze, rubbing alcohol, bottled water and some Band Aids that were going to be too small to help. No matter, the kids had done great. She forced herself to stand on her left leg and spoke to Tyler. "I need you to take those scissors and cut my right pant leg all the way up the side seam here. Then cut the pant leg off. Think you can do that?"

"Off?" Tyler's eyes grew wide. In the bright light cast from the hotel fire, he looked one part scared and one part embarrassed.

No doubt he was shy about cutting off the pant leg of some strange lady. Well, she couldn't fault him for it. "It's no big deal, Ty. Can I call you Ty?"

Tyler nodded and stared at the knife handle protruding from Rhonda's leg.

"Cool. Now, I need you to cut the pant leg off so I can have a clean area around that fucking... I mean, *stupid* knife."

Rhonda tried to control her language. When was the last time she hung out around kids, anyway? Probably when she last babysat at age 16. Bad language didn't matter much in this new nightmare world, but it wouldn't hurt her to show some politeness. It was one of their last connections to the old world they'd known, when good people existed. People who possessed etiquette, who didn't prey on other people for food or sexual debasement.

Maybe there are still good people out here. Somewhere.

"When you get that pant leg off, I'm going to pull the knife out." Rhonda gestured with her hands. "Blood's gonna pour out and I need you both to get those paper towels ready with the gauze and water. Cool?"

"I'm not scared of blood." Ellen stepped closer to Rhonda. She held a roll of paper towels under her small left arm and a wad of them in her petite right fist. "We've seen lots of blood and stuff."

Rhonda was chilled, but smiled for the girl. "Cool, Ellen. Thanks for being so strong."

Ellen shrugged, her expression deadpan.

"Okay, Ty. Let's go." Rhonda extended her right leg with painful determination and gave Tyler some space to work. She swallowed, nauseated as she wondered what Randy, Patty and Roy might've used the filthy knife for.

Rhonda watched Tyler squat and hesitate before finally scissor-cutting her military pants from the hem up the front of the pant leg, around the knife, and stopping just below her pants pocket. He looked into her face. "Is that okay?"

"Yeah." Rhonda could see her bare skin as the pant leg parted. "Snip the rest of the pant leg off. Careful though, Ty. I don't want you to cut all my pants off and leave me with only my undies."

Ellen giggled as Tyler's cheeks flushed Mars red, highlighted by firelight.

Rhonda snickered. "Keep goin', Ty. You're doing great."

In seconds, he cut off Rhonda's blood-soaked pant leg and dropped it to the curb.

"Good goin'." Rhonda felt odd in her half pants. She focused on the knife handle jutting out of her leg. "You guys ready? I need those paper towels quick."

"Yep." Tyler stood close with bandages and bottled water in his hands.

"Okay." Ellen stood with her paper towels and appeared anxious to absorb blood.

"Here goes." *God help me*. Rhonda gritted her teeth and grasped the knife handle. She psyched herself up. "This is gonna be nasty."

Rhonda was far more scared than she sounded. She'd never dealt with a major stab wound before. Where was Doc Brightmore when she needed him?

142

Rhonda braced herself where she sat and withdrew the knife with a steady and clean pull. There was a sickening wet sound, and then a spray of red arced from her unplugged wound into night air. She ripped paper towels from Ellen's hands and pressed them into her bloody wound. They were quickly saturated with blood. Crimson fluid oozed up and in between her fingers.

"Ty. Pour that water on the wound when I take these towels off." Rhonda lowered her tone; she didn't want to bark orders at these young soldiers. *Just like Daddy.* She turned to Ellen. "Sweetie, after Ty dumps that stuff on my wound, I need you to put a bunch of those paper towels on it and press down as hard as you can. It's gonna be messy. Sorry."

"Direct pressure, right?"

Rhonda half-smiled. "Yes. Very good, sweetie. I'm gonna use that pant leg you cut off. Make a tourniquet out of it." Rhonda prepared to remove her bloody hands and towels. "Ready?"

Tyler and Ellen both nodded and replied, "Yes."

Rhonda counted to three and both kids clumsily aided her. Ty dumped the contents of the water bottle on Rhonda's wound and all over her other leg. For a moment, both wound and leg washed clean. Rhonda poured rubbing alcohol on it and had to stifle a scream. Rhonda's gash bubbled away. Ellen slammed fresh paper towels on the wound. The young girl's force and pressure surprised Rhonda.

"I feel your blood coming through." Ellen spoke without worry in her voice.

Rhonda watched paper towels absorb her fresh blood and rise between Ellen's small white fingers.

"Okay, guys, just hold tight for a moment while I catch my breath."

Rhonda didn't feel nighttime cold as Ruthie's Inn burned and gave off tremendous heat, despite being a good distance away.

"Ellen, you're doing great." Rhonda readied her pant leg tourniquet and squeezed blood out of it. "When I tell you, pull your hands and the paper towels away. Ty, give me a bandage and gauze. When Ellen takes her hands away, I'll slap the bandage on and wrap it all up. Go."

Ellen pulled away her small, blood-covered hands and bloody towels. Rhonda watched fresh blood once more spurt from the wound. She pressed a bandage on her cut then wrapped it with gauze. She tied it all tight with her severed pant leg.

"There." Rhonda finished off her tourniquet and released a heavy exhalation. She felt dizzy. She looked at both kids. "You guys rock. Y'know that? You did real good. Can you help me up?"

"Wait a sec, lady." Tyler raised an index finger and jogged toward the BP mini-mart.

"Where ya goin'? By the way, my name's Rhonda."

"Gonna get you somethin'." Tyler grinned. "Rhonda."

Rhonda watched Tyler disappear inside. She turned to Ellen. "How you doin', sweetie?"

Ellen shrugged. "Rhonda's a pretty name."

"Thank you. So's Ellen."

The roof of Ruthie's Inn collapsed with a crash. Rhonda flinched. The flames grew brighter and she felt the heat intensify. Christ, the entire place was burning so fast.

"Can we leave now?" Ellen's voice a pinch of fear. "Bad man Roy is gonna get us?"

"No, sweetie." Rhonda reached out and grasped one of Ellen's blood-coated hands. She provided a smile full of reassurance, though she doubted Roy was ignoring the massive fire at his home. "Bad man Roy isn't going to get anyone while I'm here. When your brother gets back here, we're long gone from this joint."

"Thanks."

Rhonda smiled wider and gave Ellen's hand a squeeze. Tyler returned with a large plastic bag full of goods, and what looked like a long stick.

"Here ya go. This might help." Tyler handed his mystery item to Rhonda.

"A walking cane?" Rhonda grabbed it awkwardly. It looked like a golf club.

"Yeah." Tyler's dirty face beamed. "Found it next to a dead guy behind the counter."

"Thanks... Ty." *I think?* Rhonda turned it in her hands. It looked much like a cane her grandpa, Colonel Driscoll Sr., had once owned. She had to credit Tyler; the ugly thing might help keep her on her feet, and perhaps, even bash in a head or two.

"I also grabbed all of the snacks and bottles of Vitamin Water I could carry." Tyler shook a plastic bag at Rhonda.

Rhonda smiled. "Were you in Boy Scouts?"

"Sure was. Well, I was in Webelos. Y'know, Cub Scouts."

"Thought so." Rhonda stood, using her new cane to rise and support her.

"I wanna get in Junior Girl Scouts again." Ellen looked sad. "Don't think that's gonna happen, though.

Not with those things, what did you call them, Cujos? Everywhere. Cujos don't like Girl Scout cookies."

"No. They'd rather just eat Girl Scouts." Tyler spoke in a pseudo-scary voice.

"Not funny, Tyler." Ellen scowled at him. "I really liked being in Junior Girl Scouts. Mom and I..."

To Rhonda's shock, Ellen's angry scowl suddenly vanished and she put her small blood-stained hands to her face and wept. Rhonda shot Tyler a look of disapproval, but when the boy's eyes too, filled with tears, her features softened. Perhaps he felt sorry for what he said, or saddened for his sudden mention of their mother. Maybe both.

"Hey guys." Rhonda hobbled closer and embraced them with an uneasy balance. She paused. What could she possibly say to comfort them? She gave them a moment. "You're in good hands now, okay?"

Tyler gave a weak nod and wiped his eyes while Ellen shuddered with sobs.

Rhonda stepped with uncomfortable effort, and with cane in hand, she limped over to the kids. She bent at her waist and tied a length of fresh gauze around Ellen's shaky body.

"There ya go, sweetie." Rhonda smiled, and knotted the material across Ellen's chest from shoulder to hip. "You have an official Girl Scout sash now."

Ellen took her hands from her face and looked at her new, makeshift sash. She touched it and sniffled, then looked at Rhonda with moist eyes. Her lip trembled. "I just need... need some merit emblems 'n stuff."

"We'll work on that, Ellen. Your first emblem's gonna be for first aid." Rhonda hugged her and Ellen embraced in return. "Okay, let's get."

They moved to the exit ramp as fire roared behind them. They stopped and turned around once, halfway up the exit ramp, to gaze on the hell below. Ruthie's Inn and the BP station, and all the neighboring businesses were in flames.

All those poor souls. How many unnamed people had been butchered, or worse, by Patty, Randy and Roy? She hoped every victim found rest in their cremation.

Rhonda turned away from sights below and her own macabre thoughts. "C'mon. We gotta be quiet and careful while we walk."

Tyler and Ellen walked in silence on each side of her while she moved in slow, stiff, and painful strides. She didn't like this. Was Roy watching them right now? Their silhouettes must stand out sharp and clear against the blaze of firelight behind them. She imagined Roy, waiting above in darkness, prepared to strike them all. Rhonda shivered and squeezed her .45 and cane tighter.

Both kids walked a few steps ahead. "Hey, guys. Stop." She motioned them to her. "Get behind me. We don't know what's up there."

The siblings' dirty faces expressed fear. They obeyed and stepped behind her.

Okay, just breathe deep and let it out slow. Calm the nerves.

She limped to the top of the ramp and led her newfound kids into darkness.

Chapter Eighteen

On her way up the ramp, Rhonda spied the Volkswagen Passat-trap and passed it cautiously. Nothing jumped out and she continued hobbling up to I-95 with kids in tow. Damn, she could've used Tyler's Maglite. Then again, a flashlight beam would give her away to Roy or any other predator out here.

In the vast blackness of the night road, Rhonda spotted her Humvee's boxy shape, parked right where she'd left it. She suddenly realized that she still had the keys in her remaining pants pocket. She raised her gun and limped with caution toward her vehicle. Her leg throbbed with sharp, achy pain, like someone had donkey-punched and shanked her at once. She felt wetness. Blood seeped through her bandages and trickled down her leg like warm honey.

I ain't got time to bleed.

Rhonda drew closer to the Humvee as her eyes slowly adjusted to darkness. A series of explosions, like smothered burps, sounded from the road below. She ignored them. Brad's door was wide open and a body lay on the road next to the open Humvee door.

"Oh no. God no." She told the kids to stay put. She ignored her damaged leg and shambled quickly toward the motionless corpse sprawled on the pavement.

Near the open passenger door, Rhonda heard a sound from within. Was Roy rustling around back there? Scavenging for something useful after killing Brad? The idea enraged her.

"You're dead, asshole!" Rhonda whipped around the open door, prepared to blow the bastard's head off. Instead, she found Brad. Still sitting quietly buckled in and patient.

"Rrrrnnndaahh."

"What?" Rhonda exhaled steamy breath and lowered her gun to her side. She stared in disbelief at Brad. She'd been so certain he was dead. *Dead*-dead. With immense relief, she realized the body on the highway must belong to Roy.

Rhonda knew Roy would have come up here to see who waited in her Humvee. She imagined him opening the passenger door to find Brad alone and complacent in his seat. Roy probably thought he hit the jackpot; finding a docile hunk of a Cujo just waiting to be turned into their new pet. But good 'ol Roy got too close and careless, and complacent Brad turned mean.

Though relieved and impressed with how Brad had killed Roy, still seated, Rhonda almost wished Brad didn't do the prick like this. Messy and gory... the Cujo way.

What if he hurts the kids? Or if he turns on me?

Rabid is rabid. She shunned any thought of Brad

being a creature who might hunger for human flesh. Part of her knew her fiancé likely attacked and ate normal people before she found him in Levendale. He wasn't acting rabid now, though. He only showed aggression when she was being menaced or if someone fucked with him, like poking at a mad dog.

Get rolling, worry later. Keep the kids safe.

Rhonda looked at Roy's corpse at her feet. Her eyes adjusted to the dark and made out Roy's large mass: he rested, belly skyward in his dirty green coveralls. What was that smell? B.O. mixed with sharp odors of excrement and tinny blood nipped her nose.

Roy's ample gut rounded upward in darkness like a small hill. Rhonda didn't want to look, but she did. She made out a wide and murky pool that collected on Roy's chest and soaked through his coveralls. His fat neck had been torn wide open, a puddle of blood glistening where his trachea once resided. Above Roy's ravaged neck, Rhonda noted his long beard was now gone, along with his chin and cheeks, lips and nose. She made out Roy's eyes, open with a dead glint, but she couldn't see blue or any other color in them.

"Rrrrnnndaahh."

Rhonda closed her eyes. Could she feel any more exhausted or sore? Images of this day wore on her. Hearing Brad's voice raised her spirits, but also brought new weight to everything. She had to look after Brad, and more importantly, she realized, these kids needed safety. On top of all this current shit, she knew one hell of a long drive remained in front of them.

I'm tempted to go back to Fort Rocky.

Rhonda wanted to cry, nothing felt right. Maybe sleep would help. If she could just rest, maybe, just maybe, she'd feel better about her place in the universe.

"Rrrrnnndaahh."

"Yes, baby. I'm coming."

Rhonda opened her moist eyes and folded her arms tight to her breasts and turned from Roy's corpse. She limped to Brad. Good God, his mouth and cheeks were smeared dark, like a child's face after a messy battle with a Hershey bar. But this wasn't chocolate on Brad's mug.

"Rrrrnnndaahh."

Brad cracked a Cujo grin and rocked in his buckled seat with excitement. Long strands of hair stuck to his lips. He reached blood-covered hands out to Rhonda, each one holding a fistful of blood-crusted beard whiskers.

"Ughhh. Really, baby?"

She stared at Brad's polluted face. Shit, she had to clean him up before the kids saw him like this. Tyler and Ellen would flip when they found a Cujo in their car. No doubt about it. She couldn't allow their first introduction to her fiancé to be a greeting from a gore-glazed monster. How could she get two traumatized kids feeling warm and fuzzy about her Cujo-fied fiancé? It felt freaking impossible.

"You did good." Rhonda smiled at Brad. Cujo or not, he had prevailed and that piece of shit Roy was in Hell. She didn't know what she'd do if it had gone the other way.

"Gotta get you cleaned up quick. Kids are gonna be comin'."

Brad didn't reply. He sat and waited for her to do her thing.

Rhonda groaned and worked Brad's bloody shirt off of him. She turned it inside-out and using the back of the shirt and her own spit, she wiped Brad's face and hands clean, as best she could.

When she had finished, Rhonda tossed the shirt and bloody whiskers to the wind. She shut Brad's door and leaned against it as hard pain owned her leg.

Time to get the kids and pile everyone in and hit the road for Florida. A vacation. Stick to the original gameplan. She felt an urge to laugh but fatigue and pain kicked and killed the impulse. Somewhere in her mind she heard her father's voice asking her what the hell she was doing.

"I don't know, Dad." Rhonda's words traveled into night and dropped on I-95 where Colonel Driscoll wouldn't hear them.

Rhonda called over to the kids. "C'mon, guys. Roy's dead and we gotta get out of here." She felt a greater determination to get to Florida, into warmer weather. Maybe she'd take them all and live on an island. She caught herself on this thought.

I've gone cuckoo. Thinking I got me a ready-made family.

"What happened to that bad man? Roy?" Tyler's tired voice was fearful.

Rhonda thought about the faceless lump lying next to the Humvee. "He's dead, I said."

"You mean dead? By-bye forever?" Tyler's voice sounded hopeful.

"Yes, Ty."

"Good." Tyler looked at Rhonda in darkness. "Where we goin'?"

"Florida. Where it's way warm and sunny." Rhonda crossed her arms and massaged them. The night and the things in it chilled her flesh. Her eyes followed the exit ramp's grade and she looked below. Fire ate it all and shat everything to embers. She watched, transfixed and fantasized. Wouldn't it be nice to be down there? To warm herself next to the blaze? Huge flames danced and invited her in. Maybe she and Brad and both kids could go down there and rest...

... while the world turned to cinders.

Shapes of the curious walking dead emerged from dark of night and moved before bright fires below, snapping Rhonda back to reality. They needed to move.

Pronto.

"Can you carry me to Florida?" Ellen tugged at Rhonda's hand.

Rhonda smiled and put a gentle hand to Ellen's sweet and soiled face. "Sweetie, I can't carry you to Florida. I can't even carry you to our new ride on account of my leg." She moaned as she put weight from her cane on to her bad leg by accident. "We're gonna just get in my car here. Then we'll take off."

Ellen sniffled. Her voice carried an exhausted child's tone. "I'm tired. Tired of everything."

"I know, sweetie." Rhonda put her left arm around Ellen's shoulder and rubbed her. "We all need a good sleep. I promise, when we get to my wheels, you can both sleep and by tomorrow, we'll be in a better place. We'll find breakfast and get cleaned up."

"Can I have Skittles for breakfast?" Ellen looked at Rhonda hopefully. "Mom and Dad wouldn't mind."

"Yeah, and I can eat cookies." Tyler waved bags of junk food.

Thoughts of Tyler and Ellen left behind and orphaned on this planet terror broke her heart. Rhonda's breath quavered. "You guys can have whatever the fuck... I mean, whatever the *heck* you want."

When had they last eaten anything decent? What had they been forced to eat? She made a mental note to ask them about it sometime.

Tyler and Ellen blurted out excited cries. Rhonda suddenly feared their squeals might draw attention from the fire-mesmerized undead below.

Oh, shit.

Her fears were validated when dozens of Cujos looked away from the giant blaze and turned curiously toward them. Rhonda didn't like this one bit.

Slowly, a cluster of Cujos moved away from the fiery display below and began making their way toward the exit ramp. Rhonda watched their backlit numbers move on the nighttime incline, and she heard them, louder with each step, closer and closer. They sounded like steam pipes.

On a normal day, she'd take on gangs of Cujos with her M4, or just her .45 and her Ka-Bar knife. But nothing about this shitty day and night was normal. She'd been abducted and stabbed with a dirty knife. She felt sick and weak. Her knife, and M4 with six 30-round magazines waited in her Humvee and she had Tyler and Ellen to protect.

Rhonda turned to both kids. "Move your little asses into the car. Now. We got company."

Tyler and Ellen looked at Rhonda. Their twilight features changed from quizzical to terror-stricken when they followed her gaze to the scores of nightmares coming toward them.

The kids shrieked, hustling to the Humvee, where Rhonda ushered the siblings into the front passenger seat and buckled them in together. She made her bad leg cooperate and hurried to her driver's door. She tossed her cane in between the front seats and climbed in.

Rhonda fumbled for the keys and got the car started. In the headlights, Roy's reanimated corpse stood and Rhonda and the kids screamed at the same time. Roy's egg-colored eyes met Rhonda's. He hissed from a hole where his face had been.

"Nothing stays dead for long." Rhonda revved the gas and her leg screamed. How would she accelerate and brake without full use of her right leg? Fuck it, she'd deal with it.

Behind Roy, the first few Cujos crossed in front of her beams, leading an undead throng onto the highway. Rhonda shifted into drive as the rotten group followed, materializing from the darkness like specters. Every tattered horror made straight for them. No doubt her Humvee's bright headlights attracted them like mosquitoes to a bug-zapper.

"Go, go, go! They're so close! So yucky!" Ellen pogoed with frantic energy and hit her brother while she stared with giant eyes through the shattered windshield.

"Owww! Ellie! Quit hittin' me." Tyler grabbed Ellen's small arm and turned to Rhonda. "Get us outta here, please!"

"I'm on it." Rhonda stomped the gas pedal and swallowed a huge bolt for her effort. "Sit back!"

The siblings pushed into their shared seat while Rhonda rolled over zombie-Roy and one Cujo after another. The animated carrion made it easy; they moved into Rhonda's lane and came at her head-on. Undead, rotten, and rabid, every Cujo she struck added *mangled* to their character flaws as three-tons plus of unstoppable US armor crushed them.

They finally reached a clear and open southbound highway ahead. "Ewwww! That was gross." Ellen sat forward and peered around her brother. She smiled at Rhonda in the cab's dim light. "Gross, but it was good what you did."

"Yeah, that was cool." Tyler spoke with new enthusiasm. "Kinda like *Grand Theft Auto* meets *Left 4 Dead*."

Rhonda half-smiled. Her pain combined with a new, jacked-up rush as they fled. But her rush didn't last long and weariness set in after a few miles. How much longer could she drive like this? Maybe 30 minutes? Tops?

"Rrrrnnndaahh."

Rhonda heard Brad's voice in darkness behind her. *Uh, oh.* She grimaced. Damn it, she'd forgotten about *that* problem.

"What was that?" Tyler bolted upward. He tried frantically to turn around but his seatbelt restrained him.

"Yeah. What?" Ellen looked uneasy.

Rhonda sighed and glanced at them. "That, my dears, is my fiancé. His name's Brad. You can meet him tomorrow. He's tired."

"Hi Brad." Ellen reclined and closed her eyes. "I'm tired, too."

Tyler also relaxed and put his arms around his little sister. He yawned. "Fiancé? Cool."

In minutes, Tyler and Ellen fell fast asleep in their seat while Rhonda drove south with great care.

Rhonda looked in her rearview mirror. Brad's

static silhouette sat in darkness behind her. She drove and wondered what was at work here. Fate? She certainly knew that if she hadn't found Brad and fled Camp Deadnut, then she would've never found these poor kids. The things she did for love, the thing she knew she'd done out of her crazy impulses, had brought her to this place and time.

He's cool to the touch but he's hot. He's kinda dead and he's all mine.

Rhonda laughed at herself then grimaced as her leg pulsated with pain. She glanced around at the kids and Brad, and in the dim light, she frowned at her bad leg oozing more blood through her bandages.

Fear seized her. She shook her head, knowing she wasn't fooling herself. She got herself into one bad fuckup after another in just a short time out here, jeopardizing her grand plans and her life. And with two kids and a Cujo she loved all under her watch, keeping her neck intact was more paramount than ever.

Rhonda knew her neck could get cut tomorrow— from ear to ear. Anything good or bad was possible out in these feral lands, and the way she looked at it, odds were that the bad was going to keep on coming her way.

Chapter Nineteen

Several miles down the road, and with her gas tank nearly empty, Rhonda thanked the god of fuel stops when she encountered an on/off exit with a mom-and-pop gas station.

Tyler and Ellen weren't wearing suitable attire for fall weather. Poor kids. They had woken a few times and complained about how cold they were. October's frigid night air blew into a Humvee open to the elements. Rhonda hoped she'd find jackets or maybe sweaters at another store somewhere along their route. At this little gas station, she didn't find jackets or sweaters. She did, however, find some dirty moving blankets. She covered Tyler and Ellen and left the kids to sleep.

The station only had two disused gas pumps and they sat dead and dry as tombstones. Just as Rhonda was beginning to despair, she located a 55 gallon drum of gas behind the station, fitted with a hand pump-lid.

She located a gas can and filled the Humvee's tank in several painful, leg-tearing trips. She strapped a full can of gas in the rear cargo area.

Exhausted, she sat in the driver's seat for a moment while her leg throbbed. Finally, after some time, she forced herself to drive again.

Onward to Florida.

Rhonda lasted another 45 minutes before she had to stop. The smashed windshield was affecting her vision and speed. Her eyelids threatened to shut every quarter mile.

A Coca-Cola billboard erected in a field off to her right caught Rhonda's attention. She slowed and steered through a ditch and through tall and withered field grass. She pulled behind the billboard and parked in a patch of tall weeds. It looked good enough to conceal their vehicle. Confident, she killed the lights and engine and fell asleep within seconds.

* * *

"Zombieeeee! Rhonda, wake up!"

Rhonda heard the voice through deep slumber.

"Wake up! Wake up! WAKE UP!"

Little hands shook Rhonda's shoulder. She woke and jumped in her seat. Her knees smacked hard into the steering wheel and fresh pain jolted her wounded right leg. "Fuck! What? What is it?"

Tyler and Ellen huddled together, unbuckled, and stared with wide eyes between Rhonda and the backseat.

"There's a zombie behind you." Ellen pointed with her chin while her hands clasped tight to her chest. "C-c-cujo. Look at his eyes."

"He's wearin' a seatbelt." Tyler sounded panicked and bewildered.

Click it or ticket, she thought, blearily. "Chill out, guys. That's Brad. My fiancé. Remember?"

"No." Both kids spoke together.

Rhonda directed her face to the siblings with a lazy turn. "Tell ya what. Let's all get out of the car and stretch. We should take a potty break, anyways, before heading out again."

They stared at Brad and didn't move. Ellen broke her gaze to look at Rhonda. "Why's his name, Brad?"

"That's the name his parents gave him." Rhonda exited the car. "C'mon."

"He had parents?" Tyler wore a skeptical expression. His eyes darted from Brad to Rhonda and to Brad again.

"Yes, he did."

"We had parents once." Ellen gazed at her feet. She shrugged and followed Tyler outside.

Rhonda grabbed the keys and shut her door. What could she possibly say to that? Tyler seemed to handle it well, but Rhonda wondered what demons might loiter inside him. How could Rhonda help them cope with everything? She hoped Florida would help them all heal.

"C'mon, sweetie. We'll do our business over here." Rhonda waved toward some tall grass on the billboard's other side. She hobbled through weeds and glanced at Tyler. "If ya gotta go, do it now on the other side of the Humvee. We're hittin' the road soon."

Tyler stood behind the Humvee. He nodded. "What about your dead boyfriend?"

"My fiancé, you mean. What about him?"

"Doesn't he have to... you know?"

160

"Pee?" Rhonda didn't want to think about it. She shrugged. "Don't think he does that."

Tyler tilted his head. "Huh." He walked around the Humvee to relieve himself in private.

When Rhonda and Ellen finished, Rhonda helped the little girl adjust her makeshift Junior Girl Scout sash. A package of Skittles appeared in Ellen's small grip. She ripped open the package and chewed on a handful of candy.

"Think I'll get more badges like you promised?" Ellen looked at Rhonda.

"Absolutely." Rhonda limped along and placed a hand on Ellen's head. "We have miles to go and things to see. Nothin' but a lot of time ahead to earn lots of merit badges."

"Okay. I like that." Ellen looked at Rhonda with concern. "Your leg's bloody and drippy wet. It smells funny."

Rhonda knew her leg had worsened; noxious now, fucked good and proper from little Randy's filthy knife. She'd better hope they ran into a pharmacy soon, or she'd have more than a bad smell to worry about No use freaking out the kids. "You and Ty ever been to Florida?"

"Nope."

"Well, there's lots of sun and water and fun."

"And Cujos?"

These kids were smart. No way she'd fool them into delusions of a nice family trip to Disneyland. Surely Florida hosted its own bipedal horrors. "Maybe. Ain't nothin' we can't handle."

Ellen looked at her solemnly and stuffed another handful of Skittles in her mouth.

Rhonda knew it was time to address the "Brad situation." She gathered the kids by Brad's open door. He stared at them as he sat shirtless, buckled in, and well-behaved with a thin string of drool dangling from the corner of his mouth.

"Brad he's different, guys. I know it sounds crazy, but he's not like other Cujos. He's not aggressive unless he's threatened, or unless I'm threatened." Rhonda looked at the kids as they studied Brad, wondering if they were buying her explanation about why she was rolling with a zombie. "But I want you to keep some distance from him, okay? I don't want you scared of him, but I'd hate to see you... um, y'know, get drool on you."

The kids took a step back. Ellen looked up at Rhonda. "So he's your boyfriend?"

"Well, technically, he's my fiancé."

"So you're gonna get married?" Tyler started to laugh. "You'll be *Mrs. Cujo*."

"Good one, Ty. Not gonna happen. There was a time—"

"But you love him, right?" Ellen blurted.

Rhonda paused. She looked at Brad, the ghoul, but remembering him from the life before, when things were normal and they were mad in love-lust for each other. Her devotion hadn't changed. "Yeah. I sure do."

"We're good." Ellen handed the Skittles bag to her brother.

"We're good." Tyler concurred and tipped his head back and emptied the bag into his mouth. He tossed the crumpled bag to the ground.

"Pick that up." Rhonda pointed to the Skittles bag. "We don't shit in our nest, Ty."

Tyler gave a Rhonda a quizzical look before stuffing the bag in his pants pocket.

* * *

Rhonda got both kids buckled in. She was impressed with how sound their minds and attitudes were. She hoped to keep them that way. She checked on Brad. Nice. He seemed content and passive. She limped to her driver's side door. God, every step caused her grief. How long could she take this? The tainted matter that glazed her seat scared her. Her bandages were soaked through and she had to agree with Ellen, her leg did smell funny for sure, funny like month-old deli meat left in a refrigerator drawer, not quite rotten, but nowhere near edible.

Rhonda sucked in a groan. Behind the wheel, she wanted to roar. Dizziness blasted her. Spots and stars popped in front of her eyes. Would she faint or hurl? One or the other might make her feel better.

"Are you okay?"

Tyler's voice cut through Rhonda's lightheaded spell. Her eyes fluttered and she turned toward him. "Yeah. Just having a moment."

"Rrrrnnndaahh." Brad's voice sounded from the backseat with seemed like actual distress.

"You need a doctor, lady." Ellen blinked.

"Yeah? Well, *you* need some real food, kid. Skittles aren't going to cut it. And it's Rhonda, remember? No lady here."

"Rhonda." Ellen nodded.

"Don't worry. I'm sure we'll come across a hospital soon, and I'll take care of my stinky leg.

We'll all get cleaned up and get what we need." Rhonda winced, and her crippled leg screamed as she steered the Humvee back toward the highway, bouncing across a hard field and through another ditch. Electric zaps of agony bit her with every bump. Rhonda hoped it was true.

"Are we there yet?" Tyler fidgeted in his seat.

Rhonda released an exasperated breath. Christ, these kids must've asked the old question some two dozen times within the last hour. "C'mon, guys. I know it's really slow going, but I'm doing my best. I already told you we've got another day or more of driving ahead of us. With this smashed windshield, the going's slower than... heck. Just enjoy the ride. Look for some tunes to play or somethin'."

"Why're you driving this piece of junk anyway?" Tyler scrutinized a stack of CD's in his hands that he'd found in a car at their last gas stop. "I mean, geez, the windshield's busted up, front windows are smashed out, and there's a hole in the roof. It's cold even with the heater on."

Rhonda didn't know how to answer Tyler. He asked a good question. She was driving a catastrophe on wheels. She blamed herself for all the stupid shit she'd to get in this mess.

Why am *I still driving this wreck?*

Rhonda thought about it. The vehicle was no longer the fortress it had been. Shit, it wasn't even fast, thanks to the limitations of the smashed windshield. Did she keep the Humvee for sentimental reasons? She didn't know how to answer Tyler. She pursed her lips. "It's armored."

"Armored? So what?" Tyler shook his head. "We don't have windows. Anything could get us in here."

164

"Yeah." Ellen blurted. "And it's so chilly."

"It's not too bad right now, Ellie. Sun's out. Kinda warm today." Tyler inserted a CD and Metallica soon rocked them all. He put his arms around Ellen.

Rhonda agreed with Tyler, it was a nice day; bright and sunny and warm. It felt like the Indian summers she remembered from years ago. Warm wind blew in her face from her windowless door. Sounds of solid hard rock took her mind off her bad leg. During this blessed moment, she felt briefly felt like everything might turn out all right.

"I wish we had anything besides this old rock crap." Tyler peered into a grocery bag.

"Hey." Rhonda feigned insult. "Old rock crap? I like this. Metal. Hard rock, rocks. What're you into? Lemme guess, Katy Perry or Justin Bieber."

"Yeah! Justin Bieber!" Ellen clapped her small hands.

Tyler stuck out his tongue. "Ellie's got 'Bieber Fever' like all the girls out there, or, at least all the girls who *used* to be out there. I like Bruno Mars."

"Laaaame!" Rhonda stuck out her own tongue and giggled.

"Whatever." Tyler chomped on an Oreo. Cookie debris sprayed on the dash when he spoke. "I like some old stuff, too. Even older than this."

"Really?" Rhonda raised an eyebrow. "Do tell, Ty."

"I mean, like, I dunno. Led Zeppelin? Some Black Sabbath. Van Halen."

"Wow. I'll be damned." Rhonda was impressed. "How'd you get into those guys?"

"My dad. He was into cool stuff. He had lots of

albums, even a bunch of old vinyl records, and, y'know... " Tyler looked away and turned his face to his windy, windowless door. Rhonda heard him sob.

"Hey Ty. Shit." Rhonda turned the radio off. "I'm sorry. I... oh, man."

Ellen began crying. Rhonda knew it wouldn't be the last time tears would be shed. Whatever inconceivable things had happened to them, and whatever fate had fallen upon their parents, remained fresh and unmended in their young hearts. These kids had experienced a lifetime of terrible, traumatic things in just six short months.

Six months. It always stunned her. Six months wasn't shit in Earth's grand scheme of things.

Rhonda spoke gently. "I always feel better when I talk to friends about my troubles. When you start sharing your problems with people who care, it sure goes a long way to getting the bad stuff off the brain. You guys have a friend in me."

Tyler and Ellen didn't say anything at first. They just continued to weep, shuddering as they held each other for miles. Rhonda felt tempted to pull over and hold them. Console them. But instead, she drove on, and before long, both kids hitched and hiccupped and finally caught their breath.

Soon after, they told Rhonda everything.

Rhonda learned Tyler and Ellen's last name, "Roth," and that they had lived with their parents in Spartanburg, South Carolina. When Necro-Rabies broke and raced through Spartanburg, their father had packed them and their mother in the family mini-van, determined to make it somewhere safe.

Like Rhonda, the Roths had headed south. They

planned to hide out at their lakeside vacation cabin near Georgia's border and stay low until the pandemic died out and blew away. Right. They would've been hiding forever.

Their first three months had gone okay. Their cabin neighbors were helpful and nice. Everyone looked out for each other. Their neighbors were Mr. and Mrs. Whitman, a retired couple from Charleston, South Carolina. Mr. Whitman, a former sheriff, had some friends in the Army or something. Mr. Whitman made a call from some special walkie-talkie, and a day later, a military convoy stopped by on their way to Atlanta.

"The soldiers brought us what Mom called, 'words of promise.'" Tyler smiled. "They also gave us and a couple cases of mac 'n cheese and bottled water. I love mac 'n cheese."

Rhonda laughed out loud. "I bet. Y'know, I like mac 'n cheese, too. Brad and I ate a lot of it at our old place. But we got tired of it real quick, too."

Tyler's smile faded. "We did okay for a while. But nice things don't last long anymore."

Rhonda didn't reply. She only nodded and listened. She learned Tyler's good times at their cabin were coming to an ugly end.

A night attack unfolded through Tyler's testimony. Horrible events. Ellen burrowed into her older brother and didn't say anything. Their family awoke to sounds of gunfire followed by shouts and screams from the Whitman's cabin.

Tyler and Ellen's dad told them and their mom to stay inside while he went next door to see what happened. Tyler said their dad marched outside in his boxer shorts with a shotgun in one hand and a box of shells in his other. He and his sister sat in darkness on a twin bed with their mother and watched horrors unfold through a window.

At this point in Tyler's story, Ellen started to whimper, and she pressed the palms of her small hands flat against her ears.

"I need a sec." Tyler paused and exhaled a long and shaky breath. He rested his head against his seat and turned his face to the wind.

"Take your time, sweetie." Rhonda stared through smashed glass and as miles rolled by in silence.

After a long time, Tyler finally turned back toward her. "Your parents still alive?"

Rhonda pressed her lips together, unsure how to answer. She flicked her eyes at him and blinked to the road. "My own mom died with my sister when the Necro-Rabies killed our town. Lost lots of friends. My dad, well, he's out there somewhere."

"He is? Don't you wanna be with him?" Tyler raised his eyebrows.

"Not really. Well, I mean... " Rhonda hadn't wanted to get into this. "What I mean is, we disagree on a lot of things and it's not fun for us to be around each other."

"But you only get one dad and mom," Tyler said quietly and dropped his gaze. "My parents always reminded me of that."

Rhonda reached her right arm out and gently touched his cheek with her fingertips. What Tyler said was true. She felt a sudden paternal void open beneath her. Her Dad, the Colonel, her only living family member, should mean everything to her. He did, actually. But she was just... just so angry. She was tired of being angry. And she suddenly missed him and it hurt.

Rhonda couldn't deny her father loved her to no end and only wanted her safe and happy. When she ran away from Camp Deadnut, she had taken joy in anticipating Dad's surprise and anger, and the excitement of her bold exit with Cujo-fied Brad. But he sent her down this path, didn't he? He tried to euthanize Brad, after all. She pondered a new possibility; perhaps had truly been trying to protect her, his only living child. After all, she was all he had left. In her heart, she wanted to believe this.

Too late now.

"Hey, you're crying." Ellen's voice was shocked.

"Ahhh, it's nothing." Rhonda tried a nonchalant delivery, but the quiver in her voice betrayed her. "So what happened after your dad went outside? I mean, only tell me if you feel like it."

Tyler sighed. When he spoke again, he didn't look at her.

Rhonda listened with great attention. Even Brad seemed to lend an undead ear from his seat. Tyler explained how his father, a big and strong man, went next door to investigate while Tyler, and his mother and sister watched through the bedroom window. Their dad walked to the Whitman's cabin and knocked on their front door with his shotgun barrel.

While he and his family watched, they saw the Whitman's back door burst open. Lights from inside Whitman's cabin illuminated the wooded backyard, and old man Whitman flew out, ass-over-tea-kettle into the night, thrown out by unseen hands.

Whitman, shot in the legs and unable to stand, fell to his knees again and again. He wailed at his assailants in pain and rage.

Tyler told of a large, shadowy figure who walked out the back door with a pistol in hand and stood before Mr. Whitman, who kneeled in fury before this invader.

Two additional dark-silhouetted intruders dragged Mrs. Whitman out of their cabin by her hair. They joined the first formidable intruder in front of Mr. Whitman. In a dead voice, Tyler mentioned how Mrs. Whitman didn't make a sound as they dragged her into the woods and out of sight.

Ellen continued to press her palms against her ears and hummed to herself. It seemed she'd do anything to guard her little ears from horrific details. Rhonda couldn't blame her. What kid or adult would want to relive such harrowing incidents?

"At first Mr. Whitman shouted after the two men who took his wife away into the trees. Then he just stopped and hung his head in front of the first big man." Tyler paused and gulped. "That big guy raised his pistol and shot Mr. Whitman in the head. The top of his head went flying off and spinning across the yard like a hairy Frisbee. Or like he had one of those wig things. Y'know... a teepee?"

"Toupee?"

"Yeah. But it wasn't that. It was a real part of his head." Tyler took in a deep breath.

"Okay, Ty. Take it easy." Rhonda rested her fingers on his shoulder. "We can talk about other stuff."

Tyler shook his head. "Naw. I'm fine." He paused

and dry-gulped air before taking a sip of bottled water. "My dad came running around to the rear of the house when the big man shot Mr. Whitman. The big man turned fast just as my dad came 'round the corner. My dad shot that big jerk with his shotgun and killed him, but the guy pulled a lucky shot and hit my dad. I think he got my dad in the shoulder 'cause my dad whirled around and dropped his gun. He was still on his feet though, grabbing his shoulder and bending to get his shotgun. But then another bad guy ran out from the front of the house and... and took him down."

Ellen hummed frantically.

"After that those bad men killed our mom. Then they kidnapped us... and later, they got killed by those midgets and Roy and that's how we wound up with them."

Rhonda looked at Tyler. He rocked in his seat and held Ellen close to him, his bottom lip trembling and his sweet eyes filled with tears. Rhonda grasped at words to save him from this moment. But what could she say?

She drove on knowing for certain, no matter how far she ran away, the past was never going to be far behind.

Chapter Twenty

They didn't see many signs of life in their travels. Sometimes red tailed hawks, or what her dad called, "chicken-hawks," circled overhead. Perhaps these birds of prey flew with virus crammed in their guts. After all, small mammals were raptors' exclusive food source. And all small mammals, Rhonda assumed, came chock full of Necro-Rabies.

Cujos popped up along the roadside and many set themselves right on the highway, static like statues, in states of suspended animation. Others ambled in highway lanes or shuffled aimlessly through the lands she passed. In the urban ruins of mankind's recent past, she caught glimpses of undead movement. But wherever these Cujos moved or laid themselves, they always snapped to rabid attention at the sight of Rhonda's Humvee moving on the road.

At times, Brad pressed his face against his window and hissed at transient Cujos from his seat. To

Rhonda's embarrassment, she couldn't help being reminded of a dog defending its territory.

Death was everywhere they looked.

We're the only living people left. Us and Fort Rocky's survivors.

It took all her strength to keep her foot firm on the gas pedal. Rhonda feared she was getting gangrene or something. Worse, what if she died and fucking turned Cujo?

Then what would these kids do? What would Brad do?

These kids needed her. Brad needed her. They all came first. She'd fight off sickness through willpower, then, right? No, she knew her boast was filled with bullshit. No matter how powerful her resolve, infection was stronger; and creeping deeper in her flesh by the hour.

Rhonda figured Florida's state line wasn't much farther. She vowed to stay on course and see it through. Somewhere, there must be a hospital full of medicine. Perhaps, maybe real food and secure shelter.

At a steady 40 miles per hour, Rhonda thought they'd made good time today. They had passed Georgia towns like Darien and Dock Junction hours ago. A new quiet settled inside the Humvee and Rhonda found peace within it. No music played, only a semi-warm wind provided background noise.

Rhonda glanced at the kids. Ellen had passed out in a deep sleep a few counties ago. She didn't stir, not even when Rhonda hit two Cujos who charged her from the middle lane, sending them flying over the Humvee with a thump.

"That was cool." Tyler yawned at Rhonda.

Rhonda glanced at him. The boy had been sitting silently with his face turned toward the window for miles, unmoving. "What? Hitting those Cujos back there?

"Yeah." Tyler stretched and presented a half-smile.

Rhonda smiled. "Yeah, it *was* kinda cool. Running over Cujos is fun... but messy."

"Yeah. But it feels good."

"You should have seen it when I hit a bull." Rhonda shook her head. "Trust me on that one."

"A bull? Y'mean like a big boy cow?"

"Yeah. A big boy cow the size of a tank." Rhonda's mind drifted back to that North Carolina county road. "It made a helluva mess."

"No way." Tyler's eyes widened and his mouth hung open.

"Yeah way. Imagine hitting a two-ton side of beef at warp speed. It's a miracle I'm alive. That big boy cow is what totaled our car here."

Tyler glanced around. "I know I asked you before, but really, why would you wanna keep driving this thing? It's so awful."

Yeah, it was awful, and she knew Ty's question was reasonable. "I dunno why I kept this thing, Ty. I'm pretty dumb for sticking us all in it."

Tyler snickered, but then said seriously. "Y'know, my mom told me that sometimes you just gotta let things go even if you love 'em. Like when I was all into the Wiggles and had all their DVD's when I was a kid."

"You're *still* a kid."

"Well, y'know, when I was younger." Ty laughed. "I grew out of the Wiggles but didn't want to get rid of the DVD's, even though I'd never watch 'em again."

"What did you do?"

"I listened to my mom. She was right." Tyler smiled. "I just forgot that stuff and gave the DVDs to my little cousin. It turned out I really didn't miss the Wiggles at all."

Rhonda smiled. "Your mom sounds like she was a great one."

"She was." Tyler nodded and looked forlorn. "She was."

Rhonda had steadfastly avoided thinking about her own mother... until now. Her friends, her sister, and her wonderful mother, all gone forever. She wiped a tear from her eye.

"Tell ya what." Rhonda forced a smile. "When we get to Florida, we're gonna find a car dealership and trade this piece of Marine junk in for new wheels. Cool?"

Tyler beamed. "Cool! Can we get a Ferrari?"

Rhonda laughed. "I don't think that's gonna cut it. They usually only seat two people and we've got Ellen and Brad, remember?"

"Oh yeah." Tyler nodded and looked away in thought. He faced her again and smiled. "How 'bout a big 'ol four-by-four truck?"

"Oh, yeah. Now you're talkin'." Rhonda ruffled his hair. "I like big trucks. A Dodge Ram would be nice. Jacked up high. Maybe we'll take it through a swamp."

"Awesome."

They laughed together. Despite the pain in her bad leg, Rhonda's spirits lifted. Together, they journeyed toward the promise of a new life. These three elevated her.

"Can I put the music back on?" Tyler reached for a power button.

"Go for it. Might break this dull drive." Maybe music would also distract her from the pain. "You might wanna keep the sound down a bit while your sister sleeps."

"Sure." Tyler adjusted the volume until hard rock just rose above wind noise. He leaned back in his seat and Ellen rested sleepily against him. He turned toward Rhonda. "When I get bigger, I'm gonna kill all the bad guys out there."

"What's that?"

"Bad guys. Like the ones who killed our folks and kidnapped us. They threw us into a moving truck. It sure stank in the back of that truck, but not as bad as that hotel."

Rhonda nodded and remembered the stench of Ruthie's Inn and its countless dead guests.

"Those bad guys were really mad that my dad killed their buddy. I was happy about that." Tyler's eyes narrowed. It was real dark in the truck all the time. All us kids were crying. I held Ellen real tight and promised her we'd make it."

"And you did." Rhonda smiled. "I understand, Ty. I'd wanna end 'em all, too."

"That's why I hit Patty. That little bitch... sorry."

"You can call her a bitch, Ty. She *was* a bitch. A small nasty one, and you earned the right to call her whatever you want." Rhonda gave him a thumbs-up. "You did real good hitting her. You saved our lives. Shit, *you* deserve a merit badge."

Tyler grinned crookedly. "Thanks. I was sick of being scared and hiding under a bed and putting up with the threats 'n all. I promised Ellie we'd make it and I promised Mom we'd take care of each other."

Rhonda nodded her approval and suddenly lightheadedness and a wave of sickness hit her. She focused on the road and then on the gauges. The gas tank dipped to a quarter full, and if she didn't fuel this shitbox soon, they'd be forced to hoof it. She'd never make it anywhere on foot.

Rhonda looked ahead and her vision blurred on a sign for a Kingsland, Georgia exit. Another unclear sign appeared with gas station logos. What was Tyler saying? She couldn't seem to hear very well. What was happening? Ty's voice, along with sounds of rock music and wind, all faded away.

Her eyelids fluttered as she merged onto the Kingsland exit. They fluttered once again and closed for good.

Chapter Twenty-One

A screech of metal on metal. Hard and painful jolts kicked her eyes open.

"Look out! Rhonda!"

Tyler yelled, his voice cracking. Her eyes widened. Christ! How'd she lose control of the car? It careened and jumped a median, taking out every sign in its way.

Rhonda pushed both her feet into the brake pedal. Tires squealed on pavement and everyone flew forward against their seatbelts. She'd bitten hard into her bottom lip and tasted blood. Breath locked in her lungs as the Humvee stopped only inches away from hitting a 16-foot livestock trailer beneath an overpass.

"What happened?" Rhonda held the steering wheel in a white-knuckled grip. Her heart in her throat.

"You like, totally conked out." Tyler's voice rose, full of frightened excitement. "You were laughing one minute and then your skin turned green and you shut your eyes. Lucky for us this heap stayed on the road all the way down the exit."

"Yeah. Lucky."

Rhonda caught her breath and stared at the livestock trailer just ahead. In the open spaces between the slats, Rhonda saw heaps of bones, the remains of abandoned animals left inside when their owners fled or were killed.

"Are we there yet?" Ellen batted her sleepy eyes and yawned.

Rhonda laughed, hard and loud. She felt slap-happy and ridiculous all at once. She leaned her forehead against her white knuckles and shook with hysterical laughter.

Startled, Tyler and Ellen stared at her and then joined in. The kids laughed harder as Rhonda did.

"Why are we laughing?" Ellen looked at Rhonda and at her brother while she surrendered to giggles.

"I don't know." Rhonda lifted her head and snorted once. "It's just one big silly day."

Rhonda reversed and drove the exit road. Time to find one of those gas stations she'd glimpsed on the vendor sign. The pain in her leg sobered her. Nausea crept up and she began to sweat, dizzy.

Tyler and Ellen watched her and their laughter died.

Ellen blinked. "You need medicine."

Tyler leaned close to Rhonda. "You're turnin' green and really white... like back and forth. Are you okay?"

Rhonda nodded. She swallowed and focused on the large blue and red logo of a Chevron Food Mart ahead. She wanted to get there more than anything.

Maybe, she kidded herself, everything might be fine if she just got a breather.

Rhonda parked and scanned their surroundings. A large alligator crossed the road and disappeared on the other side. Were there rivers or marshlands around here? Maybe a swamp? They were near the Georgia/Florida state line after all. Other than the lone gator, she didn't detect any movement in or around the Chevron lot area. Everything looked zombie-free, but Rhonda knew she couldn't stock in first impressions. The undead could appear out of nowhere. She turned to the kids. "Okay, we really gotta get some gas. Potty break, too."

Tyler and Ellen left the Humvee and ran around to her open door. Tyler eyed her anxiously. "Need help with the gas?"

Rhonda didn't answer right away. She felt hotter than ever and ready to puke. She closed her eyes, swallowed, and mustered a smile. "That'd be great. Check the pumps while I get my cane."

Tyler looked concerned. "You're not doin' good, are ya, Rhonda?"

"Just a little under the weather. Don't worry 'bout it right now." Dots floated in front of her eyes. She blinked several times and tried to clear her vision.

"Maybe they got medicine in the store." Ellen pointed to the Chevron Food Mart beyond the pumps.

"Maybe. Let's check it out." Rhonda bent and nearly swooned as she pulled her M4 and magazines out from under the seat. She tucked mags into her belt and strapped the M4 over her chest. She reached in again and retrieved her cane. Moving with a shaky hobble she spoke to Tyler while he tested the pumps. "I'm taking Ellen with me. We're gonna check this place for stuff."

"Okay. I'll find us some gas." Tyler grinned. "I wanna get to Florida."

"Me, too." Florida, she figured, might as well exist in another solar system. She exhaled a long and joyless breath. "Me too."

"Yeah, me too." Ellen said and leaned into Rhonda's hip.

Rhonda swayed and placed a shaky hand on Ellen's blonde head. "Careful, Ty. Keep your eyes open."

"Will do." Tyler returned to the pumps.

Rhonda walked Ellen toward the Chevron Food Mart. The station stood quiet, imbued in red and gold from the sky. Every window was covered in grime, and the blackness beyond revealed nothing. Everything was a tomb.

Home to ghosts now. Her mind drummed up imaginary monsters of all kinds. *Or more frightening things.*

"Where do zombies come from?" Ellen chirped beside her.

Rhonda produced a weak laugh.

"Why're you laughing?" Ellen stopped and looked at her.

"It's funny a kid your age is asking about zombies rather than asking me where babies come from."

"Oh, I already know all about *that*."

"I see." Rhonda wasn't up to getting into a Sex-Ed talk with a fourth grader. "Well, about zombies. They're the result of... "

Uh, ohhhhhhh...

Her world spun. Rhonda watched little Ellen blur

181

and wash into the reddening sky and distorted Chevron station. Everything revolved faster and out-of-focus. She closed her eyes and hoped it would stop. She swayed on her legs, and closing her eyes helped nothing. Her head felt swollen with fever. She opened her eyes, stepped away from Ellen, and vomited violently onto pavement.

"Rhonda?"

Rhonda bent at her waist and retched. Her right hand clutched her cane and her left arm shot out with palm out to keep Ellen away. She heaved and spit out long strings of bitter saliva. "I'm okay. Jus'... gimme a minute."

She gasped. Her stomach clenched and she tasted a mixture of bile and blood in her mouth. Sweat poured from her and she blinked at the puddle of watery puke on the parking lot in front of her. Her head cleared for a moment and she stood straight. She looked at Ellen's worried face. She wished she could raise a smile to reassure the girl, but it was beyond her.

Ellen asked Rhonda something, but Rhonda didn't hear. Her full attention was on the Chevron Food Mart's front door. Horror filled Rhonda's heart. Her voice cracked hoarsely from her raw throat. "Oh, God, not now."

Rhonda's peripheral vision caught Ellen's movement; the young girl's blonde hair twirled in slow motion as she whipped around to see what Rhonda was blubbering about. Ellen screamed and ran behind her while Rhonda dropped her cane and unslung her M4.

Five Cujos shambled out of the Chevron's doorway a few yards away and made straight for them. Whatever small amount of adrenaline remained within her, Rhonda's body tapped it and pushed it into her veins for a slight boost.

She'd never get used to the sight or smell of them. Undead terrors scorched with putrefaction. Yolk-colored eyeballs jittered as they found her. Rotten rags hung off their limbs and festered torsos. They hissed.

Rhonda aimed her gun burst at their rotting heads. Zombie skulls blew to pieces like rancid fruit while Rhonda swept the M4 from right to left in one smooth motion.

Every Cujo fell... then she followed their lead. Her head gyrated in a sea of sickness and her legs gave out. She landed on her knees and fell forward on her belly. Her descent stopped on the left side of her face, her M4 now pinned between concrete and her breasts.

Flat on pavement, Rhonda's vision fluttered in and out of focus. She *couldn't* pass out, not now.

Gotta get up. Gotta keep it together. For the kids.

Hard as she tried, Rhonda couldn't summon any strength to rise. So this was it?

Rhonda panted. Fucking helpless. She burned from the inside out. Both kids yelled her name and ran to her. Through her fuzzy gaze, she stared straight ahead at the Chevron Food Mart's open doorway. There, she caught movement, outside of daylight; fuzzy things writhing on the edge of darkness. Rats. Fucking rats, she realized... lots of them inside the gas station store. Each one packed full of Necro-Virus.

Long shadows were setting in. Rhonda watched curious rat noses poke out into cool October air. Did they catch her scent? Something large moved behind the rats. What in the hell was that? She observed a tall profile rising past the rats and doorway. It moved inside the building, outlined against the filthy windows of the station store's far side. Whatever it was, she must've woken it from a squalid slumber, thanks to her explosive appearance. From inside the store came a series of loud crashes. All the vermin in the doorway scattered. She prayed they'd hide and stay put in whatever offal-stuffed recesses they dwelled in.

"C'mon, Rhonda! You gotta get up!" Ellen tugged at her arms.

"Please, get up. Somethin's comin'." Tyler sounded frantic.

Gotta stand up.

She knew she *must* get her ass off pavement and protect these kids from whatever was banging around inside this little pit-stop of nightmares. But she couldn't do it. She only wanted to rest just for a moment. Just a short break to catch her breath.

Okay...

Again, Rhonda's eyelids fluttered and she felt herself drifting away. A heavy and merciless sickness overpowered her. But before she succumbed, she smelled the thing. Then she saw it in all of its hideous glory. It emerged, glacially slow, from Chevron Mart darkness and entered into afternoon light.

No. Gotta make it... make it go away.

But Rhonda couldn't do anything about it. Neither wishes nor wasted prayers would send this shape back to the hell from which it had surely come.

This decayed thing, like all of them, wasn't supposed to be animated. But a new world turned, didn't it? The improbable walked.

Rhonda panted and strained to move her head for

a better look. Sharpened by terror, her vision took on a new clarity as she absorbed every morbid detail of this unmentionable. She stared at it from her snake's-eye-view as it dragged itself on rotten legs.

Good God, how it smelled. An absolute carrion reek of a hundred combined road-kills emanated from every molecule of its moldy form. It lagged and inched along and pushed a primitive terror button deep in Rhonda's brain. It should be interred 100 feet below ground where larva and bacteria and time could do their work. But here it stood before her, trapped in a horrifying state of suspended death and prolonged putrefaction.

The ultimate zombie, Rhonda thought. An über-Cujo if ever one wandered terra firma.

Those first five Cujos looked like healthy, young things with dark suntans next to this bipedal atrocity. Never had she seen such a horror. Across its unclothed body, she noticed exposed bones poking through deteriorated flesh.

To her disgust, Rhonda also saw internal organs in full view. Gray and shriveled lungs hung from the creature's bare ribcage, jiggling in a distended ball near its lower abdomen. This putrid mass swung like an obscene pendulum, just barely held in place by a fragile and transparent wall of decrepit belly skin. This abominable paunch looked ready to rupture and spill its contents with every zombified step.

She gasped and gawked. Ferocious dread bit into her. She scanned its yellow and black-spotted flesh, the disintegrated tissue clinging to its skeleton like a maggot-laden sheet of linen. Where she saw countless divots throughout this fetid flesh, she imagined rabid station rats had taken their chances and bit away rotten morsels from every available inch of this super-Cujo.

Perhaps, she wondered in her hot and infected mind, *this was why its genitals are gone. The rats...*

Countless flies orbited and lit upon its head. Her soul released a silent scream. She thought her entire world would end here as she took in the thing's contorting, abominable face as its cankered and blighted globules twitched in their moldered sockets and rotated to stare at her.

Surely, she imagined, this thing's eyes were sightless. All these fuckers should be blind... but the walking corpse sure didn't act blind. It reacted when Rhonda's own gaze met its own. It released a shallow hiss at her before turning its hideous head and wasted spheroids toward new movement. It stared at both kids, who shouted and tugged at Rhonda's feet.

Run! This word roared in Rhonda's head, inaudible. She hoped the kids would get it and make for high ground.

Rhonda couldn't keep her neck and head off pavement any longer. Exertion broke her. Her head dropped and she landed on her chin. She saw stars, but felt no pain. On her chin, she rolled her fever-drowsy eyes upward. To her terror, she found the monster once again peered at her. It reached with a rotten crypt-hand to seize her.

"Leave her alone!"

Rhonda watched in alarm as Ellen ran at the thing with Rhonda's cane in her small hands. When she reached the Cujo, she swung and nailed the Chevron abomination in its bloated gut. The cane handle tore into thin flesh and disappeared into the rot within.

"You big nasty!" Ellen crowed as the cane pierced deep into the zombie and slipped from her hands.

"Ellen, get back here!" Tyler's voice cried out from somewhere behind Rhonda.

Rhonda watched the two-legged fiend freeze just before its rotten claw touched her face. The terrible thing paused. Maybe it had gone into shock? Perhaps whatever foul jelly sloshed in its dome was calculating its next clumsy move. To Rhonda's dismay, it shifted and rose to its full height, hissing and drooling like some rancorous reptile.

It peered down at the cane impaled in its swaying bag of guts. Rhonda watched its threadbare bottom jaw ratchet and flop open wider, as if with surprise. Reaching down with both hands, it pulled the cane from its bowels with a slow drag. Its lower abdomen opened into a wide gash and eviscerated the monster right where it stood.

Rhonda viewed everything from her prone position. All of the creature's tainted innards, green with rot and slick with the marinade they'd soaked in for months, slopped out in coils and lumps and threatened to baptize Rhonda's head.

Rhonda squeezed her eyes shut just as liberated internal organs landed with a vile splatter next to her face. Something nasty and wet peppered her left cheek. Between this repulsive scene and overwhelming stench, her stomach rolled again.

Rhonda felt herself slip into a fevered stupor. Above her, she heard king Cujo's relentless hiss along with terrified cries of her foster children.

And then, gunshots.

Chapter Twenty-Two

Rhonda awoke to a burning in her right leg. She opened her eyes and found herself on her back beside the parked Humvee. She sat up painfully. Tyler and Ellen crouched next to her.

"What the hell's going on?" Rhonda croaked. She needed water. An unpleasant wetness spread on her right leg while Tyler knotted a dressing around her wound.

"We cleaned up your cut." Tyler wiped his hands and stood. "I had all that stuff from the other place. Y'know, the alcohol and stuff? We dumped it all in your cut and bandaged it up. I guess when I tightened the cloth, it musta hurt, 'cause you woke up screaming."

Rhonda looked at her right leg, impressed to find it cleaned and wrapped with a fresh tourniquet. A sudden jolt of panic hit her as she remembered. She put a hand to her left cheek and stared at both kids. "Where is it? That thing?"

"Tyler shot it." Ellen stood and grinned. "And I helped kill it, too. It's now just a smelly pile of yuck over there."

Rhonda looked at Tyler. "Where'd you get a gun and how the hell'd you know how to use it?"

Tyler shrugged. "We saw you fall asleep, or faint, or whatever. So when that thing lost its guts and went for Ellie, I just grabbed your pistol and started shootin'."

Rhonda sat dumbfounded. "But... how'd you know how to?"

"My dad showed me how to shoot guns. Pistols, rifles, shotguns."

"And you definitely killed it, Ty?"

"Yep. Blew its stupid head off. Blam!"

"Yeah, only after shooting its whole body like cray-cray." Ellen scrunched her face.

Tyler looked away and half-smiled with red in his cheeks. He put his hands in his pants pockets and scuffed the ground. "I kinda freaked out with all the stuff goin' on. I was shootin' too fast. Y'know... it wasn't like aiming at beer bottles and whatnot."

"Hey." Rhonda smiled at Tyler and pulled Ellen close to her. "You both did real good. And thankfully, none of us got hurt."

"I helped kill it." Ellen crossed her arms.

"I know, honey. I watched you nail that ugly fu... *fudger* with my cane."

Tyler nodded at his sister. "You're pretty tough, Ellie."

"You both are." Rhonda winked.

"Do you think I'll get a merit badge for this?" Ellen looked hopeful.

Rhonda nodded and patted the sash across Ellen's

chest. "Absolutely! Lessee, the way I figure, you got badges comin' for First Aid, Bravery, and definitely Cujo Killing."

Ellen clutched her sash and squealed with delight.

"Cool." Tyler smiled.

Rhonda felt woozy. She swallowed and her throat hurt worse than ever. She blamed this rawness on hot vomit she ralphed out earlier when they rolled into the Chevron station. Her leg hurt, too, and she knew the kids' efforts to clean her up were for naught. Sickness and infection still ravaged her.

What irreversible damage did her leg and health suffer from lack of proper medical care and rest?

I fucked myself.

"We gotta get out of here." Rhonda looked at a darkened sky. Visions of Chevron rats and yet-unseen dangers filled her head. "Help me up, please."

"You want your cane back? It's by the Cujo." Ellen stepped closer to Rhonda.

Rhonda thought of the super-rotten Cujo, turned into a "yuck" near the station mart. She pictured her bowel-ripping and gore-soaked walking stick.

"Fuck no." Rhonda grimaced. "I mean, fudge. Awwwww, the hell with it. I don't ever want that cane back."

Both kids giggled at this and Rhonda found strength to smile.

They stood on either side of Rhonda and she put her arms out to them. They grabbed her hands and grunted and got her on her feet. She swayed, intoxicated by infection and fatigue.

"Whoa." Tyler held Rhonda's forearm and steadied her. "You gonna be okay?"

Rhonda closed her eyes and nodded. Her dizziness ebbed and she breathed deeply. "I'm all good, Ty. I feel better. Just wanna get on the road. Let's roll."

Tyler and Ellen eyed Rhonda uncertainly and exchanged doubtful glances. Nonetheless, they grabbed hold of her and steadied her to the driver's door. Tyler retrieved the .45 and M4 and placed them in the passenger-side footwell.

Rhonda looked at Brad. He remained buckled in his seat, patient as an old bloodhound. He gave Rhonda all his attention and stared into her face, unblinking.

Tyler and Ellen helped Rhonda into her driver's seat and agony bombarded her leg. She stifled a moan. Both kids got themselves into their front seat and buckled in.

Tyler turned to Rhonda. "Aren't you gonna wear your seatbelt?"

Rhonda closed her eyes and began to shake. Christ, she'd never hurt so badly. Never felt so weak and sick. She hung her head while hot sweat broke out across her upper torso. She opened her eyes and stared at the center of her steering wheel. "Yes I am. You... you and Ellen keep yours on."

"She's looking really, really green and white again." Ellen sang girlishly.

"Yeah. I'm not feeling so great." Rhonda turned to both kids. "Ty, you got a soda or anything with caffeine in those grocery bags?"

Tyler rifled through plastic bags on the floor next to the firearms. He pulled out a can of Red Bull and held it out to her. "Will this work?"

Rhonda nodded and grabbed the can. "Thanks."

The Red Bull hurt her raw throat. She hoped it would kickstart her body and keep her alert.

"Do we have far to go?" Ellen looked at Rhonda.

Rhonda finished her Red Bull and belched. Tired and sore, she didn't care to excuse herself. "Well, we've still got a lot of driving ahead if we're gonna make it to the Gulf coast."

Where was a hospital when she needed it? Where would she get gas now? Time ticked on while her health and gas burned away. The Chevron station, what a fucking waste of time. She could've gotten them all killed. That was old news now. They were almost to Florida. Rhonda prepared to drive.

This journey had turned out to be one fucked-up trip. No Chevy Chase vacation here. Just a hell-ride through zombieland with her Cujo-fied hubby-to-be and new kids. She crushed the empty Red Bull can and tossed it out her windowless door into the Chevron lot.

"Hey, that's littering." Tyler frowned disapproval. "No pooping in the nest."

"Yeah!" Ellen shook her head.

The kids were right. What of Rhonda's determination to hold on to the manners of their old lives? "We shouldn't litter. Sorry 'bout that. Won't do it again. 'Kay?"

Ellen smiled. "Okay. Good."

"Let's get out of here." Tyler gazed out his window. "The rats are moving."

Rhonda looked past Tyler and beyond motionless Cujos spread about Chevron pavement. She watched Necro-Rabid vermin pour out from the station doorway. Sunlight dropped and rats moved fast throughout the dark lot. They sniffed and nibbled at deactivated Cujos. They scurried toward the Humvee and Rhonda shifted and drove away.

"Just sayin'... I hate rats." Tyler folded his arms with an air of disgust and stared westward. "Rats are why everyone's a zombie."

"Why do Cujos eat people?"

Rhonda swallowed warm spit. "I'm not sure, Ellen. They're cannibalistic, but not with their own, undead kind. Maybe 'cause we're warm and fresh, they want us. They'd eat other large and healthy mammals if they could get their hands on 'em."

Ellen's question was one Rhonda asked Doc Brightmore before. Doc said Cujos ate healthy human flesh, but never attacked and ate their own "walking" kind. How they knew the difference between regular, living people and the newly undead, she didn't know. Perhaps they possessed a zombie sense of smell or a special visual ability? Who cares? Myriad reasons why rot-walkers worked, remained, as always, unanswerable.

"I heard zombies don't poop." Ellen offered her bit of hearsay while she inspected her sash. "If they don't poop, where does all the stuff they eat go?"

Rhonda choked on this nauseating idea. She thought of the giant Chevron station Cujo... that horrific specimen of decay with its pendulous sack of vile entrails. Those same putrefied bowels stuffed with decomposing human meat.

At 45 miles per hour, and crossing the state line into Florida, Rhonda leaned out just in time to disgorge small amounts of Red Bull and whatever snacks remained in her sensitive tummy. Her Humvee veered for a second before she straightened it out.

Again she gagged and hurled red and green vomit out her window.

"Ewwww, gross." Ellen scrunched her face again and pinched her nose.

"Pull over, please?" Tyler looked concerned. "You probably shouldn't drive like this."

Rhonda blinked her watery eyes. She coughed and cleared her throat. "I'm gonna be fine, Ty. The sign ahead says Jacksonville is coming up in 20 miles. I've never been there, but it's gotta be big enough to have everything we need. Can't waste any more time."

Tyler didn't say anything, just stared at Rhonda silently. The kids seemed to be waiting for Rhonda to say something... or maybe puke again.

Rhonda coughed and hacked and glanced between their faces and the road. "I'm fine. Just talk about things that won't make me hurl, 'kay? Can I get some water?"

Tyler turned away and reached into one of his grocery bags. He pulled out a bottle of Poland Spring and gave it to Rhonda.

Rhonda drank and washed bile from her raw throat. She set the bottle between her legs. "Thanks for that."

"No problem." Tyler half-smiled. "Want me to put some music on or somethin'?"

"Not right now, Ty. I need to focus on the road and have you guys keep me alert."

"Okay."

Rhonda turned on the high-beams and spit a nasty-tasting wad of phlegm out her window. "Just need a decent hospital with supplies and I can get fixed up. And get you some real food."

"Real food would be nice." Ellen sounded excited.

"And maybe we'll even get showered and get new clothes. I could do your hair, Ellie." Rhonda glanced down and saw the gas gauge needle on empty. "Guys, we really need to find gas."

"I'm sure Jacksonville will have gas." Tyler gripped Rhonda's forearm gently, smiled, and let go. "Even if we gotta go from house to house and take gas cans from garages."

"Oh, is that how you'd do it?" Rhonda smiled.

"Sure. My dad told me to always use my brain whenever I'm in a jam."

"Daddy also said we had to stay away from big cities because they're filled with lotsa Cujos 'cause lotsa people lived there," Ellen interrupted with a worrisome expression. "We're going to a big city, right?"

Rhonda flicked her eyes to them. Damn, they might be smarter than her at this point. If she'd taken the time to scour towns she passed for a CVS or a Walgreens, she might be in better shape already. But she just had to insist on rolling, didn't she? She should've taken her chances many miles ago, but now she was rolling the dice in a large city with a lot of area to cover, and she didn't even know where to start looking for anything.

"Easy, guys. We've all made it this far through other Cujos and worse. If there's Cujos in Jacksonville, we'll deal with 'em... deal with 'em all with extreme prejudice."

"What's that mean?" Ellen looked puzzled.

"Prejudice isn't good." Tyler piped in. "It means you hate someone of a different color or religion. Least that's what Mrs. Bernd taught us last year."

"You're right, Ty. But that's not what I mean."

Rhonda thought she smelled her bad leg again and it wasn't pleasant. "I'm basically saying that we're not gonna tolerate any Cujos givin' us a hard time. We'll take 'em out with a cane if we have to. Right, Ellen?"

Ellen giggled and Tyler snickered and nudged her.

"'Sides, maybe by now all the Cujos have skated outta town and Jacksonville won't have any Cujos left to worry about."

Tyler and Ellen both gave her identical, skeptical stares from their shared seat.

No. She couldn't bullshit these kids. She knew she couldn't bullshit herself. They were all in jeopardy and she couldn't go back to make up for it no matter how hard she wished. She was already imagining armies of Cujos in Jacksonville. And she didn't just need medical supplies from a drug store; she was way beyond that, she needed an actual *doctor* now. And in her estimation, the only doctor existing on the planet was Doc Brightmore, and he was states away in lifetime long gone.

Rhonda stewed in her own hell. Jacksonville neared.

Chapter Twenty-Three

An official welcome sign for Jacksonville, Florida came into view. Population 1.3 million. This figure made Rhonda's stomach roll. How many of them were now Cujos?

She choked back bile. There was nothing left to fucking puke up. She steadied herself.

"I saw a sign for Downtown and stuff." Tyler looked out his window and stared at a dark river underneath their wheels.

Rhonda found it hard to multitask. She processed Ty's words as she weaved in and out of abandoned and smashed cars and human roadkill. Before her, the evening road blurred and darkened.

"I'm... " Rhonda croaked her words. "Just skirting the city... looking for a hospital. Gonna get off here and find something."

They exited the bridge and rolled on solid ground. The Humvee shuddered and Rhonda's weary eyes found the gas gauge needle buried in red. She'd run the tank dry.

"What's wrong with the car, Rhonda?" Ellen looked worried as they all jostled with each Humvee hiccup.

"We're running out of gas, Ellie." Tyler straightened in his seat.

It took so much strength to say anything. "Sit back guys. Just sit back... I'll get us as far as possible."

Ellen pulled her feet and legs up on her seat, put her face into her knees and whimpered.

"What's that?" Tyler pointed out to their left. Huge banks of bright lights lit the evening dark about a quarter mile ahead.

Rhonda saw it at the same time he did, surprised to see all these intense and close lights. She felt delirious.

"It's a stadium." Rhonda's raspy voice tumbled from her.

"A stadium? Wow. I've only seen them on TV." Tyler leaned closer toward the smashed windshield.

Rhonda gave a drunken nod.

Tyler beamed with excitement. "If there's lights on over there, then maybe regular people are over there and we can get help and we won't be alone."

"Ty, I'm not sure that's... "

Rhonda's words dribbled into nothing. Those lights didn't necessarily mean any normal people were there. Bright lights could also mean swarms of Cujos drawn like rabid moths. But her stamina plummeted and Rhonda didn't have the energy to find the words.

"We gotta get over there." Tyler's voice grew louder and more urgent.

Again and again the Humvee jerked its occupants

back and forth in their seats as the last drops of gas were sucked up.

"Rrrr-rrr-rrrckkk," Brad stammered from the backseat.

"Please, Rhonda." Ellen uncurled herself and sat straight. "Let's get over there. We need people."

Rhonda didn't want to argue. They were trapped like sitting ducks in their dead Humvee. No choice now but to get out and make for new ground. Where was fresh gas? Shit, where was a reliable vehicle with a full tank? No wheels, no hospital nearby. She knew she couldn't move anywhere far on foot in this condition.

Rhonda steered the dry Humvee closer to the lighted stadium. Time to admit her luck ran out. She clutched one final hope that the stadium would provide help... would have unzombified, normal people waiting for them.

Please tell me I did something right.

"Hang on." Rhonda wheezed and cranked the wheel. She punched the gas, hoping the last ounce of fuel would propel her Humvee closer to the stadium.

Both kids and Brad rocked in their seats as Rhonda dodged dead vehicles with feverish coordination. They sped faster, a miracle of some sort, she thought, and crossed a huge parking lot filled with palm trees and row after row of parked cars. Her heavy eyes rolled and refocused as she pushed on toward the stadium.

"EverBank Field." Rhonda knew this place from watching football games with Brad in the old days. "Home of the Jacksonville Jaguars."

"This place is gi-normous." Tyler looked upon it with wide eyes.

"I don't like sports," Ellen offered, but she appeared to be as fascinated as her brother with the stadium before her.

Exhausted and dizzy with pain, Rhonda put her foot to the floor... but the Humvee wouldn't move. The engine growled once before her Humvee died. Rhonda shifted into neutral and coasted into a crowd control barrier. They stopped several yards in front of a tall, three-story column filled with escalators, adorned from top to bottom with tattered banners for Pepsi and the Jaguars.

"Let's go." Rhonda spoke with her voice strained. As she opened the door and shifted in her seat, she accidentally beeped the car horn.

"Rhonda, maybe we should be a little quieter in case there *are* Cujos here." Tyler looked around nervously.

Ellen nodded in agreement.

"I'm... sorry. Shit!" Why would she make noise like that? She'd definitely lost it. She knew better than anyone that you *never*, *ever* make unnecessary noise in Cujoland.

Rhonda got out and frowned at the stadium. She turned and looked at Brad. He gazed out the window, his face illuminated by the stadium glow.

Is EverBank Field Cujo-free?

Brad moaned in distress and strained in his seat. Rhonda and the kids looked in the direction of Brad's agitated gaze and watched numerous Cujos appearing in the parking lot and from around the building.

Mistake.

Fuck me.

"You should'nt've beeped the horn." Tyler shook his head. "We gotta split."

Ellen released an unhappy squeal.

Rhonda knew she should be terrified. There was no way she could outrun hungry Cujos on foot. She just wanted to sleep. She felt done and over it.

Put a fucking fork in me.

"C'mon already! We gotta go." Tyler unbuckled himself and Ellen from their shared seatbelt and grabbed Rhonda's .45 and M4. He pushed the carbine at Rhonda. "Here. Let's get!"

Rhonda looked at her M4 dreamily and reached for it in slow motion. Lightheadedness swept through her. Who stole her body? Some bastard had tricked her. Stuck her in this useless shell. She groaned again and checked the chamber. Empty. Grunting, she ejected the spent mag. With a mixture of hazy feebleness and sharp discomfort, she pulled another loaded magazine out of her belt and locked it home. She pulled the slide backward and a fresh bullet filled the chamber.

"Ty, jump in the backseat and unbuckle Brad. Then get back here and grab the .45 and your sister." Rhonda looked at a column of escalators in front of them. "Make a run for those escalators and take 'em to the top. I'll cover you. Meet you up there."

"But what if he tries biting me?" Tyler frowned at Brad. He turned to Rhonda and blinked. "And you don't look good enough to move. We had to help you walk before."

"Just get him unbuckled. He won't bite. I promise."

"Hurry, Ty!" Ellen's face transformed into an expression of terror.

"All right, all right." Tyler jumped into the backseat, and within seconds, he climbed to the front. "He's loose. Didn't even look at me."

"Good, Ty. Take the .45 and Ellen. Go! Shoot anything you have to."

Tyler nodded and grabbed Rhonda's .45 automatic. The siblings exited the vehicle and ran toward the escalators. Through her overstrained eyes, she watched Tyler stop twice to shoot a couple of quick Cujos who charged him and Ellen. Ellen screamed and covered her ears while Ty wielded the large handgun like a pro. He took his time.

Like shooting beer bottles, Ty.

Rhonda huffed and readied herself to move. She screeched in agony as pain shot through her leg. Her wound opened wider and a surge of hot liquid poured from the gash, soaking her entire leg. With some type of superhuman determination, she moved herself past the Humvee and stood on her good leg. No time to faint or vomit now, not while a pair of fat and shirtless male Cujos trudged toward her. They lurched with outstretched arms, their wide, rotten mouths hanging open in a hiss. Were they painted? Their upper torsos appeared smeared and streaked in washed-out colors. Perhaps from some long-forgotten game-day body paint job. Behind them, more Cujos were approaching, some faster than others.

"Football season's cancelled this year." Rhonda's sepulchral voice preceded a peal of explosive gunfire from her M4.

Rhonda tottered on her left leg and pointed her weapon with her deadened right arm. A *bratta-brap-brap-brap* of her M4 echoed through the parking lot. She hit a few in the head, but the gun-bunny that Dad and Sarge once applauded was off her game. She watched with an indifferent eye as bullets blew into the painted chests and ample bellies of the Cujos nearest to her, while other rounds entered doors and quarter-panels of nearby cars.

Rhonda limped to Brad's door and pulled him out with what little strength she gathered.

"C'mon babe. Move it." Rhonda's voice wheezed out of her as she tugged Brad into the parking lot by his shirt.

Brad hissed angrily as he glared at the Cujos approaching them. Rhonda switched her M4 to her shaky left hand and clutched his shoulder with her right. She used her undead boy-toy as a walking stick.

"Fuckers." Rhonda fired awkwardly and hit everything except Cujos. She saw the kids had leapt on an escalator and were ascending. Like the lights here, the escalators had power. Her heart banged with fear and she croaked, "Wait! *Don't go up!"*

The kids didn't seem to hear her. With great difficulty, she shuffled along and led Brad toward the escalators. Brad walked alongside her, obediently, stopping twice to protect Rhonda from Cujos who got too close.

"Hurry up!" Tyler yelled from above the first level of escalators.

Rhonda jerked her heavy head toward the sound of his voice and reports from the .45. Ellen screamed, somewhere out of sight near her brother.

Rhonda watched Ty fire on a group of Cujos on the first escalator. The undead ascended, and in her dizzy mind, Rhonda realized this entire freaking stadium was running like it was showtime.

Escalating Cujos fell backwards as Tyler dropped them like pins on a firing range. His shots remained steady and dead accurate while his grade-school hands flew upward from recoil. Ty cleared the escalator as Rhonda and Brad reached the bottom. Ahead of them, head-blasted Cujos rode to the top in slumped heaps.

"We're coming." Rhonda didn't think Ty heard her weak voice. She stepped onto the moving staircase and started to fall backwards, but Brad grabbed her in time and held her in place. She held Brad's shoulder and looked into his sweet, pale face. "Thanks, babe."

"Look out!" Tyler's voice disappeared under the .45's boom as he fired over Rhonda and Brad's heads. "Got 'em!"

"Christ, Ty. Watch it!" Rhonda found her voice again. Something heavy fell behind her.

"Looks like I'm the one covering y'all." Tyler smiled as Rhonda and Brad reached the top. His smile disappeared as he gaped at the .45's open slide. "Out of ammo."

Rhonda checked her belt, but only one M4 magazine remained. She spied another two heaven-bound escalators in her double vision.

"We're fucked." Rhonda trudged ahead with Brad and nudged Tyler and Ellen forward. "Just get all the way up those next group of escalators. I'll do the shooting."

They didn't argue. Tyler bolted, the empty handgun in one fist and Ellen's hand in the other. With a distressed cry, Ellen ran with her brother.

Rhonda and Brad boarded a new escalator. Brad shoved undead aggressors from the second bank of escalators. Cujos tumbled to the bottom in a heap, but one of them rebounded quickly. It jumped and charged up moving steps with an eerie and furious speed. Several new terrors soon joined their quick amigo on the first escalator platform, no doubt drawn by the commotion.

"Stay put, baby." Rhonda placed Brad's cold hand on her hip as she called upon all of her mental faculties to give her steady aim. She pointed her M4 straight at the escalator as ghouls approached.

Walkin' maggot incubators.

Rhonda fired a single round. Her M4 clicked empty and the bolt caught open. Inside the pantry was bare. "Fuck me."

Rhonda felt like she was moving through molasses. She ejected the vacant mag and let it clatter to the floor. Brad clutched her while she pulled a fresh magazine from her belt. Why was it so hard to snap the mag into the M4? In a panic, she slammed it home, pulled the bolt, and armed her weapon.

A new bullet slid in place just as a crew of escalating Cujos reached Rhonda's floor. They stumbled over each other as they rushed to get their claws on her. With only a few feet to spare, Rhonda opened her gun at point-blank range.

Cujos dressed in filthy Jaguar swag blew apart as Rhonda raked them with fire. She exhaled in relief as her scatter of bullets penetrated their skulls and obliterated the rancid, convoluted meat within.

Brains. Gotta get 'em all.

Rhonda tasted something coppery in her dry mouth. Her body felt as though it was waning. She laughed.

At the big game one minute... and the next thing you know, you got rabies and a real rotten disposition.

Cujo-fied football fans fell and then her magazine went dry. Rhonda dropped a depleted mag and labored to replace it, even more clumsily than before. She suddenly realized there weren't any more magazines.

Both kids yelled for her. Rhonda shook her head and tried to clear the cobwebs. This was *hard*. No, she couldn't do it. She struggled to hold her M4 and Brad and felt failure loom. With what seemed like Herculean effort, she and Brad made it to the last escalator and took it upward. Below, she spotted dozens of Necro-Rabid pursuers clogging the motor-driven staircase.

"There's so many." It all seemed like an insane joke. "Welcome to the Cujo Bowl!"

Rhonda giggled at herself while Brad murmured in Cujo speak behind her.

"Rrrrnnndaahh?"

For once, Rhonda didn't answer him. They reached their new floor and she clutched her loverboy weakly as both kids rushed her.

Ellen was frazzled. "Rhonda! They're everywhere. We gotta run. Hide! We—"

"We'll go in one of those rooms." Tyler said quickly. He pointed toward a carpeted hallway with a bunch of doors to their left. "We can get in and hide."

Rhonda gazed at the hall blearily. What doors? She blinked and tried to focus. Christ, she hoped they weren't closets. Or worse, locked.

"Ty. Take this. Can't hold it any longer. Just carry it. It's empty." Rhonda unslung her M4 with great difficulty and handed it to Tyler.

Tyler spun and gawked with huge eyes. His voice cracked with a startled cry. "Uh-oh. Go!"

Now what? Rhonda turned to see what they were screaming at and gasped. Three huge Cujos in

Jacksonville Jaguar uniforms stumbled from the escalator and made for Rhonda's group without pause. Scuffed pads showed through their tattered and grimy teal. From their helmeted heads, each football Cujo hissed from carrion mouths. Their milk-white eyeballs fixed on Rhonda and her crew.

She twisted toward both kids and summoned her highest possible scream. "*RUN!* Get your asses in one of those rooms!"

On her final word, Rhonda herself tried to run. Instead, she fell hard and ate stained carpeting. Faintness swept her as Brad hoisted her to her wobbly feet with unexpected speed and strength.

Tyler ran past Rhonda and Brad. He sped to Ellen, who waited in the hall next to an open door.

The football Cujos kept coming.

"Hurry, hurry, hurry!" Ellen bounced halfway in and out of the hallway and doorway with anxious energy.

Rhonda heard a multitude of gridiron horrors hissing close behind them. God help her, she smelled their stench, too.

They reached the open doorway and Rhonda peered inside and found both kids inside a luxury suite. Was she seeing things? Amazing. Like all of EverBank Field, electricity worked here and the suite was filled with bright light.

Rhonda turned slowly and saw the football Cujos almost on them. New terror rode after these helmeted hulks as dozens upon dozens of undead jammed the hallway. It was like some half-time break had kicked into full swing.

Rhonda took a few shaky steps and held on to Brad

the best she could. Her right foot crossed the threshold as something pushed her hard from behind. She lost Brad and bit the floor. This wasn't her fucking day. Bright white flashes cut through her vision. She groaned.

She wanted to cry as she lay sprawled out on her raw left cheek. Rhonda got herself up and rolled over. Brad was standing in the suite doorway, blocking off the Cujo mob. He bared his teeth and held strong.

"Brad!" Rhonda watched him; strong and defiant against a tangle of pale hands that fought to rip him from the suite entrance. His jaw dropped and the corners of his mouth curled.

Is he...smiling? He's smiling at me.

"Rrrrnnndaahh." Brad's arm bolted out and he grabbed the doorknob. The suite door slammed shut in front of him as the undead hallway horde overpowered and yanked him out and away.

"Baby! *Nooooo!*" Rhonda wailed. From beyond the closed door came the raucous thumps and smashes and hisses of a heavyweight hallway fight. She imagined Brad, piled on and ripped to pieces. She sobbed. "He was just here. He... he... he was just *here!*"

Tyler ran and locked the door. He kicked a chair to the side and shoved a small table in front of the suite door as forceful bangs hit the door and outer wall.

"Move back." Tyler jumped as a powerful collision rattled the door. Pictures crashed to the floor. He bent and his face pinched tight as he strained to pull Rhonda to her feet. "Sounds like there's lots of 'em out there."

Rhonda bawled and tried to stay on her feet. She put all of her weight on Tyler. What a kid, he held her just fine. Now, she truly fell apart, wracked with sobs.

It had all finally come to a head. Just as well. She couldn't take any more.

Anything that fucking could go wrong had gone wrong.

Who had she thought she was fooling with her ridiculous fantasies of a romantic getaway? It was all her fault. She sobbed harder and wondered how soon she'd step into ceaseless darkness.

"C'mon, you need to sit down." Tyler steadied Rhonda's fragile body and walked her slowly, his arm around her waist.

She held on to his blonde head and his shoulders and pressed into his upper back. Tears saturated her vision and her body shook as she shuffled forward. She blinked her tired and puffy eyes as Tyler guided her to the front row of seats on the field-side of the suite. She sat, and here was Ellen curled into a ball near Rhonda's seat. Ellen peeked at her, apparently too scared to move.

Rhonda looked up wearily. What a view. She saw everything; a clear panorama of EverBank Field below; all boxes to her left and right; 60,000-plus stadium seats beyond; and a huge Budweiser scoreboard with a giant Jacksonville Jaguar head on it.

They had the best seats in the house. She took in the football field below, bathed in bright stadium lights. No turf remained, only a 120-yard mudhole packed with Cujos of every make and model.

"Wow. Look at that." Tyler pressed his open palms and forehead against the glass. The window fogged where he breathed on it from inches away. "Looks like the whole city is down there. Ellie, check this out."

"Uh-uh." Ellen tucked her face into her knees and squealed when another loud bang sounded from outside the suite.

Rhonda stifled her sobs. She quaked with heartache and sickness. She prayed death would deliver her soon. She prayed the kids would survive.

Rhonda spotted a millenary of Cujos gazing up at their suite. Holy shit, these rotten, life-defying bastards managed to spot her and the kids through this luxury glass; like exotic fish in a fancy glass box.

Cujos below gestured with their ragged arms and reached out toward her suite. A chill danced across her fever-hot flesh. How could they possibly know? How could they even identify her and the children at this distance and make a distinction between normal people and fellow zombies?

"Tyler. Get away from the window." Rhonda struggled to rise. Rhonda felt herself in an abyss; inside a black hole. Her wounded leg, a polluted limb slicked with gore and sweat. Her chest heaved. "C'mon, Ellen. Up. We all gotta get away from the glass and kill these lights."

Ellen didn't move. She kept her face planted in her knees and whined until Tyler pulled her to her feet. Spotting the thousands of stadium Cujos below, she screamed.

Below, the undead moved together with their faces aimed toward the lighted box where Rhonda and the kids made their stand. Every single rotten stiff with the power to move was making for their suite, no doubt in search of someone yummy to eat.

Rhonda joined the kids in the middle of the suite and tried to steady her sight. This box was a damn swank place to throw a party. Taking stock, she noted a nice wall-mounted flat-screen, a stainless-steel mini-fridge, beverage dispensers, chafing dishes and assorted catering supplies, along with a table and chairs in Jaguar colors. None of it would save them.

Hallway Cujos pounded and pummeled the suite with new intensity. Everything inside seemed to vibrate. Rhonda held herself against a chair while the siblings held each other, pale with fear. Scanning the room, she spotted a closed door she'd somehow missed. A restroom.

"Go in there, guys." Rhonda nodded toward the door.

Neither kid hesitated as they sprinted for the restroom. They ran inside and slammed the door behind them.

"Don't lock me out, now." Rhonda's voice wheezed. She tasted something bad in her mouth again.

She moved slowly along, bracing herself on tables and seatbacks for support. Sweat soaked her from head to toe and she panted like a dog. Points of light danced before her eyes.

Rhonda heard wood crack as the luxury suite door split inward. She sucked in a chest full of air and half-hopped, half-pulled herself from one piece of furniture to another until she reached the kitchenette counter. Darkness came and went as her infected body pushed itself past all physical limits.

She leaned against the counter, heaving. Sweat dribbled from her face and spattered across the granite countertop. Her head pounded. Death was close. Maybe one more breath... once last taste of air. Rhonda lifted her face and turned around. She spotted the restroom door only a few feet away.

There was a screech of metal and wood. The suite door looked ready to give way beneath the fury of the Cujos from outside.

Forget it. It's impossible.

The restroom door might as well be in Tokyo.

"Well, I can fucking try."

Rhonda expelled a meager breath and spat after it. Since when did she give up? She welled with a sudden anger and it overrode her fever and pain and the lightness in her head. She was furious. At fate, at the monsters who killed Brad, at her father, angry at the military and the government scientists who started it all, at those mini-freaks and their dirty knife.

Above all, Rhonda was furious at herself for causing the predicament they were all in, and for constantly making everything worse with each new idiotic decision she made.

She thought of the kids. Didn't she vow to take her foster kids under her little wing? To protect them at all costs? Despite all of her mistakes, she'd be goddamned to allow them to fall on *her*.

"I'm Rhonda Driscoll, you motherfuckers! Come get some!"

Rhonda wheezed as the last world left her lips. Memories of her mother and kid sister came to her. All her friends who'd passed before her. She'd survive for them all, too.

Somehow, she stood on her feet and took painful steps toward the restroom, propelled by fresh anger. But as she grabbed the knob, the suite door caved in and brought with it a capacity crowd of putrid gatecrashers.

Rhonda did a double-take as the intruders poured in. What the fuck was that? Her eyes must be playing tricks on her. Coming toward her was a tall yellow cat with black spots, in oversized black sunglasses, white shorts, and a Jaguars jersey emblazoned with a huge, embroidered paw-print logo.

Chester Cheetah? No, that wasn't right. Her mind spun and the whole scenario felt surreal.

Rhonda remembered now. This fucker was Jaxson de Ville, the Jacksonville Jaguars official mascot.

The mascot was a Cujo, no doubt about it.

"Lock the door and stay put! Stay quiet!" Rhonda's voice broke with concern for the kids.

Both kids yelled for her, but Rhonda just repeated her commands. She heard the restroom door lock behind her. She faced the Cujos with a fatal bravery. Her luck had run out for sure this time. All these Cujos and nowhere for her to run. This would be her last stand. She just hoped it would end fast.

Jaxson de Ville stumbled toward her along with dozens of his graveyard football buddies. Numerous undead Jaguar fans from home and abroad walked and crawled into the once coveted stadium box. Jacksonville's mascot reached out and tried to seize her with its soiled paws.

God, what a ridiculous way to die. Instead of screaming like a helpless B-movie actress for some sluggish creature to take her, Rhonda laughed in hoarse, broken barks. She couldn't help it. It was all so absurd.

Rhonda turned from her attackers and scanned the front row seats and mammoth window. She limped away, surprised with her own ability to do so, and made for the front row. She wanted to take her final seat and gaze upon EverBank Field and the shitty world beyond before she died.

Rhonda's sudden boost of new strength waned within seconds. Her entire body spasmed and weakness took her again. She hopped on her left foot and dragged her right leg along.

"Okay, just a little ways." She stepped to the first step of three. Stairs led to the first row of theater seats. But as she moved, she heard a muffled hiss behind her and felt a harmless swipe from Jaxson's soft paw as it brushed the back of her neck.

I'm not gonna look back.

She hopped the last steps. A strange exhilaration fused with noxious sickness inside her. Maybe she'd die right here, on the spot, before any Cujos reached her. She heard crashes behind her and aggravated growls as Cujos closed in.

She gazed into glass and saw reflected shapes of the crowd of Cujos behind her.

Holy shit.

They outnumbered her one hundred to one. EverBank Field below, and all its numerous stadium stands and seats, was filled with a sold out, undead crowd. Some appeared lost, but many stared her way and moved toward her luxury suite.

She turned from the glass and faced the crowd packing the luxury suite. They filled every available space and crammed the steps. They toppled over rows of seats and Jaxson de Ville led the way only a few steps behind her.

"Fire Marshall's gonna flip out on this shit." Rhonda released a howl of delirious laughter. She leaned into the wall of observation glass and rested her shoulder blades and body weight against it. She fought vertigo, but it proved stronger than her.

What an unholy stench from them all. But the intense and collective reek didn't faze her. Nothing mattered to her, well, she thought, nothing except for the kids. Way to go with her shitty efforts. She'd brought Tyler and Ellen this far only to fail. They deserved better than her, no doubt. She hoped they'd stay put and wait it out. Maybe they'd make it out of here alive. Then what? No, she couldn't fool herself that the kids would live some happily-ever-after. Not in this terror-world full of Cujos and predators lying in wait.

"I'm sorry guys." Rhonda's voice sounded strange to her. She looked at the undead mob as they shoved and hissed and packed themselves into the suite. Boy, a bottle of Jack would be nice about now. The Cujo in the Jaxson de Ville costume fell forward, pushed from behind by its posse. It lost balance and in seconds, the maggot-laden mascot stumbled off the steps and dropped at Rhonda's feet. She spat at its oversized Jaguar nose as it rose before her.

"Fuck it. I'm ready. Do it quick."

Her head rocked as a nearby aftershock split the air. An immediate series of intense and bright lightning flashes followed, their brilliance trumping all the megawatt stadium lights and luxury suite fluorescents. For a microsecond, the Cujos before her washed out in thermo-nuclear white before she squeezed her eyes shut.

Had someone set off fireworks? Rhonda's ears endured another blast. Maybe a natural gas blowout. But this felt way big. Several blasts shook the luxury suite. Every Cujo inside froze, their bleached-out, unblinking eyes reflecting fire.

Cujos appeared immobilized by surprise, or

perhaps, the insane light blinded them. She turned and stared through the observation glass.

EverBank Field burned. Rhonda watched a pair of large and smoky fireballs roar upward into the night sky. The stadium roiled and blazed in a cauldron of fire. Goalposts burned and rose from a lake of yellow flame. Any undead on the once-muddy turf below had been turned to fucking cinders. But where had this surprise holocaust come from? Had she hit a button or something?

Rhonda got her answer when she spotted something she thought she'd never see in the sky again. A jet that looked like an F/A-18 Super Hornet screamed high above. It banked sharply over St. John's River and came back in low above the stadium to drop another large fire-egg. This bomb took out every single end-zone seat, and the scoreboard. Everything burned away, baptized by fire.

Mark 77's. What did Dad and Sarge call them? "Napalm on steroids?"

Cujos moved behind Rhonda as the jet ripped the night air. Funny, this particular jet looked identical to one of three Super Hornets at Camp Deadnut.

One of Dad's flyboys? No way. What the hell was he doin' down here? Did anyone know she was up in a suite or were they just going to incinerate her ass and the kids, too? The kids...

She heard a new sound, the distinct, repetitive *whup-whup-whup* of a helicopter rotor. But not any old helicopter: it sounded like a Black Hawk.

What a beautiful warbird. It dropped like an elegant dancer and hovered right in front of her, its metal belly illuminated from below as EverBank's stadium fire raged.

The chopper cockpit pointed at her and Rhonda figured she was hallucinating. Was her *father* in there with the pilot? But how? How did he fucking find... ?

Colonel Kenneth Driscoll produced a slight grin and gave her one curt nod. He raised his right hand in an open-palmed signal of acknowledgment.

Rhonda's mouth dropped in surprise. She raised her left arm and placed her palm against glass. Oh, how she wanted her daddy now. Weakened and sick, her fury evaporated as she stared at him. He was so goddamn close... but couldn't be farther away. She looked at her father and at her reflection in glass, and thought herself a lone seal in an aquarium full of carnivorous polar bears.

Dad Driscoll waved his hands in excited motions. He yelled words she'd never hear. Again, she caught reflected Cujos, only inches away. They reached for her, and the first to make contact was Jaxson de Ville. She heard and *smelled* the mascot's mausoleum hiss as it placed two furry paws around her neck.

Rhonda held her breath and looked at her father. She wanted to see Daddy one last time. What was he doing? He waved his arms in a frantic display, his expression alarmed. Poor Dad. She imagined his horror as he watched her, his last daughter about to fall beneath an avalanche of rabid undead.

Rhonda kept her eyes on the cockpit as Jaxson de Ville and his pals grabbed her. Her father was no longer waving his arms. His expression of alarm became an angry snarl and he made a dramatically deliberate gesture as he pointed both of his index fingers straight at Rhonda and then pointed those same fingers downward. With his fingers pointed to the floor, he spoke two, slow and inaudible words Rhonda read on his lips: *GET DOWN.*

Rhonda exhaled, and summoned a scream of defiance. She pushed off the glass and jammed both of her elbows into Jaxson-Cujo. Her blows helped loosen paws from around her neck and other unseen claws from her limbs. She spun around on her stronger left leg and hit Jaxson's arms away before she head-butted its cat-like snout. She may as well have rammed her forehead into a sofa cushion. Rhonda leaned off balance, her wounded leg useless and dead to her. With the last of her strength, she managed to shove Jaxson-Cujo into the undead bunch behind it with enough force to give herself a small amount of room to move.

She dropped fast. Rolling, she pushed herself under the seats and flattened herself there.

A metal storm cometh.

Fury and wrath: in the form of fully-auto M60D 7.62mm machine guns. They roared to life and ripped incalculable bullets into the suite. Rhonda cringed as unholy firepower blew the wall of glass into dust and tore into the animated worm food filling the suite.

Rhonda remembered being on the other end of these same machine guns, slaying Cujos from the safety and comfort of a chopper. She'd give anything right now to be on the safe side of the trigger. Glass and fleshy debris rained on her from above.

She opened her eyes and was blinded by Black Hawk spotlights and machine-gun flashes. Cujos fell in droves like putrid mannequins.

Would her father's assault ever end? Rhonda covered her ears and watched her surroundings darken as bodies piled around the seats.

This ceaseless salvo, did it mean new Cujos were flooding in? Of course, she didn't need eyes to know it. She imagined waves of Cujos, those who escaped EverBank's deep-fryer of a football field, hurrying here. She pictured herds from parking lots and hallways, all on escalators to the suite. Cujos gravitated toward fire and loud noises, but also, she wondered if somehow, every EverBank Cujo knew fresh meat was on the menu in here.

Well, Rhonda thought with satisfaction, *the undead are eating lead tonight.*

Maybe she still had part of that lucky horseshoe inside her. This heavy artillery and rescue team of Cujo exterminators was an absolute miracle, and she gave thanks. A new tide had turned Rhonda from prey into a possible survivor; though only if she managed to push herself out from under this heap of obliterated Cujos and received proper and direct medical attention.

Then she remembered the kids. She screamed their names, but only heard her own voice vibrate in her head beneath Dad's machine gun assault. How could she leave those kids to their own devices in a restroom? She was supposed to be a distraction... to lead danger away from them. But as the Black Hawk blew the luxury suite to hell, she shuddered at thoughts of the young siblings as casualties from friendly fire.

Wasn't it bad enough she'd lost Brad? Two fucking times already. If Tyler and Ellen died here, Rhonda knew she'd kill herself. She'd have nothing left to live for. Dad would've rescued her for naught. Saved from the Cujos only to fall beneath her own hand.

"Get me the fuck out of here," Rhonda wailed, and realized she could hear herself. The gunfire had finally ceased.

Dad's chopper hovered nearby, she heard it, though her ears rang. Her wounded leg opened wider, all angry with a red-hot hurt that eclipsed the pain from countless glass cuts across arms and face. The reek of putrefaction was overwhelming.

Rhonda ignored these unpleasantries. Drunk with sickness, she wriggled to deliver herself from this tangled dead mass. She pressed her hands and arms against a corpse just as someone pulled it away. Bright white light hit her eyes and a familiar face came into view above her.

"Baby-girl." Her father grinned at Rhonda. He shook his head and grabbed her right arm firmly. He put her on her feet but her legs gave out. "Whoa. I gotcha."

"Dad." Rhonda swallowed dry. "There's—"

Rhonda's voice petered out into a hoarse whisper. She felt dizzy and winded. Her eyelids fluttered.

"You just take it easy. Gonna sit you down." Dad lifted Rhonda and carried her like a bride. He kicked corpses out of his way as he ascended the steps to the luxury suite's main floor.

Rhonda's head hung limp on her dad's forearm. Her vision spun. She caught sight of Dad's Black Hawk, hanging in the air, now with yellow nylon swing-lines extended from an open side hatch to the suite. *So that's how he got in here so fast*. Rhonda's vision faded and her eyes rolled into her bobbing head. She snapped to when Dad, with gentle care, laid her backside on the kitchenette countertop.

Dad turned to three soldiers armed with M16A4 assault rifles. "Keep this room clear!"

Rhonda watched their blurry figures from where she rested. Each soldier moved through the suite in hunched, cautious strides through a gory, Cujo-littered floor.

"The... the kids. Ty and—" Rhonda's soft voice trailed off as she pointed a weak arm toward the restroom door. It looked bad. To her horror, the restroom door and suite walls looked like a target range; perforated with countless bullet holes.

"What's that?" Dad leaned an ear toward her face.

Before Rhonda could answer, the soldier on point yelled, "Hostiles!" An immediate and loud explosion sounded as the soldier unleashed a grenade on Cujos somewhere in the hallway. The other two soldiers ran to join the hallway fracas and immediate gunfire erupted.

Rhonda reached and grabbed her dad by his collar as he moved with his .45 in hand to cover his three soldiers.

"Dad!" Rhonda cleared her throat and blinked tears from her eyes. "If you see Brad's body out there, please, bring him home."

Colonel Driscoll nodded with tight lips. He spoke with a sliver of compassion in his voice. "Okay, Rhonda. Will do."

"Promise? Please."

"I promise. Brad's coming home and he'll get a real burial." He patted Rhonda's hand. "I'll be right back."

"Wait!" Rhonda tried to sit upright. Frantic now, she almost blacked out. "There're kids."

Colonel Driscoll paused. "What did you say?"

"Kids." Rhonda gasped and pointed at the restroom with a shaky finger. "In there."

Dad turned toward the bullet-riddled restroom and then faced Rhonda. He barked out to the hallway. "Soldier Sanders! Here, now!"

Rhonda started to rise and her world spun like a top. One of three soldiers entered the suite and Dad instructed him to open the bathroom door and check it. With a nod, he kicked the door open with a grunt and stuck his M16A4 into the head.

With rifle pointed inward, the soldier halted. He stepped backward with his mouth open. He shook his head fast and turned to Colonel Driscoll. "Holy shit. Colonel! You better check this out."

Rhonda gasped. What was it? Goddamn it, what had they found? Dad walked with a cautious stride. He stopped and stood in the restroom doorway and grabbed his forehead. "Oh my Jesus." He faced Rhonda and frowned. He shook his square head. "What were you thinkin,' baby-girl?"

Rhonda's universe plummeted into an underworld of despair. It devoured her entire wretched and dying heart. Her father's grim face and EverBank's luxury suite all dimmed and disappeared. Her numb head dropped hard on granite and the only mercy she received came from dreadful slumber.

Chapter Twenty-Four

Rhonda reemerged from her black hell to find herself in downtown Levendale of old, in magic days when her North Carolina hometown buzzed as a vibrant and active community.

Levendale sure felt real as she walked and looked around. Yet, in her subconscious, Rhonda knew her old town wasn't genuine. She knew she couldn't be here. How could she be? Levendale was a zombie town. But if she wasn't there with warm fall sun upon her skin, and with sounds in her ears—like her heels on a downtown sidewalk, then...

Where am I? Really?

Rhonda pushed the questions away. She didn't want to know what reality, or mortality, looked like. For now, she just wanted to remain here, in her beloved town.

She walked along Main Street with her mother and younger sister. Oh, how she loved them. Rhonda laughed and greeted friends along her way. Poking her head into Sylvia's Salon, she said hello to the girls and pecked Sylvia's cheek on her way out.

Then she found herself all alone.

"It was all great once." Rhonda hugged herself in the middle of Main Street. The old thoroughfare now sat empty and dark before her. An October breeze rustled the leaves as her words echoed through a ghost town. She wept.

In this bygone version of Levendale, Rhonda wiped tears from her eyes and found Brad. She gasped with joy and entered their candlelit living room to find him waiting.

"C'mere, babe." Brad pulled her toward him on their couch. Rhonda smelled him. Christ, this felt so real. "I love you, Rhonda. I love you so much."

Rhonda put her arms around Brad. Love welled inside her. She looked into Brad's cupid face and never wanted this to end. Her heart ached, and inside it, she knew a final conclusion to this enchanted moment waited... just beneath the surface.

Just a little longer. Please.

Rhonda smiled at Brad and put her hands to his face. "I love you, too, baby. I love you forever."

On her last word, Rhonda and Brad kissed, and her flame for him burned hotter than the fever propelling her into this wonderful illusion.

For a while, and on some far side of truth, Rhonda enjoyed happiness, and then her perfect world turned on its axis.

Chapter Twenty-Five

"Okay, now. She's comin' round. Rhonda? Y'hear me?"

In darkness, a familiar voice spoke from above her. Though her eyes were closed, she knew her father spoke to her.

"Hang on, Doc." Dad sounded happy. "Rhonda. Open those pretty eyes for me. You're all good now."

Her dream evaporated. She squeezed her already closed eyes shut harder, until star-like dots appeared behind her eyelids. She didn't want to wake. Only a breath ago, she had been with Brad in a happier place. Memories of his touch lingered in her sore body like residual wetness of rain after a heavy storm. And like rain, or some post-tempest moisture in the air, Rhonda smelled him.

With a weighty sigh, Rhonda opened her watery eyes and gave up her efforts to disappear.

Goodbye, Brad. My love.

She groaned and squinted at the bright lights and

silhouetted forms above her face. Where was she? She found herself on a hospital bed with a large pillow under her head. To her left stood Doc Brightmore in a white lab coat. He checked an IV in her left hand. Her father stood to her right in a fresh uniform, his expression anxious.

"Doc. Crank her up." Dad didn't take his eyes off Rhonda. "Be slow with her."

"Yes, Colonel." Doc Brightmore fiddled at the side of her bed and her upper body slowly rose until she sat vertical.

"We're back at Fort Rocky I assume?" Rhonda looked from Dad to Doc.

"Yep. Or, Camp Deadnut if you prefer." Doc smiled. "I operated on you a few days ago. Got you all cleaned up. You had one helluva nasty wound and a leg full of infection. I'm amazed you were even as mobile as the Colonel said you were. I debrided a lot of dead tissue from you, but I managed to save your leg. You're stitched up and you're gonna be sore for a while. But I got ya plenty of painkillers and antibiotics."

"Doc did a great job on you, sweetheart." Dad nodded, then turned toward Doc and frowned. "Lucky for him, he's more valuable to us in Fort Rocky's infirmary than in the hole. That's where his sorry ass would've stayed for tipping you off about my plans for Brad."

Doc Brightmore flushed red and he nervously busied himself around the operating room.

"Don't hold him accountable, Dad." Rhonda cleared her throat. "It was my idea to kidnap Brad and steal the Humvee 'n all. Doc was just—"

Dad raised a hand, palm out, and shook his head. "It doesn't matter now. I know why you did what you did. All is forgiven."

"Really?" Rhonda sat forward. "I really fucked up."

Doc Brightmore straightened and organized medical utensils on a nearby tray. He looked uncomfortable and gestured toward a door across the room. "I'm just gonna go out by the waiting room. Stock some magazines, maybe."

Rhonda and her father followed Doc Brightmore's hurried exit with their eyes. Dad folded his arms and faced her. "You say you fucked up? I think fucking up is something we've all managed to do—and fucking up is how we've now all arrived to live in a world of rabid zombies. Your heart is in the right place."

My rabid heart...

"How the hell'd you find me, Dad?"

He smiled. "We locked in on your GPS chip, the same one that's installed in every Humvee. We communicated with that chip every mile. Thankfully, even after six months, the satellites are still working up there."

Rhonda snorted with sudden laughter and buried her face in her hands. If this didn't take the piss out of her, nothing did. She stifled her laughter and faced her father. "That figures. Good thing I didn't ditch that damn thing, huh?"

"That's definitely a good thing." Dad nodded and chuckled. "I sure as hell didn't wanna squander manpower and burn precious jet fuel chasing ghosts. I got some resistance about this mission. I pulled a real misappropriation of scarce resources for a very personal pursuit to save just one person."

"But I was worth it."

Dad nodded again. "Yeah, you're definitely worth it, baby-girl. Tell me, just where the hell were you heading to?"

"My original plan was to head to Naples. I always liked it there and it's warm." Rhonda half-smiled.

Dad stepped forward and placed a gentle hand on Rhonda's forearm. "Y'know, I love you unconditionally. More than that, I *need* you in my life and we all want you here. You're welcome back here with open arms and no repercussions."

"I can't imagine other Deadnuts are happy about the shit I pulled."

Dad patted Rhonda's forearm. "I told you, no repercussions. I'm still running the show here. Everyone's been crazy to get you back. Really."

"Thanks, Dad. That means so much. But honestly, without Brad or those kids, this life doesn't mean much to me. Nothing makes sense anymore." She held Dad's hand in her own and smiled sadly. "No offense, Dad. I love you. I really do. But I just don't feel anything for this world anymore. I just don't."

"I get it. You're heartbroken."

Rhonda raised her eyebrows and nodded.

That's a fucking understatement.

"Well, I think me and Doc can fix that broken heart of yours." Her father released his hand and turned from Rhonda. He shouted across the room. "Okay, Doc! Bring 'em in here."

Was he deaf? Nothing could fix this heart. Then Doc Brightmore came through double swing doors and into her room.

Doc, what a nut. What the hell are you up to?

Doc ran his hands through his grayish hair and opened his arms expansively. "Presenting the Rhonda Driscoll fan club. Come on in."

No fucking way...

Dumbfounded, stunned, and ecstatic, Rhonda watched Tyler and Ellen walked through the doors... with Brad in between them.

Grinning, they shouted her name. "Rhonda! Rhonda!"

"Rrrrnnndaahh." Brad's salt flat eyes filled with recognition.

Rhonda cried out with tremors of emotion.

Tyler and Ellen rushed to Rhonda's bedside and reached for her. Brad made his way slowly to her. The kids looked brand new; showered and clean with bright new clothes. Brad also looked wonderful. Someone had cleaned him good and put him in a pair of new jeans, boots, and a stylish black sweater. He also sported a new, shorter haircut. Someone botched Brad's hair and the kids hair real good. Oh, well. She'd fix them up once she recuperated.

Rhonda blinked and wiped away tears, overjoyed to see them all. She stammered and laughed through her sobs. "I... I... God, I thought I lost all of you."

"We hid real good in that bathroom." Tyler beamed. "Once we locked the door, we saw some kinda open vent in the wall. Crawled right in."

"I was scared with all those Cujos and the shooting," Ellen admitted with a smile. "But Tyler's smart and got us a good hiding spot."

"Just as you were passing out, one of my Marines busted that restroom door down and saw the kids hiding in an air duct." Colonel Driscoll tussled Tyler's shiny blonde hair. "Kids didn't wanna come out, but we got 'em."

"That helicopter ride was a blast!" Tyler grinned at her father.

"And I got a real Girl Scout sash with all kinds of merit badges and stuff." Ellen puffed out her chest to show off her new green sash. "The Colonel says I earned all these badges 'n stuff for being so brave and doing my duty."

"That's real nice, sweetie." Rhonda smiled. "I'm really proud of you guys."

Tyler and Ellen looked like real kids now, far from the scared and grimy orphans she'd found. She wondered if the kids would feel any PTSD later, like Rhonda suffered. They seemed strong and happy. They were safe, and she was grateful.

This place ain't so bad.

Rhonda put her hand to Brad's face and traced his handsome features with her fingertips. He had a muzzle over his mouth. He stared at her with his Cujo eyes. She didn't see one spark of light in his white-washed eyes, but something lurked there, some part of his old self.

Her heart pounded. She remembered the agony of seeing Brad disappear beneath a crowd of Cujos. Then the kids... she'd been sure they were dead. God-fucking-damnit, she had thought her heart ripped to pieces along with Brad and the kids.

Rhonda turned from Brad and looked at her father, standing behind Brad and the kids at the foot of the bed. "Where was he? I thought for sure you'd be bringing his dead body back for a funeral."

"You asked me to bring him back, Rhonda, and I was gonna do that no matter what." Dad raised his eyebrows. "My Marines cleared the room, the hallway, and then a couple thousand rounds and a few grenades later, a shitload of Cujos were permanently dead and all was quiet. We found Brad at the end of a hallway beneath some linebacker."

"Not a thing wrong with him?" Rhonda scanned Brad, looking for cuts or anything broken.

"Besides the obvious?"

"Not funny, Dad."

"I'm tryin' to lighten up, sweetheart." Dad chuckled. "No, nothin's wrong with him. Looks like he made out just fine despite lookin' like any other undead target out there. My soldiers identified him, held back, and we brought him home, still moving."

"He's sure different. Nothing like the typical Cujo-zombies." Doc Brightmore spoke from Rhonda's left and pointed at Brad with a ballpoint pen. "I've spent time with him. He displays no aggression toward anyone, but we gotta keep him muzzled." Doc winked at Rhonda.

"Just can't hang loose without a muzzle, especially near the kids." Colonel Driscoll set his eyes on Brad. "Not once has he snapped or attacked anyone or shown any typical Cujo violence. He hasn't even hissed. But he's still a Cujo. Rabid as all get out and capable of anything."

Rhonda recalled how Brad had attacked Teddie Fitch and how he had torn Roy apart. She considered his protective aggression toward other Cujos who menaced her. It sure seemed like Brad knew good from bad. Also, he didn't seem hungry for human flesh like all Cujos. She looked at Brad and found his unblinking gaze on her.

Dad placed his hands on his hips and looked serious. "We need to have a *talk*."

"Yeah?" Rhonda didn't look at her father. She stared at Brad. Her mind filled with hope. She relaxed against her raised bed. "What about?"

"We'll keep Brad in quarantine until it's time." Dad's tone sounded strange.

"Until it's *time?* You can keep Brad away from the people here at Camp Deadnut, but let me be clear, Dad, I'm staying with him all day and all night." Rhonda sat up in her bed. Her heart fluttered fast and she felt her anger welling up. "You brought Brad back here and I love you for it. But I don't like what you're saying."

"C'mon, Rhonda. Get up so we can go play." Ellen gripped an edge of Rhonda's bed and smiled big. She looked up at Brad's face and tugged at his arm. "Even your boyfriend, 'er, fiancé wants you to. Right, Mister Brad?"

Brad looked at Ellen and gave her a slow and uncommon blink of his eyes before he turned to Rhonda. "Rrrrnnndaahh."

No one laughed. Rhonda felt the tone and temperature of the room change.

Doc Brightmore cleared his throat. "Kids. Rhonda needs some rest for a good while... and needs time alone to talk to her daddy. How about I bring you to the mess hall for some lunch?

"Can we have peanut butter sandwiches again?" Tyler looked hopeful.

"Absolutely." Doc smiled. "Follow me."

"Not before we say goodbye." Ellen got on her tiptoes and kissed Rhonda's cheek. "Bye Rhonda."

"Awww, thanks sweetie. Sorry I can't play for a while." Rhonda turned from Ellen and looked at Tyler. "Do I get one from you?"

Tyler blushed. He reached Rhonda and gave her a peck on the cheek. "Thanks for saving us, Rhonda. We love you."

Rhonda smiled and touched his cheek. "Love you back."

She watched Doc leave with the kids. Brad stood on one side of her bed and her father stood on the other. She flicked her eyes back and forth, looking at them both. Dreading whatever words her dad was going to say, she began wishing the world would disappear.

"Rhonda... " Colonel Driscoll straightened. "It's important that you understand—"

"You have to kill Brad." Rhonda closed her eyes and tears ran out the corners and down her cheeks. "I get it."

Colonel Driscoll squeezed her arm and moved her IV to the side before kissing her forehead. "I don't have to. You can do it."

Chapter Twenty-Six

Several weeks passed as Rhonda healed and tried to put her life in order at Camp Deadnut.

One day Rhonda acquired a truckload of hair products and salon supplies—thanks to a platoon who found an Aveda store full of inventory. By Christmas, she was walking again, but not 100 percent normally. On New Year's Day she opened her own Camp Deadnut salon and worked on hair daily. She offered free haircuts and color for everyone on base who wanted her services.

Rhonda didn't barter anything and she refused all offers for her gratis hair work. She felt she needed to make amends for the ruckus she'd caused when she made her big break from Fort Rocky. When Doc first discharged her with good health, she visited each and every Deadnut and apologized in earnest for any unease she created across base. She apologized for her Humvee theft and for Brad's original, surprise arrival.

She went out of her way to extend a special olive branch to Sergeant Harris. He welcomed her with warmth, and sure seemed to turn over a new leaf. He told her, "Everyone here at Fort Rocky understands the world as it is now, a clusterfuck of a nightmare, and that, Driscoll, makes it hard for anyone to keep it together. No one blames you for going AWOL. I sure don't."

Sarge took a sly second to whisper in Rhonda's ear and tell her how he knew anyone else would've done what she did for someone *they* loved. Moreover, being the full-bird's daughter wasn't a cakewalk.

Rhonda hugged Sarge with all of her strength until she thought shed pass out. "I love you like an uncle. Y'know that?"

* * *

Rhonda had asked her dad for more time with Brad. Just let her heal up and spend Christmas and New Year's with Brad and then...

She agreed with Dad when he said he didn't want her to put off the inevitable. Rhonda didn't want to, either. She visited Brad every day, and though he didn't harm her or act out toward her, she observed a noticeable difference in Brad's disposition when other people were around. Brad was muzzled and locked away in an empty room in Fort Rocky's hospital. He'd become more aggressive. As of late, he hissed at nearly anyone who moved near him and he swiped at Doc often. Colonel Driscoll didn't want Ty and Ellen near Brad anymore, or anyone else for the matter. And her fellow Camp Deadnutians had become more vocal about their unease with Brad. She understood.

Rhonda knew everyone had put up with her bullshit for too long already. She had played her "Colonel Daddy Driscoll card" into the ground. Anyone else who would've tried pulling the same shit would've been thrown into a stockade or booted on their ass outside the safety of Fort Rocky.

She had thoughts of how she delivered Ty and Ellen from evil; and Rhonda knew both kids also saved *her* life, too, in some crazy way. For them, whatever she had done was worth it. And with these thoughts, she often fantasized about life being normal and being Brad's wife and mother to these children.

But things were much different, weren't they?

This is no world for normal, or for fantasies and hopes.

She quietly cried herself to sleep in the single bed she was given in the barracks. *Oh, Brad. I'm so sorry. Mom. Sister Beth. Kids, I'm so sorry.* The kids... they were now the only things keeping her from killing herself.

* * *

It was a cold morning in late January when Rhonda limped toward her father as he sat drinking coffee in his command-post. She'd been using a crutch for over a month. Today was the first day she moved without anything aiding her.

It was a day of new starts she guessed.

Colonel Driscoll smiled as she approached. He took a sip of coffee and set his mug down. "God help us when we run out of coffee."

"End of days for sure if that happens." Rhonda

mustered up a smile though her heart felt heavier than a tank. "Dad. I'm ready."

Colonel Driscoll lost his smile. He stood and hugged her close. "You're extremely brave. I'll send someone to let Doc know we're coming. I'm with you all the way on this."

Rhonda held him tighter. "Of course you are, Dad." She leaned forward and smelled his aftershave. She kissed him on his leathered cheek and smiled. "Thank you."

They walked from the command-post to the hospital. Several residents of Camp Deadnut greeted them, soldiers and civilians waved or saluted as they passed. The entire compound operated at a quiet murmur, most people were staying indoors to avoid the lower-than-average chill outside.

Doc Brightmore and Sarge were waiting for them when they entered the operating room where Brad was strapped down to a hospital bed. A stainless-steel surgery table was next to the bed with a lone piece of equipment on it that looked like a black handgun.

"He's been this way since Sarge and I took him out of confinement." Doc motioned with his hands as he stood over the hospital bed. Brad was hissing and *growling* and straining against the straps that held him down. "He trashed the other side of that door to the room we've been keeping him in."

"He's ornery as all get out." Sarge frowned. "Lucky Doc had me here to help get him strapped down. He threw a tantrum and could've done some real damage to one of us."

Rhonda nodded. She could see Brad had gone full-blown Cujo—nothing docile about him, no selective aggression. Drool and foam spilled out from beneath his muzzle. *Necro-Rabies*. She hung her head forlornly.

"Like taking Old Yeller of the corn crib to put him down." Sarge shook his head.

Rhonda's raised her head. "What's Old Yeller?"

"Sarge, please." Colonel Driscoll frowned. "Never mind, Rhonda."

"Right." Sarge eyes turned sad. "Sorry."

Rhonda stepped up to the surgery table and lifted the gun-looking thing off of it. It was heavy. "What's this?"

Doc cleared his throat and stepped around the hospital bed to her. "That's a spring-driven bolt-pistol. It has an automatic bolt-retraction system. They use it on cattle and whatnot for a humane death." Doc Brightmore folded his arms and paused. "I found it in the armory. Some knucklehead probably got it on a mission somewhere and thought it was an actual firearm. I thought it would be a quieter, faster, more merciful way to... you know... Brad."

As if hearing his name, Brad hissed louder and fought his straps.

Rhonda looked down at the bolt-pistol for what seemed like hours. How did she think she'd be able to do this? To put Brad down like a sick pet? Didn't he deserve better? Yes, he did. And that's why she was here, she realized. She looked up at Doc and slowly exhaled as she fought from breaking to pieces. "What do I do?

As Colonel Driscoll and Sarge looked on, Doc showed her how she'd place the barrel of the bolt-pistol to Brad's forehead, Brad lunged at Doc as the metal barrel touched Brad's forehead, and simply pull the trigger. A retractable bolt would go in and out of Brad's head and permanently destroy his Necro-Rabid brain.

"You good, sweetheart?" Dad put his hand on her shoulder. "We're right here for you."

Rhonda nodded and didn't turn around. She walked up to where Brad lay and looked down at him. Her gaze met his pure white eyeballs, and when they did, he calmed. All his hissing and growling and thrashing stopped. He seemed happy to see her.

"Rrrrnnndaahh."

She lost it. She shuddered and wept and then quickly sucked it up. She stood over him and gently caressed his face. "I feel that all I do is say goodbye to you, baby. Well, I have to say goodbye to you for good this time. You deserve peace and something better than this place. I love you so much."

She pressed the bolt-pistol to Brad's forehead. She closed her eyes and pulled the trigger. There was a sound that reminded her of a hole punch going through paper. And then it was over.

Brad lay perfectly still without a hiss to be heard. There was silence, but only for a moment before Rhonda dropped the bolt-pistol to the floor, fell to her knees, and erupted with wails of grief that sang through the hospital.

Chapter Twenty-Seven

It was two weeks since she put Brad down and had a funeral service for him. It had also been two weeks since Dad and Sarge, almost booted Marine Chaplain Johnson's fat ass.

Rhonda recalled with displeasure how the chunky Marine priest threw a fit when she first approached him in his chapel office the day she set Brad free. She asked, with all politeness, if he'd preside over Brad's funeral. She wanted Brad to have a holy sendoff and she wanted to give a eulogy. Chaplain Johnson, who'd always seemed nutty to Rhonda, and grew weirder each passing month, threw himself into a loud and frenzied rant when asked to do this honor. Outraged and offended by this request, he sprayed spittle and bared yellow teeth as he bolted from his desk chair. Veins popped out of his forehead and coursed beneath his gray flattop. He jabbed an index finger at her while his jowls shook and his eyes went wide. His creased face strained into a mask of trauma during his loud tirade.

That fucking prick.

Rhonda remembered how Chaplain Johnson screamed at her. "A funeral for a Cujo? How about a funeral for a dead rat, too? This is an affront to God! How dare you!"

She kept her cool during this acidic diatribe. She walked away and got Dad and Sarge involved. They agreed to have a chat with Chaplain Johnson. They approached Chaplain Johnson at his pulpit and Rhonda tagged along, but kept her distance among rear pews to allow these men to talk amongst themselves.

Chaplain Johnson walked from his pulpit and greeted Dad and Sarge. They all shook hands. Chaplain Johnson walked his military colleagues to a Nativity diorama made of olive wood, arranged on a nearby table since Christmas. He spoke of the Nazarene's birthday and the holiday's importance. Yet, when Colonel Driscoll personally asked for Rhonda's funeral request, all Christmas spirit went out the chapel's stained glass windows.

"It's an unholy request." Chaplain Johnson began barking at Colonel Driscoll and Sarge. Rhonda winced when both men wiped their faces from Johnson's point-blank spittle assault. Chaplain Johnson jabbed a finger at Colonel Driscoll's nose and told him he should've gelded himself decades ago to prevent his daughter, a *succubus*, from being conceived. Chaplain Johnson went on, and referred to Rhonda as a necrophiliac who should be burned alive.

On this last statement, Colonel Driscoll lost all cordiality and told Chaplain Johnson, "You're just a cunt-hair away from having my sidearm jammed into your big, fat mouth."

Sarge's restraint, however, didn't last. He grabbed Chaplain Johnson by his throat and slammed his holy head into the Nativity diorama. The right side of Chaplain Johnson's face crushed the olive wood manger and his head scattered miniature angels, shepherds, Joseph, Mary, three kings and baby Jesus across the chapel floor.

Colonel Driscoll pulled Sarge away and stopped the beatdown of the blessed Lieutenant. Chaplain Johnson tottered with a bruised and bloody head and Rhonda's dad grabbed him by his clerical collar and shoved him.

Rhonda walked away with her father and Sarge. She no longer cared about Chaplain Johnson presiding over Brad's funeral. She didn't believe in God, anyway.

Brad was buried in a cemetery located in a far corner of Fort Rocky. This cemetery was made by a group of Deadnutians who buried their own here, those who had fallen inside these gates since the pandemic had begun. A carpenter at the base made coffins and wooden crosses with the names of the dead carved into them. For this, Rhonda was extremely grateful.

Soldiers dug the grave, using a backhoe to cut into the cold ground. Colonel Driscoll was there, Dad standing straight, dressed in his sharpest, shiniest military uniform. Sarge, Doc, Tyler and Ellen, and few others joined Rhonda as she laid Brad to rest. She said a few words, cried, and sent him off.

* * *

Brad would remain her true love. Tyler and Ellen would become her kids. And time would march on.

Later, at some unknown hour, Rhonda moved beneath cozy blankets and reached out for Brad, who wasn't there. In the darkness, she heard an occasional tick from a heater. She listened to winter howl outside, the wind carrying the moans of countless Cujos who still milled about Camp Deadnut's perimeter, oblivious and immune to the elements.

Rrrrnnndaahh.

In her bed, Rhonda tossed around thoughts of a cold and dead world outside Fort Rocky's military fence and imagined an assortment of nightmarish inhabitants out there. Macabre visions of restless undead flashed in her mind and provided no comfort.

Love is like zombies... it never dies.

She slipped into slumber some time later. Her mind quieted and snuffed out reveries of the walking dead.

About the Author

New York Times Bestselling Author, Peter Straub (*A Dark Matter, Ghost Story,* and *The Talisman*—with Stephen King) says, *"Jeremy is a pretty impressive dude."*

Wagner has written lyrics to hundreds of songs spanning several albums with his international death-metal band, Broken Hope. He has a following of rabid fans worldwide, yet aside from his music career, Wagner writes dark fiction and short works full time.

His published works include the best-selling debut novel, *The Armageddon Chord,* the story "Romance Ain't Dead" for the anthology, *Hungry For Your Love* (St. Martin's Press), the story "The Creatures From Craigslist" in the anthology *Fangbangers: An Erotic Anthology of Fangs, Claws, Sex and Love* (Ravenous Romance), the seasonal bio tale "When I Scared Myself Out of Halloween" (Shock Totem Books), his horror writing essay-exercise in the *Now Write! Edition of Science Fiction, Fantasy, and Horror* (Bantam Books), and most recently, his short story "Pit Stop" in the *A Tribute Anthology to Deadworld* (Riverdale Avenue Books).

Wagner's novel, *The Armageddon Chord,* peaked at #4 on Barnes & Noble's Top 10 paperback Bestseller List and peaked at #9 on B&N's Top 100 overall Bestseller List in the first week of release. The novel also earned a Hiram Award, a first-round ballot Stoker Award Nomination, and received critical acclaim in *Publisher's Weekly* and *Rolling Stone* magazine among many other worldwide media.

The Afraid imprint of Riverdale Avenue Books will re-release a revised edition of *The Armageddon Chord* in December 2018 with new cover artwork and more.

If You Like This Title, You Might Also Like These Other Afraid Books:

A Tribute Anthology to
Deadworld Creator Gary Reed
Edited by Lori Perkins

Gone with the Dead:
An Anthology of Romance and Horror
Edited by Lori Perkins

Still Hungry for Your Love
Edited by Lori Perkins

Servant of the Undead
By Isabelle Drake

An Outcast State
By Scott D. Smith

Evoluzion:
Smarter Zombies, Smarter Weapons, Vol. 1
By James V. Smith, Jr.

Redemzion,
Vol. 2 in the Evoluzion Military Zombie series
By Axl Abbott

Stepford SoldierZ
By Axl Abbott

Demon with a Comb-Over
By Stuart R. West

Capricorn: Cursed
Book One of the Witch Upon a Star Series
By Sephera Giron

Aquarius: Haunted Heart
Book Two of the Witch Upon a Star Series
By Sephera Giron

Pisces: Teacher's Pet
Book Three of the Witch Upon a Star Series
By Sephera Giron

Aries: Swinging into Spring
Book Four of the Witch Upon a Star Series
By Sephera Giron

CPSIA information can be obtained
at www.ICGtesting.com
Printed in the USA
LVHW040012090119
603252LV00002B/146/P

9 781626 014640